MW01255221

EVERY TIME WE SAY GOODBYE

READERS LOVE LIBRARIAN-TURNED-TIME-COP BERYL BLUE (AND SULLY TOO!)

"I want to be Beryl Blue when I grow up!" – Lea Kirk, *USA Today* Best-Selling Author of Sci-Fi Romance

"A perfect blend of historical fiction, a bit of sci-fi, and wonderful romance. A really fun read, I can't wait to see what next is in store for Beryl." – Goodreads Review

"A fun, exciting, wild travel-through-time experience with the best characters, Beryl & Sully. You'll lose track of everything around you. I can't wait for the next adventure." – Amazon Review

"Janet Raye Stevens IT'S BEEN A LONG, LONG TIME is funny, romantic, sexy, adventurous, clever, and driven by the big-hearted, saucy-mouthed, wise-cracking, and delightful Beryl Blue. Bonus: Hot Guy Sully is in it. Swoon." – Suzanne Tierney, Amazon Best-Selling Author of *Art of the Scandal* & *Blooms of War*

ALSO BY JANET RAYE STEVENS

Beryl Blue, Time Cop – *Beryl Blue, Cop Book I*

Feisty librarian Beryl Blue is hurled from 2015 to WWII, tasked
with stopping an assassin from killing a soldier on leave and
changing history forever. The bad guy is one problem, his
target is another. Beryl's stunned to find herself falling for the
sexy, stubborn Army sergeant Tom "Sully" Sullivan, who makes
it abundantly clear he can take care of himself. With an
assassin on their heels and all of history on her shoulders,
Beryl scrambles to figure out how to protect a man who refuses
to be protected—and keep her heart intact.

It's Been A Long, Long Time – *Beryl Blue, Time Cop Book II*

Beryl Blue's second adventure in time takes her to the New
England seacoast in the summer of 1946—and straight into
Sully's arms. A jewel heist, explosive secrets from Beryl's past,
and the new woman in Sully's life all come into play as Beryl
struggles to catch a time-traveling thief, evade a killer, and keep
her beloved Sully from falling victim to his fatal destiny.

A Moment After Dark – A WWII paranormal suspense

Addie Brandt considers her ability to predict the future a curse.
But when her power of second sight shows her a terrifying
attack on the Pearl Harbor naval base in Hawaii, the horrific
vision is too big to ignore and she sets out to raise the alarm.
Can she stop the tragedy in time? Will anyone listen?

EVERY TIME WE SAY GOODBYE

A BERYL BLUE, TIME COP NOVEL

JANET RAYE STEVENS

GREAT BROOK PUBLISHING

First printing, 2023

ISBN: 978-1-7373103-8-9

www.janetrayestevens.com

To my friend and mentor Kari Lemor, who loves a happy ending as much as I do

1

The temporal vortex spit me out on the side of a steep hill. Already wobbly from the time skip and my own perpetual inability to stick the landing, I smacked the ground then pitched downward at top speed. I tumbled ass-over-teakettle through brush and brambles all the way to the bottom like both Jack and Jill in the old nursery rhyme. I didn't break my crown, but I did roll into a tangled mess of yellowing weeds that stopped me cold.

I sat up, every part of my body throbbing in pain and cursing myself for ever venturing into a time cop career.

Not a great way to start this mission. A mission I so desperately wanted to succeed. *Needed* to succeed. I had to catch Niels Rasmussen this time. It had been six months since that time-traveling assassin had slipped through my fingers. Six months of searching temporal time ripples and wisps of DNA signatures without a single ping, blip, or a hint as to where he'd gone. Six months of chewing my nails and keeping myself occupied by doing mundane tasks and routine extractions any junior time cop on their first mission could've handled.

And six months since I'd said goodbye to Sully in 1946 and returned to the twenty-second century. A short span on the scale of time itself, but to me, those six months had felt like an eternity. Yeah, I know, a cliché. But clichés stick for a reason. I missed Big Red so, so much, but until I figured out a way to beat whatever gruesome fate the universe had in store for him, I had to stay away.

The natter of voices and horses whinnying drifted through the trees from the nearby road, bringing me back to the present, or, in this case, July of 1882, on the road between LaPorte and Oroville, California. I had to get back on mission and stop wasting precious minutes lingering on my regrets.

I picked myself up off the ground, adjusted my Stetson cowboy hat with the tall crown and sombrero-like brim, and followed a narrow footpath toward the road. The day was hot and clear, and except for the distinct aroma of cattle, the air here in the country was clear too, free of the smoke and toxins that choked most cities in this booming industrial age.

I reached the path's end and ducked behind a thick California oak to scope out the scene ahead. A stagecoach with wooden side panels, steel-rimmed wheels, and *Wells Fargo & Company* painted below the rooftop cargo area stuffed with luggage had stopped on the dirt road, heading southwest. A team of horses snorted and pawed the ground in impatience. The leather traces harnessing them together creaked. Two burly men in gauntlet gloves and tall boots sat on the drivers' box with their hands up.

Why? Because my target, Niels Rasmussen, sitting

astride a muscular, chestnut-brown quarter horse, held a Colt .45 pistol pointed right at them.

Niels edged his horse closer to the coach. He wore a knee-length linen coat known as a duster and a bowler hat perched on his sandy brown hair, like Black Bart, the real-life 1880s stagecoach bandit he pretended to be. With a note of triumph in his voice, he ordered the passengers gazing fretfully out the large windows to toss their valuables onto the ground.

"Anyone hesitates, shoot 'em, boys," he called toward the trees that bordered the road. "Shoot 'em full of holes."

A woman wearing a hat with so many feathers I suspected every ostrich in Australia had been left bald wailed in terror but did as she was told. She flung a necklace sparkling with green and gold gems out the window. The other passengers followed suit. Coins, gold timepieces, and bulging billfolds soon littered the ground.

I doubted Rasmussen had any "boys" lurking in the woods. It was a bluff. The kind of subterfuge the real Black Bart had employed to terrify the victims of his numerous stagecoach robberies. Unlike that so-called gentleman bandit, who'd never fired a shot in his twenty-year crime spree, I knew Niels would shoot without hesitation. He'd proven that time and again as he travelled across the centuries, stealing gold and jewels, and killing anyone who got in his way.

I eased my electrical pulse weapon known as a stinger from the leather holster on my hip and gripped it tight. Did I have a plan? No. No, I didn't. But whatever I was going to do, I had to do it fast. Niels wore a TDC wristwatch, a Time Displacement Catalyzer, a fancy moniker for a portable time machine. The second he spotted me he would pound the controls and vaporize into thin air.

I had to time this perfectly. I didn't want to lose the chance to nail the bastard who'd murdered my parents and so many others. I looked down at the weapon in my hand, facing a hard choice. Would I follow Time Scope's orders and simply stun him, so I could bring him in bruised but alive? Or would I give in to the dark and bitter lust for revenge that simmered deep within me—and kill him?

Niels soon gave me an opening to find out. He slid off his horse, holstered his weapon, and squatted to scoop up his loot, stuffing the treasure into a burlap bag. I burst from the path onto the road and ran toward him. My legs pumped and my feet barely touched the ground as I closed in. I'd be on him in a moment. I armed my weapon. The horses' ears twitched at the high-pitched squeal of the stinger powering up.

My finger hovered between the weapon's *stun* and *kill* function keys. Whatever my choice, this time I'd stop him for good. *This* time he'd pay for murdering my parents. This time he'd—

The fierce rumble of hooves cut through the air as a massive quarter horse shot out of the woods and slammed into me like a battering ram. My body snapped to a halt and I herked back, sprawling flat on my back in the middle of the road. The rider hopped off the horse and clomped over to me in a jingle-jangle of spurs and swish of leather chaps.

A woman. A pretty woman and exactly Rasmussen's type, dark hair, doe eyes, plump lips, curvy figure, and smooth skin the color of fresh-fallen snow.

Shit. Ras didn't have a team of boys with rifles waiting in the woods. Just one woman, clutching a deadly-looking shotgun. She pointed the weapon between my eyes and jerked it to the left, the slightest twitch, but I got the message. I tossed my stinger. It thumped as it hit the ground several feet away.

She grabbed me by the shirt collar and yanked me to my feet. She looked toward her boss with a grin of satisfaction. Instead of rewarding her with the *way to go* she seemed to expect, Rasmussen ignored her and focused on me.

"Beryl Blue," he said with some surprise. He snatched up the last of his ill-gotten gains and stood, facing me. "An unexpected pleasure. How did you find me?"

Really? He wanted to have a debrief here and now? With the teamsters and half the stagecoach's passengers hanging out the windows, listening in? With wannabe Annie Oakley holding a shotgun to my head? And me, standing here in my circa 1880s linen shirt and tweed trousers, humiliated and frustrated as hell at being caught.

I gave a *whatever* shrug, determined not to show him my inner turmoil. "The real Black Bart was afraid of horses," I said, like he totally should've known that. "He committed all of his crimes on foot."

"Ah, my mistake. You continue to impress me with your cleverness."

Yeah, I couldn't take credit for that. I was a relative newcomer to the search for this jerk. Time Scope had been on the hunt for him since he'd murdered half the team of scientists who'd invented time travel then vanished into the past. A sharp-eyed researcher named

Dolores had discovered Rasmussen's Black Bart blunder and brought it to my attention. I'd set out after him right away.

"Why don't you come along and travel with me?" he said, with a genial smile that made my skin crawl. "We'd make a great team. You could be the Bonnie to my Clyde. You've got the brains and spirit I like in a companion."

I risked a glance at his current companion. Not something I wanted a woman with a weapon trained on me to hear. And seriously, this creep killed my parents and he thought I'd happily fly off with him to rob the past. That I'd trust him enough to even contemplate traveling with him. I'd been the queen of cynicism my whole life. With the exception of Sully, I didn't trust anyone. I certainly wouldn't follow this time-traveling murderer down trust alley. He'd cut my throat in an instant.

"Thanks for the job offer, Niels, but I have to decline. We wouldn't be a good fit."

"Nonsense. We'd work well together. We're so much alike. Smart, fierce. Driven."

If my skin crawled any further, it would leave my body. In what world could I ever be even remotely like this greedy, narcissistic revenge monster?

I replied to his dubious compliments with a frosty frown and he released a theatrical sigh of regret. "Such a pity," he said. "With me, you could've had all the riches you could ever want. Instead, you choose to waste your life chasing time runners and petty thieves."

"Not *all* those thieves are petty."

He nodded in a touché kind of way. "I'm pleased you recognize my talents." He slung his bag of loot over one shoulder. "Well, I must leave you. This is the second time you've interrupted my procurement activities. And the second time I'm getting away."

"The third time'll be the charm," I said. "I'll catch you. Count on it." A bold statement from someone on the losing side of this time travel version of *The Amazing Race*.

He laughed accordingly. He had a mean laugh. The thing that had rankled me most about him when we'd first met. Mean and mocking. "Sorry, Beryl. I don't think I'll give you the chance."

He drew his weapon and fired. For once in my life, I'd anticipated his treachery. I dove for the stinger the second he reached for the gun and the bullet whizzed by me. The bang of gunfire boomed through the air, spooking the stagecoach's team of horses. They reared up then bolted. Their hooves kicked up a cloud of dirt as they pounded down the road—straight at us.

Wannabe Annie Oakley grabbed her horse's reins and whisked the animal, and herself, to the side of the road and safety. I snatched my weapon off the ground and followed her as the terrified team thundered by, dragging the stagecoach and its shrieking passengers behind them.

By the time the dust cleared, Niels had powered up his TDC. A gust of wind and a stream of blue light shot out from the device, and he prepped for a time skip.

His companion spat a creative collection of curses, finishing with, "Wait for me, you bastard!" as she dashed toward him.

I ran after them both. It took a frustrating two seconds to rearm my stinger and I fired as soon as it pinged *ready*. Electricity burst from the weapon with twice the power of a TAZR-meets-*Star Trek* phaser, a sizzle of juice that smelled like rotting eggs and hot enough to burn a person's insides to cinders.

If I had clicked *kill*.

Had I rejected my bloodthirsty impulses and hit *stun* on purpose? Or had the memory of Sully begging me not to give into revenge steered my finger—and conscience—toward the less deadly option? Or maybe I'd just hit the first button I could find.

I didn't know. I only knew I missed. Now, I'm a librarian by birth and training. Books and knowledge were my weapons of choice, and even though I'd been dragged from 2015 and into the wonderful world of time copping and fully trained, I still had trouble operating one of these futuristic weapons, especially while running. My shot went wide. Like, way wide. The laser pulse pinged the dirt a hundred miles away.

Gritting my teeth, I aimed for Niels again, but too late. He gave his lady friend a *sorry, babe, gotta go* shrug then he and his bag of loot jumped into the temporal vortex. Wannabe Annie Oakley caught up to him as the wind died and the time tornado fizzled out. She released another barrage of colorful vulgarities at the empty space where he'd disappeared.

I scooped off my cowboy hat and slapped it against my thigh, raising a cloud of dust. I cursed too. Several times.

I'd lost him again.

I ENTERED Gloriana Evelyn Reid's office on the twentieth floor of Time Scope's HQ an hour later and flopped into a chair.

"That bad?" she said. "I can hardly wait to read your mission report."

A petite Black woman with light-brown skin, a toned figure and determined chin, Glo wore a beige jumpsuit and sat behind a small desk in a far too small office for someone in her exalted position of director of the time cop division. A stark, uncluttered place that matched her no-nonsense personality, though she'd added some homey touches since I'd come on board. A dozen framed pictures hung on what used to be bare walls. Some were 3-D digipix of friends and her main squeeze, Wesley, a bald, brown-skinned man as broad-shouldered as Sully, but most were old-school snapshots of her family members from days gone by.

"Rasmussen got away," I said. "Mission report complete in three words. No, five words. I *let* him get away." Glo lifted an eyebrow, expressing her doubt. She had more faith in my skills than I did. "Okay, he had help. I might have caught him otherwise. A woman again. From that era, as far as I could tell."

Like the last time. In Point Bailey in 1946, Sully and I had found ourselves entangled in a jewel robbery that postwar housewife Dorella Murphy had helped Rasmussen plan and execute. She'd gone along for the ride out of love for him or pure greed or maybe both. With predictable results. Rasmussen's betrayal had shocked Dorella then as much as his abandonment on that dusty California road had stunned wannabe Annie Oakley a little while ago.

"He'll slip up again," Glo said. "You know he likes to take risks. We'll find him."

She sounded amazingly chipper for someone whose go-to expression was a gloomy, *the end is nigh* scowl that always reminded me of Sully.

"What's going on, Glo? Why do you sound like Cathy Cheerleader?"

She eyed me for a moment then stood and came around her desk to sit on the edge, close to my chair. "I've got a new assignment for you."

"I'm not interested in more busy work and routine extractions. After today, I want to focus on Rasmussen twenty-four-seven."

"You'll be interested in *this* assignment."

Both dread and hope swirled in my belly. "Is it Sully? Did you hear anything new about what happens to him? Is there a way to save him?"

Regret and a bit of pity flashed across her face. She'd never tell me outright, but I knew she believed my efforts to prevent Sully's death were futile. According to the temporal tea leaves, he was supposed to die, saving me. No matter how much anyone wanted to, no matter how much *I* wanted to, that fact could not be changed. Fate was a remorseless bitch and always got its way.

At least, that's what I'd always been told.

"No, nothing to do with Sergeant Sullivan," she said. "Not directly, in any case. Remember that thing you've been nagging me to find out about all this time?"

"The thing?" I said like I didn't have the faintest idea though my nerve endings tingled with sudden excitement. I'd recently learned I was the daughter of time travelers who'd fled into the past to escape Rasmussen's rage.

An escape attempt that had failed, leaving them dead and me an orphan with a target on her back large enough to necessitate me being extracted from 2015 to here.

Complicated? You bet. And only one person could tell me the whole story—the person who'd arranged to move me in time.

Glo stood and reached across her desk to pick up her commpad, a thin, lightweight tablet device in a silver case. "I'm sending you on a mission." She tapped a button and a million pixels swirled up from the commpad's screen to form a 3-D image with several paragraphs of data and a photo of a pasty-faced woman with dishwater hair. "A fake mission, with realistic details to throw anyone snooping off the track. The mission specs will say you've been sent to 1925 to keep time tourist Gertrude Fleck from getting into trouble in a Chicago speakeasy."

"But I'm really going to meet with... who? What's their name?"

"You'll find out soon enough." She tapped her tablet and the TDC strapped to my wrist shimmied as the mission specs found their way from her device to mine. She stood and gazed at me solemnly. "You're ready for this, aren't you?"

Ready? For months and months, I'd bugged Glo and her right-hand man, Jake Tyson, to introduce me to the mystery person who'd ordered me to be hijacked from my going-nowhere life in 2015 and thrust me onto the road to time cop success. I had a zillion and one questions needing to be answered, and only half of them about how I could keep Sully from meeting his fate.

Now it seemed someone in Futureworld would *finally* answer my questions instead of sidestepping them. Or lying. I'd had my fill of lies and obfuscations and was ready for a large dose of the truth. I stood, pushing back my chair, startled, stunned, and a little shocked by this development.

But totally, completely, and absolutely ready.

"When do I leave?"

2

"**P**assword?" the guy at the door demanded, giving me a liberal whiff of the kielbasa and onions he'd scarfed at dinner.

Password? I didn't have the slightest clue, and no warning from Glo that I'd need one. I stood at the side entrance of a sooty brick building in a narrow, grimy alley on a drizzly June night, trying to get into a Chicago speakeasy called *The Gin Joint*. I couldn't just look up the magic word that would get me in, and I doubted I'd get any *forgot-my-password* assistance from the hulking slab of beef guarding the door.

"Uh... swordfish?" I said, gamely giving it a try.

The brute looked me up and down, taking in my blue-green chiffon drop-waist dress, my tan leather shoes with double straps and delicate buckles, silk stockings rolled down to expose my rouged knees, and the heavily-sequined bandeau—a fancy word for a headband—doing its best to corral my unruly chestnut-brown hair. I thought I looked fetching, but the bouncer's sneer told me he thought otherwise.

"Go back to your mama," he said. "She shouldn't of let a hick like you out in the big city."

Rude, and seriously, I was not going to leave. Of all the gin joints in all of prohibition era Chicago, I had to get into this one. All the answers were in there.

"Look, mister. I'm not a naïve girl out for a lark. I've got business to conduct, so step aside."

He stepped, but not aside. He shifted right and fully blocked the entrance. I weighed my options. The door was pretty solid and so was the gorilla guarding it. Brute force wouldn't work. I reached into my leather pouch handbag. Not for my weapon. For something more persuasive—some good old American cabbage.

I held up a five-dollar bill and the gorilla went all smiles. The bill disappeared into his pants pocket, and he disappeared from the doorway.

I swept inside and down a narrow corridor with a scuffed wood plank floor. The scents of perfume, cigarettes, beer, and the mouthwatering aroma of tonight's blue plate special, spaghetti and meatballs, greeted me at the main ballroom.

Nearly a hundred people filled the spacious area, seated at small wooden tables or mingling at the bar. A quartet of young Black men on a variety of horns played jazz way hot, to the delight of the crowd doing the Lindy Hop on the dance floor. Could've been a nightclub anywhere in any era, except for the preponderance of flapper dresses, Great Gatsby-style tuxedos, and hip flasks.

I waded into the mob, hunting for a place to sit, when

a man of about thirty lurched into my path. I perked up. If this was the person I was supposed to meet, he'd gone all-in on the jazz age cosplay. He wore a tux, wingtip shoes, and his hair slicked back with a gallon or more of that greasy stuff men of the olden days thought made their coiffure the cat's meow and not like an oil tank had sprung a leak.

"Wanna dance, beautiful?" he said, addressing my breasts.

Oh. Not my mystery date. Just a guy hitting on me. "Sorry, sonny. The girls are spoken for, and so am I." As in, Sully. I was his, now and forever. Right now, Sully was six years old, living with his parents and baby brother Patrick in a South Boston tenement. A tough guy kid who'd grow up to be an even tougher guy sergeant in the US Army during World War II and a police sergeant afterward, until...

Well, this was neither the time nor the place for me to delve into that sticky mess.

I sent my would-be dance partner on his way and found an open table in a corner. A waitress eventually made her way over. She wore a sleeveless, backless, and nearly frontless dress sparkling with more sequins than a Las Vegas drag show. Fun fact, when archaeologists had cracked open King Tut's tomb in 1922, they'd found the motherlode of sequins inside, setting off a spangly fashion explosion throughout the 1920s.

I shouted over the music to the waitress, a drink order that earned me the most derisive eyeroll I'd seen in a long time.

"You came to a juice joint for coffee?" she said, snapping her gum incredulously.

Yup, coffee. Not bootleg gin or beer. *Coffee.* My drink of choice when time traveling. Sad reality of the twenty-second century, the double whammy of crop blights and climate change left coffee in painfully short supply. Oh, you could still get the real stuff. Like these enterprising prohibition era folks, people in Futureworld found a way to get their daily cup of joe through a thriving black market. But lowly time cop me didn't have the cabbage or moolah to afford such luxury, so I made do with the fake stuff and indulged copiously in the real stuff when on a mission.

Minutes later, the jazz band launched into a frantic version of "The Charleston" and the waitress returned, holding her tray containing my precious liquid over her head. I sat back, sipped my coffee—lukewarm and weak but one hundred percent real—and took in my surroundings as I waited for my mystery date to arrive. There were a lot of pros and cons to time travel, but the chance to sightsee in the past hit the top of my *yes, please* list. I'd never been to the 1920s or Illinois, and I'd certainly never been to a "blind pig," what some people in the know called a speakeasy.

Time passed, I drained my cup, and my mystery date was still a no-show. I thought of ducking into the powder room to put in a call to HQ when the waitress strolled by to refill my coffee—and handed me a note. I glanced around for gawkers or temporal spies before unfolding the small sheet of paper and scanning the page. Written in pencil, the missive included nothing but an address and instructions to slip out the side door and turn left. No signature.

Seriously? All very *Tinker, Tailor, Soldier, Spy* meets

The Alice Network, or some other cloak-and-dagger thriller. Was I supposed to eat the note for secrecy's sake too? I tucked it into my handbag instead and squeezed through the undulating crowd toward the side door, convinced someone was pulling an elaborate prank on me.

Out on the street, I turned left as instructed and moved briskly up the dark city sidewalk. A light drizzle misted the midnight air. Shiny new Model T cars chugged along the wet street and the beam of the streetlights I passed reflected in the puddles along the curb.

My excitement and anxiety ratcheted up as I reached a stout, two-story brick building with what looked like an apartment on the second floor and a bakery on the ground level. A rolled-up awning stretched above a large picture window with the generic *Corner Bake Shop* stenciled onto the plate glass. I approached the door and frowned at the sign in the window.

Closed.

I double-checked that I had the right address. *What was going on?* This frustrating runaround reminded me of the day I'd been thrust onto this whirlwind through time, when Glo had unceremoniously dropped me in 1943, told me saving Sully would save the future, and left me to figure out the rest on my own. Turned out, the mission was a test to see if I had what it took to join her team as a time cop. I knew that now, but at the time I'd quaked in terror, a stranger in a strange land.

Was this another test? If so, did my mystery date allow extra credit, or had they set me up to fail before the exam had even begun?

Anxious and a tad angry, I reached for the brass doorknob. My fingers brushed air as the door creaked inward, as if someone had left it ajar. Waiting for me.

Inside, a single overhead bulb cast an eerie mixture of light and shadows over the spacious room and the wooden tables with chairs tucked neatly underneath. My shoes clacked in the stillness as I crossed the tiled floor to the cash register and the bakery display case in the back. The shelves were empty, but a thousand tantalizing smells lingered—bread, buttery pastries, raspberries, and a hint of chocolate. Plus, coffee.

"Hello?"

I peered into the shadowy area beyond the display case, seeing two ovens, a wrought iron baker's rack, and a long, waist-high table used for packing up orders. A large Kelvinator refrigerator stood against the rear wall, the electricity humming with a low, ominous buzz that added to the creepy feel.

A door next to the fridge creaked open. I expected zombie Al Capone to burst out, not a generic-looking white man of about seventy. An inch or two taller than my five-foot-eight, with a thick build, roundish face, and copious hair more silver than black, he wore a long-sleeved white shirt and pants, and a dark necktie tucked under a white bib apron that reached his knees.

"Beryl," he said, breaking into a majorly toothy grin. "I'm so happy to see you."

"Yeah, likewise." A sense of déjà vu tugged at my brain, but I dismissed it. I'd never met this guy before, never been in this bakery, or Chicago, or even 1925.

"Won't you sit?" His gaze dipped to the stool next to the broad table then to the glazed Brown Betty teapot sitting on a nearby counter. "Have some tea."

I didn't want tea or even coffee at the moment. I *only* wanted answers. I was impatient that way. In fact, the world's most impatient woman. Sully had mentioned that more than once. But I sensed my silver-haired friend needed to conclude my bizarre visit to this toddling town in his own way, so I accepted his tea party invite with an abrupt nod and plunked myself down on the stool.

My host scrounged around in the cupboard and found a delicate cup dotted with bluebells. He placed it in front of me then picked up the teapot and poured a rich and flowery-scented amber liquid into the cup.

I watched him and that tug of familiarity pulled at me again. "Who are you? Have we met?"

He put down the pot and met my gaze. "I'm Henry Gill. I run this bakery."

I looked him over. He wore a convincing uniform, with the apron being an extra persuasive touch. He smelled persuasive too, like jelly donuts and sugar. Flour caked his knuckles and under his fingernails. All signs he told the truth. But I'd also caught a vague yet familiar aroma wafting off of him, the odor of cheap perfume mixed with tar.

The scent of time travel. *Recent* time travel.

"Who are you *really*, Mr. Gill?"

"I'll tell you, Beryl. I'll answer all your questions." He opened a deep drawer below the table and pulled out a hunk of dough, tightly wrapped in a thin cloth. "But this meeting, and our conversation, is off the record. What I tell you here doesn't go in your mission report."

"It's a deal. I hate doing those reports, anyway." A necessary but *the* most mundane part of the time cop business.

He put the dough down and sprinkled flour on the tabletop like a light dusting of snow. "I'm going to work while we talk if you don't mind." He peeled the cloth off the dough, releasing a fresh, yeasty, and slightly sharp smell. "I'm the type that has to keep my hands busy. Working also helps me to focus my thoughts."

"Sure, have at it." I sipped my tea while he punched the dough as if it had insulted him then began kneading. "Why don't we start with who you really are."

He'd bent his head and focused on his work, but I caught the smile that twitched his lips. "You sure do get to the point."

"And *you* are avoiding the point."

This time he laughed. A fond cackle that ended with a sigh. "Alright, Beryl. I won't delay anymore. You deserve to know, after all that's happened. To everyone in this time period, I'm Henry Gill. My real name is Hank Gillespie. I'm responsible for moving you about in time. I'm also the man behind Time Scope, Incorporated." He looked up and offered me another toothy grin. "In other words, I'm the company's founder and CEO."

I BLINKED HALF a million times as this news penetrated my brain.

I'd always wondered how high up Operation Extract Beryl went. I figured some executive paper-pusher in some office had brought me to the future as a sick practical joke. Or had sent me to 1943 on a dare, putting me through that ludicrous test to see if I would actually kill someone who I believed threatened the timeline. And that same paper-pusher had decided to raise the stakes by throwing Sully and me together to see what happened.

I *never* expected to discover that the person in charge of the entire time travel show would be the culprit.

"You're what now?" I said when I found my voice.

He stopped kneading and gazed at me. The light beaming from behind him haloed his head, brightening his silver hair. "I'm the one in charge. I own the company."

"You? Own the company? A pastry chef?"

"I wasn't always a baker, but it's such a rewarding change of pace. I used to sit in a big office, worrying about temporal shifts and paradoxes and time runners trying to change the past. Now, I delegate those tasks. All that concerns me these days is how to make the perfect loaf of sourdough bread. It's tricky, you know." He frowned at the dough, his breezy manner dropping a notch. "Working here also keeps me out of harm's way."

I was usually slow on the uptake, but the truth got to me eventually. "Or to keep harm from finding you. In the form of Niels Rasmussen."

His chin dipped in the barest of nods. "How much do you know about Niels?"

I calmly sipped my tea, as if the world hadn't just tipped on its axis. As if the mere mention of Rasmussen's name didn't set my blood on fire. "I know he worked at Time Scope in the early days until an accident got him kicked off the project and cut out of the profits." A *lot* of profits. Turns out, time tourism was mega-lucrative and Niels, already unstable, blamed his fellow scientists, and the company, for cutting him out of his share. "He went on a murder spree. His coworkers fled into the past to escape him. The lucky ones have stayed hidden. The unlucky ones, like my parents..." I shrugged. "Is that about right, Mr. Gillespie?"

"Call me Hank." He reached for a rectangular metal loaf pan and fit the dough inside. "Niels resented me for my decision. Railed about my stealing everything he'd ever cared about and worked for and vowed to get back at me. I didn't take him as seriously as I should have. Only when the team members started to die did I understand the depth of his mania."

Hank pushed the bread pan aside and removed another cloth-wrapped dough package from the drawer. He spread more flour on the table and began the kneading process all over again.

"The Temporal Twisters we called ourselves," he said. "I brought them together, nurtured minds far more brilliant than my own, encouraged them. Came to care for them as family. Niels knew the one way to get back at me."

"By killing your family. *My* family." A bald statement laced with anger and more than a little grief. I'd never really known my mother and father. Only six when they died, they existed in my mind as vague images, snatches of sights, sounds, and moments I couldn't quite recall. Strangers, really. So why did it sting so much when I thought of them?

"I grieve their loss every day." Hank dug his fingers into the dough, kneading with vigor. "Your parents were special. They met in the lab. Mabel was with us from the beginning, Felix came along later. Right away, he was smitten. They fell in love. We all knew, though they thought they hid it from everyone. Young people in love think no one notices." He paused and stared at a point over my shoulder with a wistful expression, lost in his memories. "We were a small group back then. Close, tight-knit, full of energy about our inventions. Then..."

A cloud of sorrow closed over me. "Then, the accident."

He released a remorseful sigh. "I took Niels under my wing. He was so brilliant and promising. If anyone could make a breakthrough with the temporal tech, it would be him. I was right, but at what cost? He was arrogant, daring. He took too many risks. He *thrived* on risk."

"He still does."

"Yes. I know about his robberies throughout time, the jewel theft he dragged you into."

"Tell me how it began."

"Niels worked closely with your mother and Oliver Bishop. They made a breakthrough. They managed small time skips and increased the jumps with each test. Niels was eager to forge ahead but I didn't think the tech was ready. He pushed the issue. He was involved with a young woman, a lab assistant. Claimed to be in love with her, though I don't think he understood what love is. He's a greedy, possessive man who saw Lexie as a means to an end, nothing more. He convinced her to help him test the oscillator before it was ready. Your mother and Oliver fought him. Your father and Niels came to blows. Niels accused them of jealousy and trying to steal his work. He went ahead with the test in secret. Oliver and Mabel found out and rushed to the lab to stop him but got there too late."

My stomach clenched. "What happened?"

He stopped kneading and looked up at me, his expression angry and wounded. "He managed to send Lexie back ten minutes, but something was off, as if her cognitive functions didn't quite—" He laced his flour-coated fingers together like puzzle pieces. "Didn't quite mesh. Worse, when he returned her to the present, her atoms failed to reconstitute. She was just... not there."

I suspected he sanitized this description. *Good.* My imagination worked on overdrive most of the time. I knew the poor woman had died. I didn't need the graphic details to confirm it.

"I fired him on the spot and contacted the police. Niels flew into a rage. Not about facing the law, or even Lexie's horrific death, but the loss of his status and his share of any profits we might realize from our work. The money." Hank sunk his hands into the dough again, working it with vengeance. "He was arrested but released pending trial. Then he disappeared. That's when members of the team began to die. I figured it out, but not fast enough. Niels had cobbled together his own oscillator. A crude device that enabled him to escape to the past after each murder he committed, so he wouldn't be caught. Four people lost their lives before I understood—"

He turned away and swiped his arm over his teary eyes.

"It was your plan for them to go back in time," I said gently. "My parents, the others."

He nodded with a rueful smile. "The baker tidying up his workspace after he made a mess. As soon as we perfected the tech, we made a plan. Each team member chose where and when to go. They did *not* share that information with anyone. For their own safety."

"Except for my parents. You knew where they went. How else would you have known to send Jake to watch over them?"

"Your parents were the most vulnerable. They had a child. Or were about to have you when they fled."

Well, well. Another piece to fit into the puzzle of me. I hadn't been born when my parents left the twenty-second century. They'd managed to keep off Rasmussen's radar for a little more than six years before he caught up to them. I hadn't been given access to the classified incident report Jake had filed so I didn't know the full details. I only knew the date and time they were murdered, and that Jake had mistaken Oliver Bishop as the killer. And that their child—me—had escaped the attack unharmed.

Physically unharmed, anyway. The mental harm had lingered for years.

"Why did you wait so long before moving me to the future?"

He avoided my gaze. "It's... complicated."

"Oh no you don't. Tell me the truth."

He sighed as if the truth was the last thing he wanted to share. "I thought you were safe, but in 2015, we got a ping on Niels within ten miles of your location. That was too close for me. I'd already moved you once, so I decided to extract you after that. Niels never knew Mabel and Felix had a child, but if he ever figured it out, I thought the last place he'd look was the era they had all fled. I took a risk and brought you forward."

"But not before giving me a test first. Was it your idea to send me to 1943 and throw Sully and me together? You had Glo tell me Sully was being threatened by a time-traveling assassin and I had to kill the guy to prove I was worthy of being a time cop."

Hank looked me in the eye for the first time. "Using Sullivan wasn't my idea, but I signed off on it. We needed to have you willing to take a tremendous risk for a good cause before moving you forward."

"And by we, you mean...?"

"Jake and Gloriana. And, to some extent, Sullivan himself."

"Sully? Are you talking about how he's supposed to save me and then..." I couldn't bring myself to say the word *die*.

"You know his character. He will step up when the time comes and fulfill his destiny."

My chest squeezed so tight I could barely breathe. "Does he have to? Can his fate be changed?"

He hesitated. Far too long. "Maybe. I don't know." He chuckled softly. Sadly. "You look like your mother when you glare like that. I'm telling you the truth. I honestly don't know. It hasn't happened yet in the timeline, so there might be a chance."

I sipped the last of my tea, outwardly calm, trying not to show the volcano of hope that erupted as he spoke those magic words. There might be a chance to save Sully. I'd glossed over the doubtful and anemic way Hank had uttered the words *might* and *chance* and went straight to *save Sully*.

"Why have you done all this? Why do you care so much about me? I mean, sure, my parents worked for you, and you feel kind of responsible for what happened. But all the other stuff. Moving me in time, making me a time cop, even providing me with a place to live. You've been protecting me through Jake and Glo and training me so I can protect myself. Why?"

Hank didn't answer. He crossed to the oven and opened the door. A wave of heat flooded the room. He picked up the loaf pans and put them in the oven. He came back to the table and swept the scattered flour into a small pile with his hand.

"Come on, Hank," I prodded, peeved that he'd clammed up after being so chatty. "Why have you helped me so much?"

"Let's just say I have a vested interest in you." He leaned a hip against the table. "I made sure you can defend yourself, not just because of Niels, because..." He met my gaze. "Because I've already lost so much. I couldn't bear to lose you too."

Too? "What does that mean?"

"I thought you might have figured it out by now."

"Figured out what?" I had to ask the question, though deep down I knew. I guess I'd known since the moment Hank had stepped through the door. The feeling that we'd met before, and why his golden-brown eyes and pleasant smiles seemed so familiar. The way he'd cocked his head. I knew but needed to hear the words from him.

"Your mother was my daughter, Beryl." He offered the toothiest of toothy grins. "I'm your grandfather."

3

Jenjen meowed. Well, howled actually. A monstrously large and fluffy gray Maine coon cat with giant paws, Jenjen could wail at the ear-splitting volume of a heavy metal band determined to blast every note into the far corners of Madison Square Garden. I winced accordingly.

"Oh, are you trying to tell me you want breakfast?" I muttered. "I had no idea." I got another eardrum popping *feed me now, I'm dyyyyinggg* howl in return.

I opened a pouch of Impossible Salmon, squeezed the gooey stuff onto Jenjen's plate then fed the empty pouch into the reclamation tube. Where it went from there and what would happen to it, I had no idea, except that it would be recycled like most of the other waste products we humans liked to make. Score one for the environment, courtesy of the twenty-second century.

I cleaned up my own breakfast dishes using the water-saving super-heated steamer then got ready to leave for my morning shift at the west side branch of the city's public library. I'd been working there ten hours a week since I'd come to live in this time period. Some kids dream of growing up to be race car drivers or movie stars. I'd always dreamed of becoming a librarian. I loved the thrill of being a time cop and wouldn't change that for anything, but being a librarian, working in the place where books lived, and people came to learn and schmooze and connect... *Nothing* beat that satisfaction.

Well, one thing would. Seeing Sully again. And to find a way to do it *without* risking his life.

I crossed my apartment to get my daypack from where I'd left it on the bookcase by my bed. The trip was short. My studio apartment was barely big enough to hold me, Jenjen, and my few sticks of furniture—various tables, two armchairs, and a sofa that Jake called vintage and quaint and I called old and saggy.

I picked up my bag and eyed the photos hung on the wall above the bookcase. Not those new-fangled digipix like Glo had, with moving parts and eyes that followed you around the room horror movie-style and creeped me the hell out. These were real pictures in old-timey frames, including a black-and-white snapshot of my parents picnicking in a park, me sitting on Sully's lap at a Ballard Springs bar, and a photo booth strip of Sully and me cuddling and smooching during our last adventure in the summer of 1946.

My gaze settled on the newest picture in my photo wall, Sully in his policeman's uniform, scowl firmly in place, his hat brim pulled low on his forehead, hiding his thick, copper-colored hair and those expressive eyebrows. The picture had been taken when he'd joined the Ballard

Springs police department after he came home from the war.

I touched two fingers to Big Red's scowling lips. His fate was to die, to sacrifice himself to save me. Such a Sully thing to do. How and where I didn't know. I only had a vague idea of when, somewhere between 1947 and the mid-1950s. I'd stayed away from that era until I could figure out a way to prevent his death. And now, according to my newfound grandpa, there might be some way for me to succeed.

It'd been three weeks since I'd met Hank. Three up-and-down, emotional weeks since I'd learned the stunning news that I had a grandfather. I'd lingered in the bakery for hours, sipping a gallon of tea while Hank baked bread. We'd talked, *he* talked, mostly about my parents and their life before time travel. Before me. As the sun rose, he sent me home with a loaf of fresh-baked bread, a promise he'd tell me more the next time we met, and one tantalizing tidbit that blazed foremost in my mind.

There was a chance to save Sully. A slight chance, but a chance nonetheless.

But how?

A glance at the time-ticker function of my apartment's Interface told me I was running late. Really late. I'd have to grapple with those questions later. I slung my bag's strap over my shoulder and hustled back to the kitchen island to swallow the last of my triple-synth latte before leaving. It tasted exactly like what it was, fake espresso with a splash of caffeine and a boatload of steamed soy milk.

A bell chimed. "Jake Tyson is at the door," the Interface announced. The east wall of my apartment swept away like dust blown in the wind, replaced by a high-res image of Jake, standing outside in the hallway. Tall, slim, and muscular, he looked like Jake Gyllenhaal's earnest younger brother, with his chiseled features, thick black hair, cobalt blue eyes, and a pair of dimples that could disarm the frostiest curmudgeon at twenty paces.

When he smiled. Which he decidedly did *not* do today.

"Admit," I told the Interface. The door swished open like something out of *Star Trek* and Jake stepped inside, bringing with him the scent of soap and the sulfur mixed with nail polish remover remnants of a recent time trip. He wore Time Scope's required uniform of blah beige jumpsuit and an equally dull windbreaker jacket.

"What's going on?" I asked.

Must be important. Futureworld had all kinds of remote ways to communicate with each other, including full holograms that made you think the person was right there in the room, pretty awesome for someone whose VR experience growing up was playing a mid-1990s version of Oregon Trail on a desktop Dell that froze constantly. For Jake to come all the way over to my side of town to see me meant he had big news.

"Glo wants to talk to us," he said. "Alice has found a lead that could be our suspect."

Ooh. *Really* big news. I hadn't expected a ping on Ras so soon after I'd lost him. "How strong a lead?"

"Strong enough to call a meeting."

So, more than a ping. A temporal hit. "Great." I shifted my handbag strap from one shoulder to the other and nodded to the door. "I'm ready."

"Wait. Before we go, there's something I want to talk with you about."

"Okay," I said warily. He'd activated his serious voice. Jenjen heard it too and pulled his nose out of his dinner and looked up, ears twitching. "What is it?"

A pregnant pause. Like, nine months long. Jake's signature thought-gathering habit that drove me bananas. I got it. He wanted to make sure his words were precise, but he also wrestled with precisely which words *not* to tell me. How much info to share.

That was Jake to a fault. Stingy with information, obsessive about secrets. After my visit to 1946 when I found out my parents were time travelers, I'd demanded he tell me everything he knew about them and my grandmother, about the woman he'd loved and lost, and... well, just about every other secret he'd been keeping from me since he and Glo had brought me on board the security division.

He'd obliged. Barely. The woman he'd once loved he wouldn't even name, but he'd confessed she'd been someone from another era, someone he would never risk the timeline to be with. My grandmother, he'd said, was a nurse who'd lived in the apartment above my parents. When they'd been killed, she'd taken in six-year-old me. As simple as that, a selfless gesture from a woman I'd believed to be my father's mom but turned out to be no relation at all. Her sacrifice had kept me safe, until Rasmussen had closed in on my location and Hank and company had decided to move me.

And... that was it. I suspected Jake still hid a *lot* about my past, but I'd given up trying to crowbar those secrets from his pretty but tightly sealed lips. Or from anybody else. Glo went all *no comment* when I asked even the most innocuous question about my past, and I had an inkling ol' grandpa kept more secrets than Jake and Glo combined.

"Just spit it out," I insisted. "It'll be healthier for both of us." But mostly for me. My blood pressure climbed as high as the clouds when Jake got all squirrelly and secretive like this.

He dragged his fingers through his thick black hair. "Uh...look... If we've found Rasmussen, I think you should sit this mission out."

"Yeah, not happening. We get a hit on him, I'm going. You know I have a personal stake in catching him." Even more personal now that I'd met Grandpa Hank, the only family I had left. I had to protect him from Rasmussen as Hank had protected me. "If you think I'm going to stay back and let you or anyone else do the job for me, you don't know me as well as I thought."

Come to think of it, I didn't know much about Mr. Dimples, either, though he'd been my mentor since the beginning and my mission partner in the early days. I didn't even know his job title. I suspected he didn't have one. Except doing whatever he was told to do. The man was a stickler for the rules. As in, following them to the letter. Probably why failing to keep my parents safe had hit him like a grand piano dropping onto his head, leaving him flattened and wracked with guilt.

"This is serious, Beryl. You didn't wait for me to get back from my mission before going after Niels in California. You know it's safest to have two on a team."

Still mad about that, was he? "I didn't have time to

wait for you. Research got a bead on him and I didn't want to lose him."

"Instead, he almost killed you." His gaze turned fearful. "He almost killed you the last time you ran into him, too. You know that's what he wants most. The man's imbalanced and unpredictable, but he's also focused on his need for revenge. He told you that himself. He would've killed you if he'd seen you in your parents' car. If he knew you were there, if he knew you existed, he would've done it when he killed them. With no hesitation. A *child*. A six-year-old child."

Damn, why had I put those details in my mission reports? Jake's protectiveness went into overdrive when he'd learned about my near misses with Time Scope Enemy Number One. "But he didn't get me, as you can see. I escaped each time."

He scraped his hand through his hair again. "Only by sheer luck."

I bristled. I understood where Jake's impulse to shield me came from. His failure to protect my parents had fueled a driving need to protect me from danger at all costs. It had even triggered what he'd mistaken for feelings for me, feelings we'd both shut down pretty quick. But seriously, his efforts to cocoon me from every little threat had gotten old and annoying.

"Listen, Jake... I hear you. Your concern is noted, but I'd appreciate you not treating me like a damsel in distress." The only man I'd let coddle me was Sully. And he knew enough not to. "I can take care of myself."

I always had, from the time my grandmother died of lung cancer when I was fifteen until I'd fallen off a ladder at work and into the arms of these meddling time travelers eight years later. Sure, I'd been kind of an emotional mess, running away from life and any semblance of a family. But I'd had no one but myself to answer to or depend on and I'd liked it that way. Until Sully had come along.

"You know, if you're going to worry about me so much, you're welcome to skip this mission."

He snorted. "Sure. And who'd watch your back? Who'd give you directions? You know you're shit with directions."

Direct hit. He'd sunk my battleship. "And who'd correct your slang? You know you're always off by decades with your slang."

His dimples put in an appearance as he flashed a smile. I was glad. I didn't like bickering with him. Especially over something I thought we'd settled a long time ago. Besides, his doubt fueled my own, and I was shaky enough without him getting all gloom and doom on me.

I followed him out the door and moments later, I sat in the passenger seat of his Total Control Vehicle, TCV for short, an all-electric, self-driving car that looked like a giant silver egg. The surface roads were crammed with TCVs, but the vehicles were so methodically timed and controlled, there was little chance of a traffic jam or fender-bender slowing us down on our way to Time Scope's HQ.

I Interfaced into the library as soon as we set out, switching my shift to another day. They didn't need me there, anyway. Shelving and most other chores were automated, so the head librarian gave me mostly piddling assignments, just to satisfy my need to putter around among the books.

"I heard you finally met your... Met Hank," Jake said when I finished my call.

Ah. No surprise to learn he knew about Hank. And no surprise to discover he'd kept yet another secret from me, though he'd probably been ordered to keep that news hush-hush.

"Yeah. Finding out I had a grandpa was quite the reveal." I side-eyed him. "What about you? How long have you known about him?"

"About you being related? Not long. Before, I only knew him as the boss."

"The boss who sent you to the past to guard my parents. Why you?"

Ten long seconds went by before he spoke. "Why not me? I was young, eager. Not very smart." He flashed a rueful smile. "I'd just saved a time tourist from getting himself killed in the French Revolution. The bonehead thought he could reenact *A Tale of Two Cities* by joyriding in one of those wagons they took people to the guillotine in. Tumbrels I think they were called. Anyway, my adventure was the talk of Time Scope. I was a rising star, impressed with myself, and when Hank came calling, I jumped at the chance."

He'd dropped a surprising amount of info about himself in the last five seconds, more than I'd learned in the three years I'd known him. All delivered in a monotone laced with regret.

"Do you wish you'd turned him down?" I prodded gently, wanting, and needing, more.

"Sure. When I think of what happened, and what you lost." He glanced at me then gazed through the windshield, focused on a point far away. "And what I lost." He shrugged. "I only wish Hank had set me straight about Bishop sooner. About my mistaking him as the killer and not Rasmussen."

The night my parents died, Jake had gotten to the scene too late. He'd seen Oliver Bishop by the car, holding a weapon. Rasmussen had already taken off into the crowd. Jake made the wrong assumption. He'd thought for years that Bishop was the murderer. But hearing him now, so cut up and full of remorse, I could understand why Hank had kept the truth from him for so long. Jake already shouldered a lot of the blame. Why burden him with more guilt?

"If you'd known the truth, would that have changed anything?" I asked.

"No. Maybe." He sighed. "I'm not sure. I think I might not have gone..." He shook himself like a dog shaking off water. "I guess that's one of those would-a, should-a, could-a things you're always talking about. I'll never know."

He fell silent and I didn't have a chance to coax any more revelations out of him. We'd reached Time Scope headquarters, a thirty-five-story concrete-and-glass monstrosity tucked among dozens of other ugly high-rises in the city center. The TCV glided around a corner and into the parking lot. The vehicle's doors whisked open and we headed into the building.

I put my questions aside and turned my thoughts back to Rasmussen and whatever surprises Glo had in store.

WE STEPPED off the elevator and entered the Temporal Research and Information department, steering toward the director's office. Four times the size of Glo's cubbyhole, Alice Ly's bright, high-ceilinged office suite featured several towering Interface screens, standalone consoles on half a dozen desks, and not one family photo to be found. Instead, newspapers and artifacts from historical events and time periods that intrigued Alice were strewn about, covering nearly every surface.

"Is it Rasmussen?" I asked Alice the second Jake and I stepped into the room.

"That's what I like about you, Beryl," Glo said, following us in. "You skip the prologue and go to the meat of the story."

So sayeth the bluntest and most direct person I'd ever met. Glo didn't dance around a subject like Jake. She got right to the point. And she got to the point now.

"Alice's team has discovered an interesting temporal blip."

Alice, a slight, brown-haired, fortyish woman of Vietnamese and German descent, beckoned us over to a table at the center of the room. She wore the same style jumpsuit as Jake and Glo, accentuated by shiny silver hoop earrings I'd picked up when I'd chased a time runner in 1973 and had given her for her birthday.

She pushed a button on the commpad on the table. A bluish beam shot out from the screen and burst into a mass of colorful pixels. They bounced off one another like bumper cars at Six Flags then eventually fused together into a solid 3-D image hovering in midair.

The front page of an upstate New York newspaper, dated August 15, 1969, took shape. The main headline read, *Crowd Gathers for Local Concert*, and in smaller type below, *Traffic Snarls Mark Festival Start*. I handed the headline writer the understatement of the year award when I saw the accompanying photo of a massive line of stopped cars snaking along for miles on a narrow two-lane highway and an equally massive mob of people surrounding the vehicles. This wasn't just any crowd, and they hadn't jammed the New York thruway to travel to just any concert.

This was Woodstock, the largest and most famous music fest of the twentieth century.

"Earlier today," Alice said. "One of my team members doing a normal temporal scan noticed an unusual blip in the timeline for this event." She nodded at the floating newspaper. "Because of its historical significance, I ordered a thorough check, searching each minute for ripples or intrusions, or some other temporal event that could have bobbled the timeline."

She waved a finger over her commpad. The image melted, replaced with a grainy black-and-white photo-graph. Dated the next day, the picture depicted a large group of men and women, mostly white and mostly young, sardined together across a section of a gently sloping hill. Several flashed peace signs at the camera, some were on their feet, swaying to the music, arms wrapped around each other, and still others lounged on the ground, sleeping or making out.

"I didn't understand why the system set off an alert." Alice flicked her finger again and the photograph enlarged dramatically, zeroing in on two bearded men sitting close together in the center of the crowd. "Until I found this."

"Time runners?" Glo leaned in for a closer look, studying the picture with a frown that turned to surprise. "No, not runners. The image is shit, but I'm close to certain that's Kip Butterfield and Jose Luis Santos."

"And they are...?" I didn't finish and didn't need to. Glo's expression answered my question.

These men weren't ordinary time runners, people who slipped away while on a temporal vacation, intending to live out their days in the past. Ninety percent of a time cop's job was retrieving time tourists who'd overstayed their extraction date, not because the company cared about them—all clients paid in full, up front—but because of the damage a runner could do to the timeline by, say, stepping on a butterfly.

I crowded next to Glo and studied the two men closely. One wore corduroy bellbottoms and a paisley print shirt, the other jean shorts, a pocket front tee shirt, and John Lennon glasses with square frames. These guys were on the run, certainly. But not out of some mistaken nostalgia for the good old days that really weren't as good as they imagined.

They were part of Hank's crew. They'd fled into the past for the same reason Hank and my parents had.

To escape Niels Rasmussen.

"But wait, there's more," Alice said, with a smirk at me. She loved tossing out slang and pop culture references of my millennial era. She was a lot better at it than Jake, who thought I'd totally get what phrases from the 1950s like *let's agitate the gravel* and *put an egg in your shoe and beat it* would mean. Seriously, as if a 1990s kid like me would even have a clue.

Alice did another finger wave, further enlarging the

image, shifting focus to the left and an extremely fuzzy man twenty or so yards away.

"Rasmussen?" Jake asked.

"I don't know. It's hard to tell," I said. Because of the blurry image and because of Niels himself. Except for his lanky build, he was a decidedly average looking white man with no distinguishing facial features.

Alice chimed in. "Even if it's not him, my temporal scanners set off a series of alarms and flares and ripples. Pointing to this day, this place, this moment. Could simply be the fact Kip and Jose Luis got caught on camera. Or could mean there's about to be a disruption in the timeline. Something's going to happen that's not supposed to. Couldn't hurt to send a team back to see if Rasmussen is there. If he is..." She waved a hand and the photograph dissolved into a cloud of pixels that fluttered down onto the table like blue snowflakes. "...he's there for only one reason."

My stomach cramped and Jake grunted. Glo muttered a curse. "How could they do something so foolish?" she said. "They *know* they're supposed to stay out of the public eye. Stay away from anything that could call attention to them."

As in, don't get recorded or photographed. That's how I'd caught up to Rasmussen in 1946. Usually camera-shy, he'd slipped up and ended up with his face plastered on the local newspaper's front page. At the time, I had no idea who he really was, and didn't figure it out until it was almost too late.

"Cut the guys some slack," I said. "It's Woodstock. They must've thought it was worth the risk. And they're in a crowd. I mean, there had to be, what, five million people there that day?"

Alice smiled patiently and dropped a *well actually* on me. "Despite claims by many people to have been there, official estimates put attendance at only four hundred thousand that weekend."

"Okay, my bad. I don't know much about Woodstock except people were told to avoid the brown acid and the whole lollapalooza turned into Mudstock because of rain. My point is, how could they resist traveling to that cow pasture to see history? Even *with* the risk. I might've done the same thing."

"And expose *yourself* to danger, as these two have?" Jake grumped. "Finding Niels in the old west was a lucky break. This—" He gestured to where the holo-image had been. "*This* seems like a set up. Like he *let* himself be caught on camera. Could be a ploy to lure Beryl into his sights. Could be a trap."

"It could be a trap, Admiral Akbar," I said. "Or Kip and Jose Luis are in real danger. Whatever, we don't have a choice. We ignore this, and Rasmussen will do what he always does. Kill. Do you want to sacrifice those men to keep poor little me from breaking a fingernail?" Jake editorialized with a snort and I rushed on. "I know that's harsh, but you have to accept I'm in danger as long as the man is at large. And for the last time, I can take care of myself. *You* taught me how. We can't pass up this chance to get him."

Jake threw up his hands in frustration and looked to Glo.

She scowled, adding a sigh. "Beryl's right. It's a risk, but if he's discovered where and when Kip and Jose Luis are, they'll need to be extracted. If you can catch Rasmussen while you're there and bring him in, all the better." She straightened. "Let's prep for a trip to 1969. Alice, map the timeline. Get it down to the second and get them there before that picture was taken. Let's see if we can trap Niels this time."

"On it." Alice waved and a new image blossomed from her commpad, a series of wavering numbers and symbols that gave me flashbacks to high school algebra class and all the tests I'd failed.

"Be careful," Glo said to Jake, then shifted her gaze to me. "Especially *you*. And don't mess up this time."

4

With Glo's dubious pep talk ringing in my ears and Jake frowning at me like an angry papa, I went to get ready for our time trip. Gerry, the company's head costumer, insisted I try on every miniskirt and pair of go-go boots in the shop, delaying our departure for over an hour. I grew impatient with Gerry's fussing. I would've gone naked if it could speed up my next chance to face off with my nemesis.

But, though the 1960s—and Woodstock—were all about letting it all hang out, going naked wouldn't cut it, so I finally put my foot down and chose a buttercup-yellow minidress with a white Peter Pan collar and short sleeves, love beads, white tights in a diamond print, and a pair of beige lace-up shoes with low heels I could do a decent fifty-yard dash in. No pockets in the dress, so I gripped the long strap of a suede shoulder bag just large enough to hold my weapon and a tube of my favorite lipstick. As usual, my hair could not be forced into any era-appropriate hairstyle, so Gerry had wisely left it alone.

Not to be outdone, Jake walked out of his dressing room decked out in a plaid shirt, jeans with frayed cuffs, scuffed combat boots, a scraggly wig of brown hair, and an even more scraggly fake mustache.

"How do I look?" he asked, popping on a pair of aviator sunglasses.

"Groovy." Hyper-groovy, in fact. We looked like cast members of the most earnest production of the musical *Hair* ever to go on tour. Even my TDC got in on the act. Gerry had disguised my portable time travel device as a Jovial brand gold-plated and oval-shaped wristwatch.

Jake's boots thumped and my love beads clicked as we trooped to the security department's temporal transfer station, a cramped hallway adjacent to the more spacious and luxurious main temporal skip area where time tourists set out on their journeys into the past.

"Headed to Woodstock?" Mortimer said as we stopped at the armory to pick up our weapons. "Sounds fun."

Sounds like a root canal, his tone said. A spare, fifty-something guy with a beaky nose, Mortimer had little interest in time travel or history. Or books, even. I'd learned that in the beginning when I'd launched a get-to-know-my-coworkers charm offensive and quickly discovered a number of them only saw this job as a paycheck, and not as the thrill ride of an adventure I did.

I kept the chitchat to a mumbled, "Yup, fun," and tucked the stinger Mortimer handed me into my shoulder bag. Jake opted for the larger and more powerful TV remote-shaped cack .22, though I preferred the smaller, easier to conceal stinger that looked like a 1950s sci-fi movie ray gun.

Paperwork complete and fully armed, we moved on to the row of temporal oscillators lined up the length of the hallway. I called the gleaming boxes time coffins, due to their grim shape and claustrophobic interior. We stopped at bay T-2, my preferred time machine.

Jake steadied me as a rumble shook the hallway, followed by the hiss of decompression. Oscillator T-3 popped open and Elspeth Holmes popped out. A relative newbie time cop, Holmes reached into the darkness behind her and hauled a jowl-cheeked middle-aged man out of the machine. Both were dressed to impress a 1910s crowd, Elspeth wearing a satin gown and white gloves, her companion in white tie, tailcoat, and waistcoat with a gold watch chain.

"Caught another time perp trying to rob the Titanic." Holmes tipped her head toward her prisoner, who walked with a telltale just-been-zapped stagger. "It's become my regular beat."

She led the woozy man past us, and Jake and I got back to work. He punched in a code, activating T-2. The time coffin's doors spread open like a hawk's mouth, eager to welcome us into its hungry gullet. We could've travelled with site-to-site temporal skip via our TDC devices, but the oscillator was faster and more reliable.

Didn't make the time skip any more pleasant. The shimmering protective shield that enveloped me the second the doors snapped shut reminded me of that. The machine booted up with a steady *clank-clank-clank*, like a rollercoaster car struggling up the tracks to the top of the first hill. I held my breath as I did when I'd ridden one of those death contraptions as a kid, both anticipating and dreading the moment we'd sail over the edge and plunge downward into the abyss.

The energy shield squeezed tighter, the clanking hammered my ears, and fire and ice chased each other through my veins. Tiny knives seemed to jab into my skin as the temporal vortex whipped up then spun and pulled like an F-5 tornado, peeling my atoms apart bit by bit into a million pieces of Beryl. A hell of a ride that ended soon, but not soon enough for me.

The tornado ebbed, my atoms slapped back together, and the vortex spit us out into the past, in a discreet location where our landing wouldn't be seen. In this instance, I flopped to the ground beside Jake behind a row of port-a-potties. I smelled them before I saw them. Going to Woodstock, I figured I'd catch the scent of sweaty bodies and cigarettes and marijuana drifting on the breeze, but this was one part of the experience I'd rather do without.

After we got our bearings and, at least for me, the world stopped spinning, we strolled into the open and a steamy and overcast day. Jake flipped open the cover of what appeared to be a hardcover copy of the book *Catch 22*, but really had a combo commpad-slash-time machine known as a Kicker disguised within. He tapped the screen and the text of American bombardier Captain John Yossarian's World War II misadventures faded, replaced with the Kicker's GPS.

"Alice's calculations give us five minutes before the temporal blip occurs," Jake said, pointing the way through the sea of bodies gathered on the hillside. "An ensemble called Santana is playing now." He jerked his chin toward the wooden stage in the distance, flanked by massive speaker towers and lights. The tiny figures of Carlos Santana and his band were barely visible. "As far as Alice could determine, a song called 'Evil Ways' was playing when the photograph was taken."

I didn't know the song, but the title seemed appropriate for Rasmussen and what he planned to do today. If we couldn't get to Kip and Jose Luis first.

We hurried to our destination, and by that I mean we slipped and slid. According to the notes Alice had loaded into our mission specs, we'd been dropped here in between Woodstock's famous rainstorms. It had drizzled through the night and into the morning, leaving the ground and grass sopping wet and churned into mud by thousands of pairs of feet. The waterworks had ceased for the moment, and the sun tried to peek through the gray clouds, but the real flood was still to come.

We sloshed past hippies, yippies, and flower children in long hair and sideburns. At least one man appeared to be naked, but most were decked out in the threads of their generation, tie-dyed shirts, jeans or shorts, minidresses and maxi-dresses. And love beads. Lots of love beads. The murmur of conversation, singing, and laughter rose and fell across the crowd. On stage, the musicians gave it their all, pumping out Santana's signature Latin-fused rock.

I wished I could take the time to soak it all in, but I had to focus. While Jake navigated our way toward the temporal ex-pats, I searched the mob of psychedelic prints and flowered caftans for Rasmussen. Not an easy task. There had to be a thousand people swarming this section of the hillside alone.

Jake looked up from the Kicker. "That way. Almost

there." He steered me upward. We stepped over a sleeping man and Jake pointed again. "Over there."

They sat on a tan blanket spread over the ground, grooving to the tunes. Both men were gorgeous—Kip, pale and blond, looked like he stepped off a yacht in Newport, and with his smooth brown skin, dark hair, and trimmed beard, Jose Luis could've been a runway model circa 1969.

We waded toward them. I kept my focus to the left and the crest of the hill where Rasmussen was supposed to appear. The muck and mud had slowed us down and we didn't have much time to reach our targets before Niels crashed the Woodstock party.

We reached the men and Jake dropped the Time Scope version of The Terminator's *come with me if you want to live*. "Jake Tyson, Time Scope security. Prepare for extraction."

Both men shot to their feet. "What the hell?" Kip spat.

Exactly what I would blurt to such a blunt command. Poor Jake. Subtlety was not in his DNA. These guys had ditched their lives in Futureworld and everyone they knew to run away from the big bad wolf's murder spree. They had no idea the time-traveling assassin had caught up to them. But we didn't have time to wine and dine them and explain the situation fully before dragging them home.

"We'll give you the details later." I raised my voice to be heard over the music and cheers and crowd noise. "But you need to come with us now."

The men exchanged fraught glances. "We're not leaving," Jose Luis said. "This is our home now." He gestured to the stage then back to Kip. "This is our place in time."

Admirable, but risky given the circumstance. "You could be in danger. Rasmussen—"

That's when I spotted him. He snaked through the crowd at the top of the hill like a python on the hunt. He wore an outfit similar to a thousand other men here, a dark blue tee shirt and a pair of faded jeans, and except for his forty-something age, he blended in. I could just make out the weapon clutched in his hand. Not the Colt he'd brandished at the stagecoach passengers. Somehow, he'd gotten his hands on a cack .22.

Jake saw him too. We acted fast to protect our time runners. I hip-checked Kip out of the way. Jake pushed Jose Luis to the ground, then cried, "Beryl, get down."

Too late. Rasmussen fired.

The laser stream blasted out of the weapon. A kill shot. I could tell by the beam's pinkish tinge, indicating a charge a thousand times more powerful than a stun beam. The searing pulse shot over the heads of the crowd and dug into the dirt between my feet. Intense heat singed my ankles, burning a hole through the leg of my tights. I gaped down at the acrid smoke coiling around my legs and my blood pressure went volcanic.

Only one thing had saved my innards from being liquefied into pudding. A young Black woman in a yellow dress and poufy Afro had bumped into Rasmussen as he punched the trigger, disrupting his aim and knocking the cack from his hand.

"Lightning!" someone shouted, and the concert crowd morphed from mellow to panicked in a flash. Screams rang out and people surged outward in a circle like when a boulder hits water. A guy with linebacker shoulders slammed into Jake, who stumbled and tripped over Jose

Luis, still on the ground. Jake fell, landing face first in the mud with a splat.

At the top of the hill, a furious Niels frantically searched the ground for his weapon, lost and trampled underfoot. Despite my trembling, I went into action. I leapt over Jake, still floundering in the mud, and dashed upward.

Niels saw me and he took off. I shoved people out of the way and raced after him as fast as I could up the wet and slippery hillside. I silently cursed him, and my own arrogance. And Jake for always being right. This whole thing was a trap. Rasmussen had deliberately caused the time ripple that led Alice to conduct a search that brought me here—so he could kill me.

If not for the young woman who'd jostled Rasmussen's elbow, he would have.

At the top of the hill, I slowed and anxiously searched the crowd, fearing I'd lost him. Only for a moment. I saw him push through the mob and onto a relatively mud-free path not far away. He broke into a run. I did too. As Carlos Santana and the band launched into their next song, and the concertgoers swayed to the music on a cloud of pot fumes and mellow vibes, I chased him. I ran so fast my lungs burned and I gasped for air. My love beads bounced, my shoes thumped the ground, and my handbag bumped against my hip.

We rounded a bend. The crowd thinned out then winnowed down to a few stragglers ducking into the woods for a potty break or concertgoers coming back from skinny-dipping in the lake just visible through the trees. I tugged my stinger from my bag and armed it as I raced along the path. The *stun* or *kill* question flashed into my mind again but I pushed it aside. I'd figure that out when I got within firing range. The important thing was to catch him.

I drew closer. Close enough to see him fiddling with his wristwatch TDC as he ran. My belly seized. He was going to time skip and slip through my fingers again. I dug down for a burst of energy and sprinted after him at a speed that could qualify me for the Olympics.

I closed the distance between us, but not enough. He pressed some buttons and a shaft of blue light shot out from his TDC, followed by a hard gust of wind that shoved me back and whipped dirt into my face. *Shit*. The vortex had already formed around him. In a moment, it would pull him in and he'd be gone.

Running hard, I activated the voice control on my own wrist device. "Sarah, initiate Tokyo Drift," I said. Sarah being my Interface connection I named for my favorite time-bending badass, Sarah Conner, and Tokyo Drift for what the crew in temporal tech called dual stream travel. If I could boot up my TDC in time, I could latch onto Rasmussen's vortex stream like surfing on a meteor's tail and skip right along with him. An impulsive move and not the best idea I ever had. I'd never tried the maneuver before, and from what I'd heard, such a jump could be dangerous.

But... I would *not* let this jackhole get away from me again.

A mini blue cyclone shot out from my TDC. My arm sagged as if a thousand-pound weight pressed it down. Threads of light sparked from my device and latched onto Rasmussen's time tornado like grasping fingers.

"Far out," a naked man speckled with mud exclaimed

as we flew past him, both of us enveloped by an undulating and shimmering blue cloud.

Rasmussen threw an angry glance at me over his shoulder, but it was too late to terminate the skip. His temporal stream surged then his entire being collapsed into nothingness as he was sucked into the vortex, dragging me along. My breath left my body. My feet left the ground. The stream held me in a choking hold. Then, a sharp tug yanked me forward and I followed Niels into the abyss.

The last thing I saw of 1969 was Jake, barreling up the road after me, and gaping in terror as the time tunnel swallowed me up.

IF A MASS of atoms shooting through the temporal void could scream, mine would have. Tokyo drifting on Rasmussen's tail was less like Wendy soaring on stardust across the sky with Peter Pan and more like latching on to the bumper of a city bus and surfing glass-strewn streets in bare feet.

Painful. Really painful.

Worse, I could feel my host's rage at my tagging along uninvited. It kicked me in the head. Repeatedly. When we closed in on our destination and our beings began to solidify, he kicked me for real, but not before he reached out with a wavering and rubbery arm and ripped my TDC from my wrist.

My vortex buckled. Our streams broke apart. I fell out of the sky and smacked against a hard surface with a painful thud. My shoulder blades screamed in pain. My head spanked the ground. My handbag's long strap had twisted around my neck and tried to strangle me. My necklace string snapped and love beads hit the floor, scattering in all directions like colorful bugs.

Great plan, Beryl.

I lay there a moment, stunned. When my head stopped spinning and my eyes uncrossed, I freed myself from my bag's stranglehold and sat up, eyeing my surroundings. I was no longer outside. I sprawled on the floor of a broad hallway with shiplap walls that would make an *HGTV* home decorator drool. My stinger had torn from my grip during reentry and landed at the foot of a pair of narrow doors directly across from me, with signs reading *Ladies* and *Gents* hanging overhead.

Also across the way—Rasmussen.

He'd burst sideways out of the vortex and skidded to a stop in a sitting position against the opposite wall. His skin had paled to a sickly white and his head lolled, his eyes unfocused. He looked bruised from our bumpy ride, but not as battered as me. My limbs ached, my head throbbed, and I panted like a dog on a hot day, struggling to catch my breath.

"I said I wanted you to join me in my travels," he said, touching the back of his head and wincing in pain. "But hopping into my stream is not what I had in mind."

"Didn't you just try to kill me like, two minutes ago?" I flicked a glance toward my weapon, on the floor about six feet away. Reachable, if I had the ability to move. "Make up your mind, Niels. Do you want to travel with me or kill me?"

"Whatever will hurt Hank the most."

There it was. Without hesitation. A blunt, vengeful

statement that would've knocked the breath out of me if Rasmussen didn't choose that moment to lunge for my stinger. Though still woozy, I scrambled to stop him. Glass love beads bit into my skin as I scuttled across the hallway on my hands and knees. Before he could grab the weapon, I seized his hand and gave it a twist that would've snapped his wrist if I had more leverage. He recoiled with a yelp. I tried to snatch his TDC, a steam-punk-ish device with a wide strap and a bulbous sphere, but he shot to his feet and bolted down the corridor into the room beyond.

Cursing under my breath, I scooped up my stinger, blinked away the last of the time skip's cobwebs, and found myself chasing him yet again.

I rushed out of the hallway and into a smoky cave that smelled like a twelve-keg frat party. A jukebox blasted a fiddle-heavy country song called "Smoke, Smoke, Smoke That Cigarette." A smattering of men of varying ages in cotton work uniforms did as the song instructed. They puffed away as they huddled over tall beers at a long wooden bar. Even more men hunkered down at tables and booths that filled the tight space. A dark-haired wait-ress in a low-cut top and tight black skirt carried a tray of beer bottles across the room.

How far had we traveled from Woodstock? And when? This sure wasn't the hippie crowd that thronged the hill at Max Yasgur's farm. These were hard hats and factory workers who shook their fists at the kids running around protesting the America they should love or leave.

Rasmussen hadn't slowed down to speculate. He shoved through the tables and raced across the room. I charged after him. The waitress and a couple of the men looked up as we flew by, but the rest were too thoroughly engaged in their liquor to notice.

The bar area opened into a larger space, a restaurant, empty and dark, not yet open or closed for the day. Wooden chairs with thick legs were upended onto the tables ranging around the room. Heavy, salmon-pink curtains were draped over the windows, giving the place a Mae West's boudoir feel.

Rasmussen slowed, his head swiveling until he spotted the exit.

"Stop!" I cried. I didn't think or strategize. I acted. I aimed the stinger in his general direction and fired. Missed by a country kilometer, as Glo would say. A blast of cold air and a burst of daylight rushed into the room as Niels threw the door wide and disappeared outside.

I groaned. My impulsive decision to ride on his vortex coattails had gone from bad to worse to the very, very worst. I should've gone after him. He had my TDC. My only way home from... wherever we'd landed. But I couldn't chase him. Couldn't prevent him from escaping again.

I had a bigger problem to deal with.

I'd missed Rasmussen, but the scorching laser pulse had found a target. A flammable target—the drapes covering the window closest to the door. Fed by the air that had whooshed in when Niels rushed out, a flame burst to life. I gaped in horror as the fire quickly ate up the curtain and licked upward like climbing a rope, searing the wall and the ceiling above.

I snapped into action. I stuffed my stinger into my handbag and snatched up a tablecloth from a pile stacked on top of a nearby chair. "Fire! Fire!" I yelled, frantically beating at the flames.

My shouting yielded results in an instant. The waitress and several men pounded over, one of them armed with a fire extinguisher, a heavy thing that looked to be made of brass. The man spared me a glare then got to work. A pale-yellow substance with a sharp but sweet odor squirted from the hose he aimed at the flames. The fire hissed its displeasure as the blaze sputtered out.

I sagged against a table and gasped for breath, coughing from smoke and the fire extinguisher's acrid chemicals. Flooded with relief.

For a moment.

The ad hoc fireman dropped the extinguisher and grabbed my arms, jerking them behind my back.

"Bob, call the police," he ordered over his shoulder. "Tell them we've caught an arsonist."

5

I had company in the jail's holding cell, a buxom blonde pushing fifty named Gladys, who wore a slinky red dress and a pancake hat perched jauntily on the side of her head. She smoked a long, thin cigarette and had to be wearing a full gallon of perfume. A delightful scent compared to the one drifting over from the grizzled man curled up and snoring on a bench in the other cell. His shabby suit smelled as if he'd rolled in dog poo. Looked that way too.

Not that I had any right to criticize. My appearance was equally disheveled—my mod minidress rumpled and dirty, my stockings shredded, hair full of soot. Plus, I reeked like a forest fire Smokey the Bear had been unable to prevent.

Seemed about right for me, Beryl Blue, Futureworld's most inept time cop.

Ten minutes ago, a burly policeman in a thick wool coat and equally thick Boston accent had clipped a pair of handcuffs around my wrists and hauled me away from the crime scene. A wall of frigid air hit me as soon as we'd stepped outside into the cold. New England winter cold. As in, temperatures in the twenties, a frosty breeze, an unsettled gray sky, and the smell of snow in the air. And me, dressed for summer in nothing but a minidress and tights. My legs instantly froze. My exposed arms didn't fare much better.

While the patrons of the bar I'd almost burned down watched from the front steps and passing pedestrians stopped to gawk, the cop gripped my upper arm and tugged me to the curb.

"Into the paddy wagon you go," he'd said, and hoisted me into a boxy police van. *Paddy wagon*. An archaic and derogatory term that would surely offend my Irish relatives. If I had any.

After a bumpy ride in that cold box, my cop friend led me into a multi-level brown brick building through a door marked *City Jail*. Inside, the entire precinct ogled my legs as I was booked and relieved of my handbag, with the stinger inside, then hustled into a chilly cell with my perfume-drenched cellmate demanding to know what I was in for.

I shivered from the cold but burned inside. What was I in for? For being really, really bad at my job, for starters. I'd been all *you go, Beryl*, when I'd chased after Niels at Woodstock. Time cop of the year, about to take down Time Scope's most wanted villain single-handed.

Satisfaction that had lasted exactly two seconds. He'd escaped, just as he'd escaped all the other times before. What's more, he'd gotten my TDC. My side still ached from the kick he'd given me when he'd torn the device from my wrist and booted me out of our shared vortex.

He'd stolen my only way home, the only way I could contact HQ. Then he abandoned me.

I paced across the cell to the barred window, eye-level with the sidewalk of a city street. Well, not exactly *abandoned*. I kind of knew where he'd left me, and I had a rough idea of when. The glimpse I'd gotten of my surroundings before I'd been shoved into the police van had given me a clue. The view outside the jail confirmed it. Women in winter hats bustled past, their spectator pumps tapping the pavement. Men in suits with baggy pants and high waists accompanied them. Old-timey cars chugged along the street or were parked in front of a number of downtown office buildings. Familiar buildings.

I shuffled over to the rough wooden bench against the wall and sank down next to my cellmate. "What year is it?" I asked.

Gladys took a long pull on her cigarette then exhaled a plume of bluish smoke straight up, like a chimney. "You don't know? You been on a benda, sista?" she said in a Massachusetts accent totally devoid of the letter *R*. She accessorized her questions with a gaze that swept over me, head to toe, taking in every inch of my groovy threads. "Musta been a dilly of binge for you to end up in the joint in ya nightgown."

"Please. Just tell me."

Her gaze turned tender, almost motherly. "Poor kid. I've had days like you're having. Couldn't even remember my own name." She brushed a lock of frizzy hair out of her eyes, scattering ashes like smoky snowflakes. "It's the year of our lord, nineteen hundred and forty-seven."

"Nineteen... forty-seven."

"Not for much longer. It's almost Christmas. It'll be the new year before you know it." She took another deep drag, another release of chimney smoke. "And look at me, none of my shopping done and stuck in the jug with a glamour puss who don't even know what day it is."

The bench creaked softly as I stood. I dragged over to the cell door and gripped the bars, holding tight. In the jail's outer room, the cops on duty went about their business. Their voices rose and fell, telephones rang, typewriters clacked, and the men clomped around like a herd of clumsy buffalo.

According to the murky data Alice and her team of research rats had assembled, sometime between the years 1947 and 1954, Sully would die, doing what he did best, protecting someone. In this case, me. Did Rasmussen know of Sully's grim destiny? Had Niels brought me here to make it happen? Possibly, though he didn't have much time to program the skip, and he was mighty pissed off that I'd piggybacked on his temporal stream. Perhaps fate or whatever force that enjoyed messing with Sully and me could be the culprit.

My thoughts turned as gray and dark as the winter day outside. Whatever the answer, I'd been stranded here in 1947, without a ride home. In Ballard Springs, where Sully lived. In the police station. Where Sully worked.

I cocked my head and listened, trying to find his deep, smooth jazz kind of voice in the group in the outer room. I knew he'd be there. We *would* meet again. It couldn't be a coincidence I'd been dropped into this time and this place. As Glo often said, there were no coincidences in time travel.

Fate made sure of it.

IT DIDN'T TAKE LONG. In only a few minutes, his voice joined the chat beyond the holding cell's door.

"Sarge, we been waiting for you to get back," one of the cops said.

"Yeah? What's the ruckus?" Sully asked. My girl parts went all tingly and alive at the rumble of his voice.

"A ruckus of the female kind," another man said. "You gotta see this doll Joe Moran brought in. She's a firebug. Nearly burned Scotty's Bar and Grille to the ground."

Not exactly to the ground, more like a seared patch on one wall. But still... I cringed at the damage, and at the thought of what could've happened.

Sully's concern didn't match mine. "Is that so?" he said with mild interest.

"Nicest pair of pins I ever seen," a cop with a squeaky voice piped up. "She's real screwy, though. Seems like we should take her up to the city nut house, not stick her in a holding cell. We figured we'd let you decide on that when you got back."

"Aren't you fellas thoughtful," Sully replied, slightly more interested in the topic. "What makes this girl so special?"

Squeaky voice chortled. "She ain't wearing nothing but a slip, for starters. Plus, she's got a toy gun in her pocketbook. Like what I seen in a Buck Rogers picture I took my nephew to. Here, look."

A heavy pause, followed by an urgent, "Is she a curvy dame with brown hair?"

Sully didn't wait for an answer. His broad shoulders

filled the doorway seconds later. Three quick strides and he reached me at the barred door.

"Beryl," he murmured.

I drank in every inch of him. In his timeline, it'd been a year and a half since we'd parted. He'd had one—no, *two*—birthdays since then. At twenty-eight, he was even more scrumptious than when we'd met. His police uniform wasn't much different from the dress uniform of his Army days, only blue, with shiny buttons and a leather belt with a strap that crossed his chest and over his right shoulder. He looked like a tough guy hero in an old movie with his strong jaw, sapphire-blue eyes framed by wisdom lines, the deep dimple in his chin, and his broad nose with a scar across the bridge.

He looked me over too, his gaze steady and cool. Sergeant Poker Face, as usual, revealing nothing. Except for his left eyebrow. It rose, ever so slightly, and... *Sigh*. I could write a sonnet about that beautiful thing if I had the slightest interest in poetry. Dark red, the color of a copper penny, the same shade as his hair, and very expressive, like some kind of emotion-o-meter. Right now, his eyebrow expressed surprise and delight. With a hint of suspicion.

He reached between the thick iron bars and took my hands. "Jesus, you're as cold as a popsicle." His gaze dipped to my short skirt and torn-up tights. He scowled. "No wonder. I suppose they've stopped wearing trousers where you're from?"

I responded with a gurgle that landed somewhere between a laugh and a sob. Oh, how I'd missed that scowl. Almost as much as I'd missed him. And I wasn't so cold now. The warmth of his hands holding mine seeped into my skin and shot through my blood, igniting that old fire that burned like an inferno whenever we touched. Whenever he was near.

"I hoped to see you again," he said, his voice tender and aching. "I'm glad to see you. Over the moon." He brushed his thumbs over my knuckles. "But why? What're you doing here?"

"It's a long story."

"It's *always* a long story with you." He squeezed my hands then let go, scowling again. "Go ahead. Spit it out."

"Well…" I looked back at Gladys on the bench. She took a long, considering drag on her cigarette, watching us keenly. "I was chasing a runner." I lowered my voice. "Not an ordinary runner."

"Was this before or after you tried to burn down Scotty's bar?"

"During. But I plead not guilty to that, with an explanation."

He laughed, a barrel-deep, whiskey-smooth sound that rumbled in his chest and wrung me out. "Oh, I missed you, Beryl." He glanced over his shoulder toward the open door and the chattering cop crowd beyond. "Let's see what I need to do to bust you out of here."

"No," I said in an urgent whisper. "You should leave me here and you know why. I'm safe here." I gave him a pleading look. "*You're* safe with me in here, locked up tight."

His left eyebrow skirted up again, annoyed this time. "You're coming with me, Beryl, no argument. None of that fate and destiny mumbo jumbo. I'm getting you out of here and bringing you home with me."

"Home? That's ridiculous—"

"You can take *me* home, handsome," Gladys said. "I plead not guilty with an explanation, too. I didn't nip Gino Tancredi's wallet. It just jumped into my purse."

"No judge is gonna buy that one, Gladys."

Sully's eyes twinkled at her. She sighed. The guy stretched out on the bench in the other cell turned over and sighed. I sighed, too, and melted into a puddle of goo. And why not? Sully had charm to spare.

"As for you, Beryl, no argument. I'm getting you out of here. Then you can catch me up on what you've been up to and why you're here."

———

Minutes later, Sully steered me across the snow-dusted parking lot behind the police station to his car. A 1941 Plymouth Super Deluxe Coupe he'd bought at a bargain, he informed me as he opened the door for me to get in. He started the engine and the dashboard heater puffed out warm air. I turned to him, but I didn't catch him up on what I'd been doing. I didn't tell him the whole tragic tale of how I ended up stranded in Ballard Springs, either.

We didn't speak at all. We had more important catching up to do, of the nonverbal variety.

If I could write a sonnet about Sully's eyebrow, nothing less than an epic poem would do to describe his kisses. When he drew me into his arms and his lips found mine, I was transported to another world, one populated by only us. He kissed me and my body woke up after all this time waiting for him, wanting his touch. Everything else melted away, all my worries and fears, and time and destiny too, replaced by need. For him and only him.

A long, long time later, we parted. But he didn't release me. He held me close with one arm encircling my shoulders, his free hand holding mine, our fingers laced together.

"I knew you'd come back to me," he murmured, his warm breath tickling my ear. "But did it have to take so damned long?"

"I missed you too," I said, snuggling against him. He'd found a woman's coat somewhere in the police station, a scratchy wool fabric in hunter green, with oversized lapels, buttons the size of salad plates, and smelling like beer, cigarettes, and the sour scent of old perfume. But it was warm, and he was warm, and I was with him and that was all that mattered.

For now.

"Tell me what's going on," he said, with a gentle kiss to my temple. "Give it to me straight down the line, no lies or sidetracks."

"I would never."

He chuckled. "You would *always*."

That had once been true. I'd lied and sidetracked and invented stories to keep Sully from learning about time travel. In my defense, Time Scope had mandated the lies. The number one rule of time travel club was don't talk about time travel club. Well, the second rule, actually. The real number one, the hard and unbreakable top temporal commandment remained the one that agonized me most. The past is a fixed event, unable to be changed. Attempting to do so risked imploding the timeline and creating a future filled with paradox chaos.

But I'd lied enough where Sully was concerned and had promised him—and myself—to tell him the truth from now on. I wasn't about to break my promise.

So, I told him everything about my recent misadventures. The whole frustrating story, from losing Rasmussen in the 1880s, to Woodstock, to landing here in Ballard Springs, and even the embarrassing stuff, like the fire, and Niels tearing my TDC from my wrist. Sully listened intently, and except to ask what a hippie was and to growl angrily when I mentioned Ras kicking me, he didn't interrupt.

My legs had all but thawed out by the time I reached the story's exciting conclusion. "He got away. Again. Where to is the question. He could've run off into the city or he could've hopped into the vortex and skipped into another era."

I tried to convince myself Niels had done the latter, and abandoned me not knowing Sully lived here, thinking I'd molder away in this time period with no allies, no friends, and no way to skip, leaving him free to plunder across time. Because if he'd stayed, the danger to Sully would increase a whole hell of a lot.

"Now, I'm here." I gestured out the window toward the busy street at the end of the parking lot. "Without a ride home, an arson charge hanging over my head, and a time-traveling assassin on the loose." Sully still had his arm around my shoulders. He squeezed me with a one-armed hug. I leaned into that hug and sighed. "If anything could go wrong on this mission, it sure has. Murphy's Law in action."

"Murphy's what?"

"Murphy's Law. Oh, never mind." Perhaps that old

saying wasn't as old as I thought. "Thanks for busting me out of jail, sergeant, but now, I don't know what to do. Unless I come up with some way to contact my friends two hundred years from now, I'm stuck."

He nuzzled my ear. "Is being stuck here so bad?"

"*Mmmm*... No." Anxiety bubbled in my belly, and I tore free from his oh-so-enticing embrace. "*Yes*. Me being here is a dangerous situation with fatal consequences. You're in danger, as long as I'm here and we're together. That's why I told you to leave me in jail."

His lips drew down in a frustrated frown, like we'd been through this too many times and he wasn't going to argue the point again. "Didn't we decide if you ever got back to me, we'd fight whatever the threat is together?"

We had. But that was at a time when I thought I could figure out what the threat was. I didn't expect to end up back here with him, emptyhanded, and without a plan.

"Listen, Beryl, in my view, you lose the war if you fear the battle. If we go into this, united, ready for anything, we'll be okay." He took my hands and held them in a firm but comforting grip. "I put my neck on the line for strangers back in the war. I took risks for dopes who didn't have enough sense to duck when getting shot at. If you think I'm gonna shy away from danger when it comes after someone I love, someone I couldn't stop loving if I tried, then you've got another think coming."

He ended this midcentury version of *do you even know me?* with a dramatic *got it?* lift of his eyebrow. I got it. Actually, I couldn't argue with it, mostly because I couldn't speak. Could there be a romance hero to be found in any book in any library anywhere who was braver or more protective than him? Or more reckless?

"You know, Sergeant Sullivan, I believe you'd pick up and relocate Mount Everest just because someone said you couldn't. You are one stubborn mule."

"Takes one to know one, Miss Blue." He released my hands and slid across the seat to settle behind the steering wheel. "Now, no more bellyaching or worry or any of your time paradox booshwa. You're coming home with me. We'll get you some decent clothes that won't cause a riot at church, and then we'll figure out a way to put you in contact with your future friends."

"Wait. Don't you live with your brother?" The last time we'd been together, Sully told me he lived with his kid brother Pat, home from the Navy and attending school at the nearby Army camp on the GI Bill. "He may not like you bringing a strange woman home with no warning."

"He'll be fine with it," Sully said with a confident wave.

I fiddled with the big buttons on my borrowed coat, weighing my limited options. I was stuck, and until I could figure out how to get in touch with Glo and Jake so they could help get me unstuck, I would need a place to stay. Sully wouldn't let me just wander off to sleep in an alley. The prospect of cuddling—and more—with him for the next day or so was tempting. Very, very tempting. Though I doubted I would relax until I had a TDC strapped to my wrist again and I was gone and Sully was safe, I had no choice but to agree.

"Do you promise me you'll watch your back, especially when we're together?"

He flashed one of his infamous *I won* grins. "I *always* watch my back. Second nature to me now. I'll watch your back too." His gaze roved over me, a slow, searing trail from my ankles to my lips. "And every other part, too."

He punctuated this ridiculousness with a smirk I suspected he thought was sexy but really made him look like a drunken wolf. Sully had a lot of skills. He could bench press a cow, he could be as gentle as a baby's breath with people who were hurting, and he could send me into dizzying heights of pleasure with a single touch. But flirty seduction? Not so much.

I reached to buckle the nonexistent seatbelt as he steered the car out of the parking lot. As his Plymouth puttered along the street, I studied him out of the corner of my eye. I loved him. Body and soul. Shocking to admit. Beryl Blue didn't fall in love. I'd always been about running away, especially from that four-letter word.

Then, along came Sully.

Our fine romance started in a typical romance novel way. I didn't like him. Not at all. He was bossy and sarcastic, a trifle sexist, and have I mentioned his bossiness? The man kept getting in my way, determined to help me out of a jam, to save me when I was supposed to save him during that godawful test Hank had cooked up. The annoyance was mutual on Sully's end. He didn't trust me. Was suspicious of me every minute. We'd bickered and bantered through that adventure, while the sparks flew faster and hotter than a final exam in welding school.

He stared ahead at the road with his jaw set firmly. Daylight waned and dusk came in. A pale blue sheen from the dashboard light brushed his face. My heart swelled, remembering those days when we'd first met and how hard and how fast I'd fallen for him. How I'd fallen for his courage, his protectiveness, and, not going to lie, for his very broad shoulders. But most of all, I fell in love with *him*. A hero. A man I could trust, a man I could count on, one hundred percent.

He noticed me looking and reached for my hand, bringing it to his lips. He kissed my knuckles softly, then murmured, "I know you're worried, sweetheart. There's trouble ahead, but you know I'm gonna do whatever it takes to fix it."

I shivered, and not from the cold. *Whatever it takes to fix it.* Sully's motto and mantra and catchphrase all rolled into one. Admirable in the extreme. That confidence and determination got him through the war. That strength and courage fueled him and sustained his one goal in life —to help.

But such a selfless philosophy could be dangerous. Especially when fate puts a target on your back.

6

Sully's car cruised along the city's streets. The headlights beamed on the darkening pavement. I nestled back against the seat, determined to follow his orders and put my worries aside and enjoy our fleeting time together. The car's heater huffed in uneven, sporadic gusts across my legs, helping me to relax.

"Ballard Springs sure looks different since the last time I was here," I said, gazing out the window.

Not an exaggeration. The city we'd seen on our jeep jaunt through downtown in 1943 had been bursting with wartime energy. Back then, patriotic bunting fluttered from buildings and blacked-out streetlights. Posters in store windows urged housewives to collect waste fats and explore the joys of canning one's own vegetables. Shoppers had clutched their ration books, hoping to get the last sack of sugar at the grocer's. And, with Camp Davis Army base not far away, the streets had been mobbed with GIs on weekend leave.

Now, all signs of the war years were gone. Pedestrians

clogged the sidewalks, but only a few were in uniform. Plows had pushed snow from a recent storm into soot-coated piles along the curb. Store windows blazed with lights, both regular and of the Christmas variety. Advertising signs touted washing machines, vacuum cleaners, and that newfangled invention, televisions, all made in the USA and all in abundant supply. Shiny new cars of every make and model rumbled by, in a variety of colors, churned off the production line in Detroit by the minute.

"The last time you were here, I thought you were a spy," Sully said, flashing me a glance. "Not a good spy, the way you lied and bumbled about."

"I did *not* bumble about." But I did lie. A lot. "Now I'm a suspected arsonist. Is that a step up or a step down?"

His eyebrow hiked up in amusement. "Don't fret over the arson charge. I arranged to have the boys lose your booking sheet."

"Won't that get you in trouble?"

"So what? Could liven things up some. Not all of us cops work a beat as exciting as yours."

"Really? I like to think being Sergeant Sullivan of Ballard Springs would be a pulse-pounding thrill ride."

He snorted. "Not even close. It's nothing but paperwork and writing reports. Settling petty squabbles, escorting ducklings across the road."

"Okay, Robert McCloskey. You're pouring it on a little thick."

He smiled. He didn't do that often. He frowned sometimes, lobbed the occasional smolder, indulged in copious eyebrow gymnastics, and of course a scowl was his go-to look, a brooding, dark, and way, way sexy scowl. But a smile? He didn't deploy that as often as I would like.

Especially a happy, somewhat content smile like this one that curved his tempting lips and softened his rugged features. It looked good on him.

"Guess I am bellyaching some," he said, easing the car to a stop at a red light. "It hasn't been a bad life. Just... dull." He glanced at me, smiling again. "Not so dull now, with you here."

The light turned green. He cruised through the intersection and steered the car into a perpendicular parking space, with the front end facing the curb. As a woman who couldn't parallel park if the devil sat in the passenger seat threatening me with a red-hot pitchfork, I wondered where this clever traffic invention had been all my life.

"I've got to pick up a few things before we head home," he said, answering my question before I could ask. He gestured through the windshield to a broad storefront with a green awning above the entrance and blocky letters etched into the granite over the door reading, *Main Street Drug & Notions*. "I need to pick up some..." His cheeks blushed as red as a ripe strawberry. "I mean, if you're staying with me, I'll need some... supplies."

"O-h-h-h, *supplies*," I said, with a coy grin. In other words, he'd stopped here to buy some condoms. Had he been... How would they put it back in these more demure and puritanical days? Had he remained true to me in the time we'd been apart? I sure had. Too hung up on Sully and the dim hope we could find a way to be together forever to open myself up to someone new.

Not that anyone could measure up to him, anyway. In any way.

He leaned toward me and ran his thumb along my jaw, mischief in his eyes. "Yeah, supplies. And coffee. I want to make sure there's plenty on hand. I know how much you love the stuff. Is it still rationed in your time? Or have they lifted the restriction?"

"Eh, no. They haven't."

And doubtfully ever would. I'd eventually have to explain about all the icky things we humans had done to the planet that caused so many problems in Futureworld, but not now. I couldn't focus now, not with the way he gazed at me and how his hand had found its way inside my borrowed coat and gently cupped my breast. A fire ignited in my core, heating me to scorching and eliminating all need for coffee or anything of the hot beverage variety.

"Buy all the coffee and... supplies you can get your hands on," I whispered, my voice going all Lauren Bacall *you know how to whistle, don't you?* husky and suggestive.

"I'll leave the car running. Only be a minute." He kissed me then leapt out of the vehicle and practically galloped into the drugstore.

Chilly air had crept inside when he'd opened the car door, cooling my raging fire a little, but not tempering my anticipation in the slightest. I sat back, waiting for his return, watching the crowd hustle past on the sidewalk. Men and women in business attire, heading home from work. Shoppers, carrying packages wrapped in Christmas paper. A woman in a coat buttoned tightly over her pregnant belly held a child by the hand. Teenagers trooped by, traveling in packs as they often do. Most of the people were white, but a few were not, reminding me of the city's pockets of diversity.

Minutes later, Sully returned, closed the car door with a decisive thump and tossed a brown paper bag onto my lap. "Coffee." He patted his overcoat's breast pocket and aimed that ridiculous wolfish grin my way. "Supplies."

"Sully, you're a real piece of work. Anyone ever tell you that?"

That earned me another grin and another kiss. "Let's go home," he said.

WE LEFT DOWNTOWN BEHIND, heading toward the west side of the city and into a neighborhood crowded with three-decker apartment houses of varying colors but identical design. The opposite of row houses found in factory towns like Ballard Springs, three-deckers were tall, detached buildings with an apartment on each floor, a gabled or hip roof, large windows on all four sides, and a small porch on each level, overlooking the street.

Sully turned a corner onto Franklin Street and the car rolled smoothly up a gently rising hill. Christmas lights blinked in the windows of the houses lined up along each side in neat rows. Two boys, one Black, one white, built a snowman in one of the tiny front yards. The boys wore scarves and wool coats with huge buttons. They'd dressed their snowman in a similar style, adding a vintage top hat, a carrot nose, and a corncob pipe to complete the ensemble.

Vague childhood memories of living and playing in a place like this swirled in my brain, coupled with an odd sense of déjà vu, like watching an old movie and thinking I'd seen it before, but unable to clearly remember anything about the plot. I knew I'd lived in one of the many three-deckers that populated Ballard Springs before my parents were killed, but I couldn't recall where. Had it been here, in this neighborhood? Had I seen these houses before?

The car crested the hill and Sully pulled up to the curb in front of a pale-blue building with lights burning in the upper windows. Snow-speckled yew bushes bordered the broad steps up to an open porch with a wooden top rail and square balusters. Thick posts on either end held up the porch's slanted roof.

"Here we are," Sully said and killed the engine. "You ready to meet the family?"

Not really. Sully may be sure his brother would welcome me with open arms, but I was not. I mean, Sully loved me, for all my faults and time traveling ways. To Pat, I was a stranger. A stranger Sully intended to have stick around for a couple of days or maybe more and possibly forever if I couldn't find a way back to the future. And why did that thought suddenly get me all giddy inside instead of terrified?

Sully hurried around the car to open the door for me. I couldn't turn back now. I had no choice but to keep calm and carry on.

He took my hand and we climbed wide wooden steps to the porch. We entered the building through a front door that opened with a squawk of old hinges—no key necessary in these more trusting times. He steered me across a cold and musty-smelling foyer with wood paneling and into the first-floor apartment.

He flipped a switch and an overhead light came on. We stood in a tiny vestibule off the parlor. More memories scratched at my brain. I knew the layout of the rest of the rooms, arranged in a tidy rectangle like dots on a domino tile—front parlor, dining room, kitchen, and a small bedroom on one side, two more bedrooms, pantry, and the sole bathroom on the other.

Sully nudged me forward into the parlor, a cozy room with mismatched furniture no doubt picked up at a secondhand store and a Christmas tree that stood by the window, tall and twinkly and completely real, nothing like the fakey fake 1990s kitsch Grandma Blue and I had put up every holiday. A hundred green and red bulb lights crowded the tree's branches and so did delicate glass ornaments, nearly buried under shimmering silver icicles that were probably ninety percent lead and absolutely poisonous.

"Home sweet home," Sully said with a shrug. "Such as it is."

"It's lovely," I said, my voice deepening with unexpected emotion.

A light came on at the back of the apartment, followed by the click of a door closing. "Tom? Is that you?" a man called, his voice as deep and resonant as Sully's. "You're home early."

Footsteps creaked across the floor and a tall man entered through the doorway from the kitchen. Patrick Sullivan, no doubt. He looked too much like his brother to be anyone else. He had the same broad shoulders and height, but brownish hair like mine and no chin dimple.

"Hey Pat," Sully said, as jovial as Santa Claus bringing gifts by the orphanage and not springing an out-of-town guest on his brother so close to Christmas. He took my hand, and tugged me from the parlor to the dining room, closing the short distance between us and Pat.

Pat looked me over, taking in my ratty coat, torn stockings, and wild hair. "Cecelia," he called over his shoulder. "Tom's home, and he's brought company."

More footsteps pattered softly on the hardwood as a slender Black woman wearing a crisp white nurse's uniform stepped into the room. A little shorter than me and in her mid-twenties, she had a heart-shaped face with a wide forehead, smiling eyes, a prominent jaw, and straight hair styled to curl under as it brushed her shoulders.

She held a baby on her hip. Well, not a baby of the infant variety. My inability to determine the age of any child under twelve was pretty legendary. I couldn't be sure, but I put this little girl's age as somewhere between expert at crawling and just about to start walking. So... ten months? An adorable ten months. Dressed like a candy cane in a red and white top, red pants, and matching booties with tiny pompoms, the sweet little thing had light brown skin, a button nose, and a duck-shaped barrette clipped to her wispy reddish-brown hair.

The girl gurgled happily as she played with the collar of her mother's uniform. Until she spotted Big Red. With a delighted squeal, she launched herself from her mother's arms into Sully's.

"Hello, Effie," he said, kissing the girl's forehead with an audible *smack* and getting her squealing again.

I would've squealed too if I hadn't dissolved into a great big puddle of mush watching them. I didn't think anything could make me fall deeper in love with Sully, but there it was. I mean, a gruff and grumpy guy like him now making theatrical chomping sounds as he pretended to nibble on Effie's adorable little fingers?

Sigh...

"Beryl, this is my brother Pat, his wife Cecelia, and..." He tossed the child into the air and caught her deftly, making her squeak in delight. "...and this is my best girl, their daughter Effie."

Okay, I'd figured that out from context clues, but hearing the words still surprised me. I mean, Pat and Cecelia being a thing wouldn't cause anyone to blink in Futureworld, or even in my old 2015 era of love-is-love except in some intractable, small-minded corners. But this was 1947. The height of Jim Crow and segregation, and though legal in Massachusetts, interracial marriage was still a big *nope* in a lot of US states.

Sully turned a loving look my way. "Pat, Cecelia, *this* is Beryl Blue."

I waved a jaunty hello. None of the usual head-scratching and confusion followed hearing my surname, so I knew Sully had told them about me. *What* he'd told them became clear when Cecelia gasped.

"Beryl Blue?" Her forehead squinched and her gaze shot to her husband. "Isn't that the girl who says she's from—?"

"Why don't you go change, hon?" Pat cut in. "I know you had a long day. I'll get suppah ready," he added, his South Boston accent even more pronounced than Sully's.

She hesitated, her eyebrow slipping upward Sully-style, doubtful and a little miffed at her husband, but she didn't say anything else and toddled off toward the rear of the apartment.

Pat centered his gaze on me. "So, you're Beryl Blue. Will you be sticking around longer this time?"

This time? *Ouch.* Not exactly welcoming. More like

guarded and defensive, a tone that got me looking toward the door for a quick exit. So much for Pat being completely fine with me dropping in without an invitation.

Sully wasn't as easily intimidated. "She's staying as long as she needs to." He kissed the top of Effie's head then handed her to her dad. "There's a problem we need to fix before she leaves."

"A problem *you* need to fix, you mean." Pat eyed Sully over his daughter's head and the two men engaged in a scowling stare down. Pat's scowl was formidable, but not as seasoned as Sully's. After a moment of strained silence, Pat capitulated with an aggravated sigh. "We'll set another place for supper. Hope you like beef stew, Miss Blue."

Sully shrugged off his coat, a policeman's winter overcoat, heavy and wool, with gold buttons. "Call her Beryl, you dope. She's not your Sunday school teacher," he added, helping me out of my borrowed coat.

"She sure isn't." Pat's eyes popped as he took in my bright, bright dress with its short, short skirt.

"Mind your manners, brother. Beryl's lost her luggage and needs a change of clothes. You think Cecelia has something she can wear?"

"I'll ask her—" Effie squirmed wildly in her father's arms, then headbutted him for good measure. Pat looked at her and laughed, joy and affection replacing the frosty wariness that had stiffened his posture and filled his eyes since we met. He looked boyish, younger than his twenty-six years, and utterly besotted with the girl in his arms. "Let me get this inchworm into her pajamas and I'll see what Cecelia can dig up."

Though Cecelia was not quite as curvy as me, she managed to find a serviceable outfit, if casual by 1940s standards—a button-down blue cotton shirt and a pair of wide-leg linen pants with a side zipper, a style known as sailor pants. I changed into my new couture in the long, narrow bathroom with a porcelain sink and a clawfoot bathtub right out of an antiques magazine.

I opened the bathroom door, greeted by the peppery smell of beef stew and potatoes that set my stomach rumbling. The sound of low male voices in a serious discussion squeezed my belly in a different way.

"Don't you think I know my own mind?" Sully said. He'd changed from his uniform into a long-sleeved shirt with big pockets and tan trousers. He aimed a fierce frown at his brother, who stood at a white enamel gas stove with an exhaust pipe that shot up the wall like a chimney.

"I trust you, Tommy. It's *her* I don't trust."

Her, as in me. Could hardly blame him. Sully knew my backstory. He'd seen time travel in action. He was a true believer. But Pat... To him, I was an unknown entity, a woman who'd dropped in from out of nowhere, claiming to be a time traveler. I wouldn't trust me either.

"You've always been a sucker for someone with a sob story." Pat snatched up a wooden spoon and stirred the source of the yummy smell in a large metal pot, intensely focused on this task. "She could be loony, or dangerous. I've got my family to think about."

I froze in the doorway, gripped by the desperation in his voice. A family he'd no doubt already gotten a lot of grief for in these intolerant times. I hadn't thought of that.

My being here could not only pose a threat to Sully, but also to Pat and Cecelia.

"I know," Sully said, his voice coaxing. "But I'm asking you to help me out. Beryl won't be here long. She's in a spot of trouble and needs my help."

Ugh. The way he'd said that, with a dangerous mix of understatement and confidence I'd come to expect and dread from him.

"Then what? She goes back to where? To when? You can't actually believe—" Pat cut off abruptly when he looked past Sully and spotted me. "Suppah's almost ready," he said, sending an uneasy grimace my way before turning to his brother. "Tommy, why don't you set the table?"

Sully eyed me, worry tightening his face. "Sure." He grabbed a stack of bowls off a shelf and stuffed them into my hands then followed me into the dining room carrying the rest of the dishes.

Cecilia looked up as we entered the small room, made even more cramped with the large wooden table and mismatched chairs, a desk, and a stout bookcase filling the tight space. A half dozen black-and-white photos stood on top of the bookcase—Pat in his Navy blues, newborn Effie, Cecelia and Pat in what must have been their wedding photo, and the portrait of Sully in his policeman's uniform I had hanging on my wall at home.

I circled the table and put the bowls in place next to the silverware and bread plates Sully laid out.

"You certainly look more comfortable," Cecilia said, running an amused glance over my casual Friday attire.

She looked more comfortable too, in a dark-green, belted dress with a button front and long sleeves. She sat at the table with Effie beside her in one of those old-fashioned wooden highchairs that had been outlawed as hazardous and extremely dangerous in my time—no safety harness, detachable tray that weighed a thousand pounds, sharp edges, easy to fall out of. Unaware of the danger, Cecelia calmly spooned what looked and smelled like strained carrots into the little one's mouth. Effie loudly smacked her lips after each bite in an enthusiastic, five-star review.

Done with his table-setting task, Sully kissed me and indicated I should sit down before he ducked into the kitchen and returned with a pitcher of milk and glasses. He took a second trip and came back with several cans of Narragansett beer.

My head was spinning by the time this domestic scene played out and we all sat down to eat. Pat took his place at the head of the table, with Effie in her highchair at his elbow and Cecelia next to her. Sully and I sat close together on the other side. Very close. Eager for some alone time, I would've suggested skipping dinner altogether and retiring to Sully's room if not for propriety and my growling belly.

I turned down Sully's offer of a glass of milk, opting for beer instead. So did he. He punched triangular-shaped holes in the tops of two cans with a can punch opener, and we dug into our meal. Effie painted her highchair tray with leftover carrot mush and occasionally splattered her dad with applesauce as we dined on savory stew and a soft Italian bread fresh from the neighborhood bakery.

Conversation flowed, with everyone speaking at once. I didn't contribute much, content to eat, sip my beer, and watch the others, their animated faces, their easy manner, enjoying the moment. I'd never been much for family dinners. Maybe we sat down together when my parents were alive, but Grandma Blue worked a lot of nights as a nurse, so I often ate alone, with Pop Tarts my meal of choice.

This... This was family. This was what I'd missed.

"I'm telling ya, the Red Sox'll make the world series again in forty-eight," Pat said, tearing into a chunk of beef. "I think they'll even win it."

"Don't count on it," I murmured, hiding a sardonic smile.

Sully side-eyed me but addressed his brother. "Won't happen unless the Sox get more muscle on the pitcher's mound. And Ted Williams doesn't slow down."

Pat scoffed. "Teddy's got years of play left. Everyone said he was washed up when he came back from the war. Said flying for the Marines took the splinter out of him and he was an old man. He got Boston to the World Series last year. He won the Triple Crown this past season. Not bad for an old fella."

Cecelia caught my eye with a *bored, much?* lift of her eyebrow. I returned a *tell me about it* grimace. I mean, the Triple Crown was baseball and not horse racing?

"Williams can't do it alone." Sully buttered a piece of bread. "The Sox need stronger pitching and even stronger bats, more than just Ted's. They need—"

"Colored players?" Cecelia offered. "There's talk of more teams desegregating after the Dodgers and Jackie Robinson. Maybe some of the greats from the Negro leagues will get a chance."

"I have my doubts," Pat said gloomily. "Some of us

may want a mixed league, but are the team owners ready to take that gamble?"

Sully looked to me for the answer, and after a moment, so did the others. Even Effie, who ceased drumming on her tray with her spoon to stare at me with large, liquid brown eyes. I heaved a mental sigh. Sure, ask the time traveler for inside info on the future. Info she's not supposed to share, not without lying or breaking a thousand Time Scope rules.

"Well… the owners *may* be ready to change," I said, going for vague. Some of them would, and some wouldn't, not for a long time. Sully's beloved Red Sox would drag their feet on integrating for a dozen more years, becoming the last major league team to do so. I sipped my beer, a pale ale with a smooth, sort of fruity taste, and changed the subject. "Pat, Sully mentioned you were in the Navy during the war."

He hesitated then met my gaze with a smile that barely reached his eyes. "Sure was. Cooped up for nearly four years on a tin can, with water, water everywhere. While Tommy enjoyed the great outdoors, fresh air, and bouncing French dames on his knee."

Sully directed a sardonic grin at his brother. "You forgot the part where I slogged through mud up to my waist while Adolf's boys lobbed mortar shells and exploded trees over my head."

He flashed a glance my way then applied himself to the last bites of his stew. He spoke with a hint of bitterness, but not as much anger as I'd heard in his voice the last time we were together, when the pain of the war was still fresh. Though I suspected from his tone and posture the trauma still stuck, just below the surface, never going away.

I steered the subject to a more mundane topic. "What are you up to now, Pat?"

"Up to?" He leaned across the table and reached for the can opener, followed by a resounding *ka-chisss* as he popped a triangular opening in a beer can's lid. "If you mean what line of work am I in, I'm a repairman at Flynn's Hardware downtown."

"A good repairman," Sully said. "He got more than a tattoo and a permanent sunburn while on that tin can during the war. He learned a thing or two about radios and receivers."

Sully's voice beamed with pride, and so did Cecelia's when she added, "He's studying at state college to be an electrical engineer. He's taking classes at Camp Davis."

"Right," I said. "Sully mentioned that to me. You're studying on the GI Bill." As were a zillion other veterans of the war.

"That's where we met. Camp Davis." Pat eyed Cecelia, his voice deepening. "Just before Cece was mustered out of the nursing corps."

I turned my attention her way. "Oh, you were a nurse during the war, too?"

"I was. I always wanted to be a nurse but didn't think I had a chance. Training is expensive, and most nursing schools have a strict quota on the number of Negroes they'll accept. Then, war came. I saw a recruitment poster for the WACs nurse corps that said, *Urgent, all women can help*. Get that? *All* women, meaning me." She wiped carrots and sundry dinner items from Effie's face with a damp cloth. "I thought that's what it meant, anyway. Come to find out, few Negro women who applied were accepted. I was one of the lucky ones. I was put in a colored nursing unit at the Camp Davis base hospital. *If* you could call what we were assigned to do nursing. Most of us pulled janitorial duty or work usually done by orderlies. KP, scrubbing floors and garbage pails, and the like."

Yikes. "I'm so sorry."

"I was sorry too, for a long while. I got the blues. I thought I'd made a mistake joining up, thought I'd never be a real nurse. All of us girls were in a tough spot. The camp's commander made it clear he didn't want us doing regular nursing duties, and we had to follow orders."

Sully snorted his opinion of that. I simply nodded. I knew a lot of racist crap had gone on in these times, but to sit across the table from a woman who'd lived it, to hear her story. Well... words were inadequate.

"We fought back as best we could." She set her jaw in a firm line. "Some of us chose to go on strike. We refused to work and instead stayed in our barracks for two days. You can imagine how that went over with the brass. They threatened us with court-martial and jail or worse. Mutiny, they called it. In the end, we had to give in, but not before our duties got amended. No more janitor work."

"But you still had to do KP," Pat said, both teasing and outraged. "And you hated KP."

She laughed, a delicate jingle bell of a laugh. "I did, and still do. That's why Patrick does all the cooking and scrubbing pans now." She gazed at her husband over the top of Effie's head. "Though, my time at Davis wasn't all bad."

"We met at the bus stop," Pat said. "My first week attending classes, Cecelia's last week in the Army."

"He offered me his seat. The only man on that bus who would," she said with another loving look at Pat. He returned an equally smitten smile. "I knew he was special right away."

"It was fate," Pat said.

"It was good manners," Sully grumped.

"Come on, Sully, even an old grouch like you can admit that's a meet cute right out of a romantic movie." I undercut my teasing with a quick peck on his cheek. Cecelia giggled, and so did Effie. But Pat's easiness dialed back, slipping into wariness again, with a side of hostility.

Great. I'd thought maybe he'd begun to thaw toward me during dinner, but clearly his mistrust ran deep. I had no idea how long I'd be here, or how to find my way back to the future. I did know one thing, though. I was going to have to work mighty hard to overcome Patrick Sullivan's suspicion—and hopefully win him over.

THE MEAL FINISHED, the dishes washed and put away, we gathered in the parlor. The radiator pinged a happy tune as steam heat made its way through the pipes to warm the room. The box-style radio on the credenza by the wall played something called *Lux Radio Theater*, featuring a production of *Miracle on 34th Street*, featuring most of the movie's cast, except for Natalie Wood. The lead icicles on the Christmas tree shimmered and twinkled in the lights.

Sully and I cuddled together on the sofa. Cecelia sat in a rocking chair. Knitting needles clacked as she worked busily on what might eventually be a scarf. Or maybe a mitten. Pat returned to the parlor after putting Effie to bed and sank into a wingback chair beside his wife. He leaned back and snapped open the evening newspaper with headlines about the Nuremburg trials and the expected increase in commercial licenses granted for television stations in the new year.

A cozy scene. Comfortable, even. Except for the watchful looks Pat snuck my way over the top of his newspaper. And Sully fidgeting beside me, eager for us to be alone and get reacquainted.

The radio show took a commercial break. A honey-voiced announcer cheerfully touted the miracles a greasy hair tonic called Wild Root Cream Oil could do for your love life, followed by a catchy jingle.

Pat abruptly folded his newspaper, tossed it onto the table between the chairs, and stood. "I'll be right back," he announced. He dug a pack of Chesterfields and a gold lighter out of his pocket as he crossed the room. Cecelia aimed a disapproving frown at his back but said nothing. He snatched a jacket from the coatrack in the foyer and disappeared out the front door.

With a quick glance at Cecelia, I disentangled myself from Sully's arms and got up to follow Pat's path.

"Hey." Sully gently gripped my wrist, stopping me. He gazed up at me imploringly. "You don't have to explain yourself to him."

"I think I do. Not everyone can embrace the unknown as gleefully as you do. I've got to give him the chance to trust me."

He grunted. Sully's version of giving in. And surprisingly quick for once.

I plucked my coat from the rack and in a moment, I joined Pat at the porch railing.

"Nice night," I said. Not really. Murky gray clouds covered the sky, obscuring the stars. I hugged myself against the frosty air. "Cold, though."

Pat snapped open the lighter and flicked the spark wheel. A blue flame shot to life. He touched it to the cigarette between his lips and inhaled deeply. "Nobody in their right mind should be out in this weather." He pulled the cigarette from his mouth and breathed out a noxious plume of blue-white smoke. "But Cecelia doesn't want me smoking near the baby."

"Wise woman." I suspected that frown she'd lasered at him in the parlor announced she didn't want him to smoke at all. "She's great, by the way, and Effie's adorable. And Sully... Well, he's your number one fan. He's so proud of you for going to college."

Pat flicked ash over the porch rail into the snow-coated bushes below and chuckled ruefully. "Tommy gave me no choice. He insisted I finish school, get a degree. He didn't want another Sullivan in a dead-end factory job like our pop."

"Sully's a smart guy."

"He is. About most things, anyway." He turned to look at me, his gaze keen.

"You're wondering how smart he is about me."

He nodded. "One thing you gotta know about my brother is he doesn't lie. Never has. He believes in the truth at all times. So, when he tells me this dolly he took up with is a time traveler, I believe him. I believe *he* believes it." He narrowed his eyes. "The question is, do *you* believe it?"

Several seconds ticked by. Pat pulled on his cigarette again. The crackle of burning tobacco filled the fraught silence.

"Well... it's complicated." Oh, how I hated that phrase. Evasive in the extreme, and somewhat condescending to the person being *it's complicated* at. I knew 1947 had been the year of Roswell and UFOs and little green men, but would Pat believe me if I told him the truth? His combative posture told me no. Even the challenging way he exhaled smoke made me doubt it. So why try?

He gave an irritated snort. "I don't think it's complicated at all. You're playing a game with my brother. You come in and out of his life like the Flying Dutchman, a ghost ship bringing a bad omen. Never staying long, but long enough to turn him upside down. I thought he'd got over you when he started walking out with Millie. Then last year, you came back, and Millie was out of the picture."

I flushed with guilt, though, really, he couldn't put that breakup on me. I'd met Millie and it didn't take a relationship expert to see how incompatible she and Sully were. She wanted marriage, a split-level in the suburbs, and weekends at the country club, while Sully... did not. He wanted something a staid, midcentury housewife-in-training couldn't give him.

He wanted *me*.

"Pat, I love how protective you are of Sully. I never had a sibling, only foster brothers and sisters. Some of them I clicked with. Some were protective, like you are." I laughed. Not amused, more like sad, slightly self-pitying. "Angry teenage Beryl did *not* want to be protected, though. Not at all. I wanted to run. I lost everyone I ever loved. Didn't want to love anyone else, ever again." I looked him in the eye. "Then I found Sully. We found each other. I don't want to hurt him for all the world."

Smoke gusted from Pat's nostrils in a frustrated sigh. "You *are* hurting him. If you care for him as much as you say, why don't you stay with him? Make a home and a family."

The words pounded into my heart, accentuating the hurt. How could I tell him about Sully's fate? "I-I can't."

"Why not?"

"I just... can't."

"Because you're a time traveler?"

I sighed. Glo would be furious if I violated the rules and said yes, but not half as angry as Jake. I sighed again. This convo would be so much simpler if Sully had kept my secret identity exactly that. A secret.

"Yes, Pat. I'm a time traveler."

His eyebrows weren't as expressive as Sully's, but their upward trajectory expressed his surprise at my bold admission. And his disbelief. "Prove it."

I frowned. He was as blunt as his brother, nowhere near as charming. And, come on, how could I prove my claim? Tell him the Boston Red Sox would finally win the World Series, but it would take a lot of heartbreak and nearly sixty years? Tell him there'd soon be a war-not-a-war in Korea, or that in a couple of decades, his marriage would finally be legal in all fifty states? Oh, and that soon, there would *be* fifty states.

All of that was in the future, but I couldn't show him, not without my TDC and a wealth of holographic head-lines from newspapers yet to come to back me up. He wouldn't believe me.

"It's not that simple, Pat. There are rules about talking about the future." Ridiculous rules, in my opinion. "There's a risk to the timeline if someone learns what's going to happen."

"That's what a con artist would say."

Sighing in frustration, I gazed out at the view, a quaint but somewhat chilly scene. An older model car wheezed up the hill and rolled past a house decorated with twinkling Christmas lights. Music from a radio or record player drifted out from somewhere, and a giddy baritone voice implored, *Let It Snow, Let It Snow, Let It Snow*. As if obeying the crooner's demand, errant snowflakes fell, twirling on the cold breeze.

Wait. *Snow*? Yes, snow. I got an idea. After Alice had narrowed down the timeframe for Sully's date with destiny to the six-year period from the late 1940s to 1954, I'd become a research rat, searching Time Scope's databases for any blip or clue that could pinpoint the actual date of Sully's death, and what would cause it. Never found a solid date, but I'd gotten mighty familiar with the events that would unfold over the next seven years.

Including one event happening only a few days from now.

"It's going to snow," I blurted. "On Christmas."

Pat scowled. "Yeah? That's news? It often snows on Christmas and most other days in December."

"Not like this. It's going to snow a *lot*. A storm that'll catch everyone along the east coast with their pants down. They'll call it the great northeast blizzard of 1947. Or something like that, I'm not completely sure. But I do know it'll be a record amount of snow, almost as big as the blizzard that hit New York in the nineteenth century."

"That's mighty specific." His expression telegraphed doubt, but his voice wavered. He wanted to believe me. For Sully's sake.

"It's specific because I know it for a fact."

Another pause, more wavering. "Christmas is in three days." He stabbed out his cigarette on the porch railing. The flame went out with a hiss like a dying snake. "We won't have to wait long to find out if you're a con artist making up stories."

"You'll see I'm telling the truth." I watched him flick the butt into the bushes at the base of the porch and immediately remove another from the pack. "Oh, and there's one more thing about the future I can tell you." I eyed the cigarette he placed between his lips. "It'll soon be common knowledge that smoking causes cancer."

I turned on my heel and headed back inside, with a cold wind at my back and Pat's curse of surprise following me into the house.

7

_____

After concluding my porch interrogation with Pat, I found Cecelia nodding off with her knitting in her lap, and Sully eagerly waiting for me in the parlor. He met my gaze, his blue eyes darker in the low light and burning with need. My nerve endings crackled with anticipation, matching his desire.

He stood and held out his hand, tipping his head toward his bedroom door. Seconds later, he led me into a small, square room with one window, a bureau, a wide bed with a wooden headboard, and a brass lamp on a bedside table cluttered with photographs, books, and a thoroughly midcentury windup alarm clock. I itched to get a look at the book titles, but Sully pulled me into his arms as soon as he closed the door.

"You're cold," he said with a scowl. "You were out there a long time. What did Pat have to say?"

"Do you really want to talk about that?" I gazed up at him coyly and began to unbutton his shirt. "Do you really want to talk at all?"

A laugh rumbled in his chest. "Ah, Beryl. My love." He shrugged out of his shirt then liberated me from my blouse and my groovy bra. "My elusive love," he murmured between kisses as his lips traveled down my neck, to the hollow of my throat then further down to my breasts, making me shiver. "My sweetheart. I missed you."

I'd missed him too. So much.

We kissed and caressed and undressed each other, exploring our bodies, getting reacquainted. I slipped off his undershirt—men still wore undershirts in these days—and ran my hands over his muscled chest and broad shoulders. I traced the outline of the tattoo he'd gotten in the war, a busty, dark-haired babe with a vague resemblance to me and the words *A Real Piece of Work* on a ribbon that wove around her shapely ankles.

I'd missed him, and I'd missed this. The physical, the connection I'd always run away from, unable to trust anyone, unable to fully open my heart. Until Sully.

He picked me up and carried me the few steps to the bed, setting me down gently. Then he was beside me, holding me, his lips finding mine in a searing kiss that robbed me of breath. Consuming me, body and soul.

The world outside melted away. Pat's hostility, the past, the future, my fears about Rasmussen and being stuck in time. There was only us. Together. For how long I didn't know and wouldn't try to guess. We were together now.

And that was all we needed.

I woke to the smell of bacon frying and coffee brewing, and daylight breaking beyond the shimmery window curtains in Sully's bedroom. I stretched like a satisfied cat. I would've purred if I had the slightest idea how.

"Sully?" I murmured sleepily.

No Sully. Not beside me, anyway. He'd slid out of bed while I was sleeping and now stood near the closet door, getting dressed.

"It's just after dawn," he semi-whispered. "Go back to sleep, sweetheart." He put on his dark blue uniform pants then buckled his belt. "You sure earned your rest last night."

He punctuated that with one of those awful and not even remotely seductive leers. I knew I needed to tell him to retire that expression *tout de suite*, but not now. I was in too good a mood.

I sat up and arranged the blankets around me to stay warm, watching him tuck in his shirt and put on his tie. I loved to watch him get dressed. And undressed. Every inch of his body was enticing, from his thick copper hair to his *yes-please* kissable lips and solid jaw, his muscled arms and chest, his strong thighs, and of course those broad shoulders that made me swoon.

"I do love a man in uniform," I murmured.

He took his coat off a hanger in the closet and crossed the room toward me. "And I love *you*." The mattress dipped as he sank down onto the bed and sealed that declaration with a kiss.

"The feeling is more than mutual." I shifted to check out the books on the bedside table. Sitting atop a stack of Dashiell Hammetts and Agatha Christies was a hardcover copy of H. G. Wells's *The Time Machine*. The fraying dust jacket depicted a man in a Victorian-style suit operating the controls of a futuristic time machine that looked like a metallic ant. "Since when do you read sci-fi? I thought you preferred mysteries."

"Are you a book critic now?" He ran his fingers through my hair. Always a tough task, what with my hair being as tangled and impenetrable as the thickets in a Normandy hedgerow. "I've been reading up on time travel. Trying to learn a little about your world."

A sweet gesture that sparked sadness in my belly. My world was so far away from his. "Spoiler alert." I forced a light tone. "That book is nothing like the world I live in. Though to be honest, class divisions still exist and probably will forever."

"Maybe you'll tell me about it sometime." The bedsprings creaked as he stood and reached for his coat he'd tossed onto the bed.

I threw off the blankets and got up, stretching again and adding a yawn. Behind the books on the table were several framed photos—a picture of Effie in a summer sunsuit, two boys I guessed to be Sully and Pat in front of a dilapidated tenement building they probably called home, the photo booth pictures of Sully and me from our last adventure, and the snapshot taken at Jonesy's nightclub in Ballard Springs when we'd first met in 1943.

I picked that one up. Sully had kept the picture with him throughout the war so it was in rougher shape than the copy hanging on my apartment wall, with cracks and smudges and frayed edges. Sully, Marco, Griff, and Stan, all in uniform, all wasted, were gathered around a tiny table filled with beer bottles and dinner plates. I perched on Sully's knee. He looked happy. I looked stunned. Probably because it was the moment I realized I'd fallen for Sully. In a big way.

He came up behind me and slipped his arms around my waist. During the night, I'd appropriated one of his undershirts, but my feet and legs were bare. I leaned back against him, savoring his warmth in the chilly room, welcoming the feel of his strength holding me.

"We were so young then," I said, smiling at the photo in my hand. "Do you ever keep in touch with the fellas?"

He glanced at the picture then kissed my temple. "No. I put that in the past. They made it out alive, that's the important thing. The lucky thing." His voice went as rough as gravel and I knew he thought of my grandmother's brother Augie, and all the other men who didn't make it.

I put the picture frame down and turned in his arms to face him. I caressed his cheek, my touch light, tender. "*You* made it. I'm grateful for that." An ironic, melancholy statement. He'd made it through the horror of war, to face an unknown end in peacetime.

He tightened his embrace, then released me. "I gotta go before I'm late." He began to button his coat. "What d'ya say you meet me downtown for lunch? Say, around eleven?"

I froze. "You know I can't."

"What? Have lunch?"

"Go out in public. With you. What if Rasmussen is still here? Lurking about, waiting for us?"

"Then I'll deal with him." He paused with the top button still undone, looking pensive. "Ever think he might not have anything to do with... whatever's to come?

Could be an accident. You could be in the path of a careening car."

"Then what? You'll jump in front of me? You won't be able to lift the car over your head like Superman, you know."

"I will if I have to." A frustrated scowl darkened his expression, but he didn't push the issue. He went back to buttoning his coat. "Alright, we'll skip lunch. What are you gonna do today instead?"

Celebrate the fact that I may have actually won an argument with him? I mean, really, Sully seemed as addicted to risk as Niels. *And what about you*, a small voice inside me piped up. Was I so scared of the vague warnings of an unknown threat that I wouldn't take a risk at all?

"I don't know," I said. "Maybe I'll go to a movie."

His eyebrow twitched in surprise, but he didn't question it. "You'll need some cash." He stepped to the bureau to get his car keys and wallet. He pulled out several dollars, came back and handed me the bills. "This'll be enough for a movie and lunch if you want. I hear the Rialto is playing the new Hope and Crosby road picture. There may be a new Three Stooges short, too."

I gave him a chipper, "I might check that out," and by that I meant I decidedly would not. Though I appreciated comedy in all forms, you couldn't pay me enough to willingly go see three grown men hit each other over the head with frying pans.

"You'll also need change for bus fare downtown." Coins jingled as Sully dug into his pocket then dropped several nickels and dimes into my palm. He waved off my thanks and took me into his arms. "I'll see you tonight."

He flashed one of those rare, joyful smiles that got my stomach whirling. "It's gonna be a hell of a long day at work. I'll miss you every minute."

He kissed me, long and slow and extra thorough, showing me exactly how much he'd miss me and fore-shadowing the million more kisses and other delights to come when he returned.

"Sully," I said when we parted, stopping him before he could turn to go. "Please promise me you'll be careful."

He flashed a cocky grin. "I always am."

I went up onto my tiptoes and pressed my lips to his. "You *never* are."

I PUT on my borrowed blouse and sailor pants, added a patterned tan cardigan I found in Sully's closet for warmth, then I followed the tempting smell of bacon into the kitchen.

Cecelia, dressed in her nurse's uniform, sat in a chair at a small, round table with the morning newspaper spread out before her and her fork poised over a plate filled with fried eggs, crispy bacon, and toast. Next to her, Effie danced in her highchair of doom, wriggling like a worm and flinging oatmeal around. I silently cheered the kid on. Not so fond of oatmeal myself, I'd be tossing it too.

"Help yourself to breakfast," Cecelia said, gesturing to the stove. "And there's coffee."

A gas flame flickered under an old-style metal coffee percolator on the stovetop, with a bubble in the lid like a crystal ball. Steam curled up from the spout. The smell got my mouth watering, as did the tantalizing scent of bacon and eggs beckoning to me from the skillet on the next burner. Not to mention the toast stacked on a plate on the counter. A sumptuous breakfast right out of an old TV show that no one ever had time to eat, though a little hard on the arteries.

I grabbed a plate and piled on the delights, then poured myself a cup of coffee. I sank into a chair across the table from Cecelia and took my first gulp of 1947 era coffee with a satisfied sigh.

"Did you sleep well?" Cecelia asked, casually turning the newspaper page without looking up.

"I slept like a baby." I crunched on the greasiest, most crisp, and most delicious piece of bacon I'd ever eaten. "Though that's a weird phrase. Slept like a baby." I grinned at Effie, who grinned back. "Babies toss and turn and wake up ten times a night, don't they?"

Cecelia glanced up this time and flashed a knowing smile. "*You* were awake at least ten times last night."

I choked on a bite of toast. Sully and I had tried to keep things quiet, but sometimes... "Oh, heh. Sorry. Thanks again for letting me stay. I know my arrival was kind of a surprise."

"A surprise for you too, I think, from the clothes you were wearing yesterday." She closed the newspaper and turned her attention to her breakfast. "It's no bother, really. For me, at least. To be honest, Pat was against you staying. He's the type who needs a lot of warning and proper orders and everything shipshape before doing anything. That's the Navy man in him. Me, I'm not so worried about who you are and where you come from. As a nurse, I see a problem that needs fixing, and I try to fix it."

"You're a lot like Sully in that department."

She laughed that jingle bell laugh. "He'd have made a fine nurse if he didn't become a policeman. And if more men were nurses. We do enjoy bossing folks around and forcing them to take their medicine."

Something Sully excelled at. Among other things.

I nibbled on another piece of bacon. "Where are you from? Did you grow up here in Ballard Springs?"

"No, I'm from Vermont, up around Ferrisburgh. My grandparents left North Carolina and moved up to there to farm after the war." She did not mean World War II. She meant the Civil War. "I reversed direction and came down here when I joined the nursing corps. And then of course, I met Patrick."

Effie chimed in with an exuberant, "Dadadadaaaa," that ended in a Bronx cheer and her spoon clattering to the floor.

Cecelia patiently picked it up then gazed at me, her expression growing serious. "Honestly, I'm glad you're here. I think Tom deserves a slice of happiness. He's such a lovely soul, but a lonely soul. Oh, I know he presents himself as solid as granite, but deep down, he seems so... lost. Like he doesn't fit, and he's searching for someplace where he will. At first, I thought it was the war. It took so much from so many men. Women too. Left them unsettled, at loose ends. Now that I've met you and seen you two together, I understand. He's found where he fits. With you. It's just, for some reason he hasn't told us about, the two of you can't be together."

I didn't get a chance to reply. Well, I was too overwhelmed to respond. But if I could speak, what could I say? She didn't know about Sully's impending doom, and I wasn't about to tell her. How would she react to hear this odd woman she'd welcomed into her home would be the cause of her brother-in-law's death?

Fortunately, any response I could cobble together would have to wait. Footsteps sounded in the back hall followed by a brisk knock on the door.

"That'll be the sitter," Cecelia said, her manner suddenly urgent. She gulped the last of her coffee. "Better get a wiggle on." She stood and carried her breakfast dishes into the pantry to put in the sink, then she hustled down the narrow, paneled hallway that led to the rear door.

With her mom gone, Effie stilled her perpetual squirming and stared at me with a wariness and mistrust that equaled and possibly even surpassed her father's.

"Yeah, I know, kid. How dare your mom leave you here alone with the scary lady with the Medusa hair."

Effie's lower lip pushed out in response. And quivered, too.

I fought a surge of panic. In my time cop career, I'd faced off with time runners desperate to escape to the past no matter what the cost. I'd chased a cutthroat band of temporal art thieves after Rembrandt's early works. I'd barely escaped capture when a time runner in Salem accused me of being a witch.

But nothing terrified me more than being left alone with this tiny girl in the blue corduroy dress and a yellow bib, her chubby cheeks speckled with oatmeal.

"Now, now, it's okay," I said, adding a nervous laugh.

Her lip pushed out some more. Her chin trembled.

Tears would follow, no doubt, and me without the skill set to deal with them. I mean, I didn't do baby. I had no experience in that department and probably would never have the chance to develop such expertise. At least, I'd never thought about embarking on that road. I'd only been focused on Sully, my jobs, and keeping my cat Jenjen happily fed because when that feline dude got hangry, watch out.

But kids? I hadn't thought that far into the future. Quite literally the future. Would there be a negative impact on the timeline for a woman out of time like me to procreate?

An academic temporal discussion that meant nothing to this little girl watching me with an expression almost as panicked as my own.

Desperate, I started to sing "How Much Is That Doggie in the Window?" A silly song from the fifties my mother would croon to me when I got anxious. Which, my fleeting memories informed me, was quite often. I guess being on the run from a time traveling assassin didn't equate to family bliss. The song always soothed me, sung by my mother in a voice as off-key as my own. By the time I got to the chorus, Effie seemed to calm down. At least her chin had stopped quivering.

Or perhaps whatever she spotted behind me had done the trick.

I stopped singing and swiveled in my chair to see Cecelia watching me with high amusement. So did the rest of the entourage she'd escorted into the kitchen—a plump woman of about forty with dark brown skin and wearing a gray-and-white striped dress with buttons from collar to hem, a towheaded white boy in knee pants, and a skinny Black girl of about thirteen, wearing the latest in teen fashion, a plaid skirt, cardigan, white bobby sox, brown loafers, and her hair in stubby pigtails.

Introductions were made. Mrs. Josephine Storms from the third floor, accompanied by her daughter Ruthie and the boy with the most generic name ever, Billy Wilson, from the three-decker next door.

"Me and Ruthie look after Effie, and also this little ankle-biter weekdays until three," Josephine said, tousling the boy's mop of curly hair. "His momma works first shift at Harrison Steel. She's lucky to still have a job there. They laid off most girls working the line as soon as the war ended." She lowered her voice and winked. "I think one of the supervisors is sweet on her." She shifted gears, looking me over, her expression curious. "What's your story, Beryl? What brings you to town?"

Cecelia stepped in. "Beryl's an old friend of Tom's. They met during the war." She shot me a sly glance. "Beryl came in from... California. Just yesterday. She's here for a Christmas visit."

Smooth, mostly true, with no secrets revealed. Jake would be impressed.

"California? Did you fly in an airplane?" Josephine asked, both awestruck and alarmed. "Lord, you're a brave one. I wouldn't travel in one of those sardine cans for anything. I'd be terrified I'd fall right out of the sky."

I didn't venture to tell her about the time skip, which literally was falling right out of the sky. "My trip wasn't too terribly bad," I offered instead.

"Except they lost her suitcase." Cecelia lifted Effie out of her highchair and wiped the girl's oatmeal-y face with the bib. "I don't have much that will fit her and all she's got are the clothes on her back."

Josephine *tsk-tsked*. "Another reason to take the train. My bag never went astray in all the visits I've made to my brother's home in Washington, DC." Air travel versus rail debate completed, she looked me over again. "You seem to be close in size to my sister. She lives nearby. I'll send Ruthie over with a note and see if she has any glad rags to spare."

"Thanks, but I'm not planning to stay very long," I said, a confident assertion from a woman who'd gotten herself misplaced in time, without a return ticket. "I'd hate to put you and your sister to any trouble."

She waved airily. "Nonsense. You'll need something to wear, at least until your luggage is found. Besides, Althea's expecting another visit from the stork in a few weeks. She's as big as a barn and her clothes don't fit anymore. She'll be happy to share. Now, let's get this little miss and be on our way."

Discussion closed, she swept Effie away from Cecelia and ushered her little mob down the hallway to the rear door. Effie peered back over Josephine's shoulder and opened and closed her chubby little fist in a wave good-bye. Cecelia waved back, a wistful look on her face.

After they'd gone, she picked up her nurse's hat, bright white and with a winged brim, and gazed into a round mirror on the wall above the handwringer washing machine.

"Jo's something of a steamroller," she said. "But I don't know what I'd do without her to care for Effie while we both work." She put on the hat and secured it with metal bobby pins large enough to double as lightning rods.

"The lord knows Jo has her own troubles. Her husband died a year ago, before Pat and I were married. He was only forty-one. Jo babysits half the neighborhood to pay the bills. With Ruthie's help."

"Ruthie? Shouldn't she be in school?"

"Yes, she should, but she can't go." Cecelia met my gaze in the mirror. "She got measles when she was younger and the disease took her hearing. She can talk some, but she's deaf and can't go to school."

She spoke clinically, the nurse recounting a patient's condition. My emotions were a tad more engaged. "That's... that's awful," I said. And infuriating. Things were so terribly backward in these allegedly good old days.

"I know. It shouldn't be that way. But special schools are expensive. Some folks even tell Jo to put Ruthie in a home and forget about her." Cecelia turned to face me. "As if a mother would *ever* do that."

My chest tightened at the anguish in her voice, and at the knowledge that some mothers of disabled children would buckle under the pressure to do just that. "It won't always be that way," I said. "Things will be better. Soon there'll be vaccines to prevent measles and polio and all kinds of other childhood diseases."

She stiffened and a mix of hope and fear played tug-of-war in her expression. "Soon? How soon?"

I immediately regretted speaking out and breaking one of Time Scope's cardinal rules—don't talk about the future. Cecelia was anxious for her own daughter's health and well-being and I'd kindled a false hope. Soon wouldn't be soon enough for Effie, or the millions of other children who'd be at risk before the vaccines would be available.

Kicking myself for being a thoughtless dope, I didn't answer, just gave a sad shake of my head that caused Cecelia's shoulders to droop.

"Well..." She ran her hands over her dress, smoothing nonexistent wrinkles, the cool and clinical nurse sliding back into place. "I suppose I should get to the bus before I'm late for work. What are you going to do with yourself today?"

Not go to a movie, as I'd told Sully. I had only one goal for today. Send an SOS to Futureworld, so they'd know where I was. There had to be some way to leave a trail of breadcrumbs for Time Scope to follow and find me.

Anyway, that was a me problem, not Cecelia's. I stepped over to the table and picked up my coffee cup. "I'll figure out something to do. After I have more coffee."

She nodded, clearly disappointed in my response. I supposed she hoped I'd confess to a packed schedule of shopping and shenanigans with all the other time travelers who'd dropped by 1947 on the eve of Christmas Eve.

After she took herself off to the bus, I drank that second cup of coffee then cleaned up. Might as well pull my weight for the short time I was here. The hopefully short time. I mulled over ideas for sending some kind of *help me, Glo, you're my only hope* message to the future as I went into the pantry and washed, dried, and put the breakfast dishes away.

I'd lost my best chance for Alice and her research team to get a ping on me when Sully so helpfully destroyed all evidence of my arrest. I could go the *Back to the Future* route. *Back to the Future Part II*, actually. Write a letter and mail it for Glo and Jake to receive in almost two hundred years. That had worked in the movie. Could it work in real life? I had no idea, and no idea how to do it. I'd hardly used snail mail in my 2015 life, and not even once in the 2130s.

Frustrated and out of ideas, I vigorously scrubbed away the mess of oatmeal on Effie's highchair tray before it could solidify into a sticky paste that could cement bricks into place. Then I moved on to organizing and shelving the books and magazines strewn about the apartment. The Sullivan family might not appreciate me going all efficient librarian on them, but I couldn't help myself. Force of habit, I guess.

I tucked *The Sun Also Rises* between two other books on the bookshelf in the dining room then added Cecelia's newspaper to the stack of magazines I'd piled on the telephone desk. *Wait.* I picked the newspaper up again as a new idea knocked on my brain. A clever scheme. Well, maybe not clever, but not as ludicrous as some of the others I'd contemplated.

Way back when newspapers were king of the media world, they offered the public more than just news and obituaries. They also featured a whole section at the back of the paper known as classified ads. Or "want" ads as Grandma Blue had called them. Small ads in a tiny typeface that offered anything a reader "wanted" to find—a job, a used car for sale, tailoring and housekeeping services, and more. And at only a fraction of the cost of larger display advertisements.

That's what I'd do today. I'd visit the offices of the *Ballard Springs Times* and place a classified ad. That would create a public record that surely my friends in research would find as they hunted through their myriad databases looking for their lost time traveler.

I finished tidying up then found a pencil and a piece of paper and sat down at the kitchen table to compose my ad. Would this plan work? Did I want it to work? After our heated reunion last night, the idea of staying here with Sully was as tempting as chocolate cake and twice as delicious. He sure wouldn't mind if I never found my way back to 2133. He'd welcomed me dropping in on him out of the blue like an early Christmas gift.

Be rational, Beryl. The risk of me staying here was too great, not just to Sully, but to his brother and Cecelia too. I owed it to all of them to try, at the very least.

I picked up the pencil and began to write.

8

I tucked my stinger and the notepaper with my want ad scribbled on it into my coat pocket and left the house around ten. I headed for the bus stop at the bottom of the hill. The day was cold and a thick cover of steel gray clouds loomed overhead. A city bus lumbered up to the stop minutes later, puffing diesel fuel and other noxious chemicals. I followed a housewife clutching a shopping bag on board, dropped a nickel into the fare-box, and took a seat.

As my rapid transit chariot waddled toward down-town, the three-decker houses with their clotheslines strung from back porches gave way to office buildings, shops, and clogged traffic. Through the windshield, I saw the newspaper building ahead, a five-story granite building with dozens of windows and *Ballard Springs Times* on a marquee sign at the top. I pulled the chord to signal the driver I wanted to get off. The bus squealed to a stop in front of Pierce & Taylor, a modern-style concrete department store that took up half a block.

Cecelia had loaned me a winter hat, a felt concoction shaped like a salad bowl. I pulled it down over my ears as I stepped off the bus and turned up my coat collar. Mostly due to the cold, but also because I felt somewhat self-conscious. In an era when men wore suits to take out the trash and women dressed in their Sunday best *and* a girdle to drop by the butcher shop, I was seriously under-dressed in my casual slacks and coat borrowed from the jail's lost and found.

I crossed the street and entered the newspaper build-ing's steamy-hot lobby, where the heavy stench of printing ink and cigarette and cigar smoke battled for odiferous supremacy. The place bustled with activity. The click of footsteps and voices echoed off the walls and ceiling as people hustled toward the bank of elevators directly ahead or veered off toward the stairs.

I found where I needed to go on an information board and opted to walk the two flights up rather than cram into an elevator with a crying baby and a dozen adults puffing away on cigarettes.

At my destination, I joined several others waiting in line. As I inched closer to the desk, I fidgeted, torn once more about whether or not I wanted this plan to work. Whether I really wanted to leave Sully. My turn came. I approached the service window and faced a portly man with blotchy pink skin who offered a helpful smile.

Too late to back out now.

Moments later and after spending not nearly as much of Sully's money as I'd expected, I pushed through the door and out into the cold. I stopped among the pedes-trians breezing by on the sidewalk and gazed around, holding my breath. I didn't know what I expected.

Perhaps Glo popping out of the vortex and chiding me for going missing and giving her a temporal headache and a paperwork nightmare. Maybe Jake rushing up to me, breathlessly demanding to know if I was okay. Or Hank, even, taking precious time away from creating his perfect sourdough bread to escort me back to the future.

The one thing I didn't expect was... nothing. No time tornado, no familiar faces from the future, no resolution. The ad had been a waste of time and money. I was still stuck, with my *should I stay or should I go* dilemma unsolved. And the risk to Sully still there.

I headed back across the street to Pierce & Taylor and instead of going to the bus stop, I followed the crowd of shoppers into the store. I still had most of the cash Sully had given me. Since I was stranded here for the time being, I decided to pick up some supplies to tide me over.

Inside, I found myself in a scene from the movie *Miracle on 34th Street*. The colorized version. The scent of hot chocolate, popcorn, and cotton candy drifted through the store. Huge red and green ornaments hung from the ceiling on white ribbons and colorful paper bells dangled from the shelves. Miniature Christmas trees dotted every free space, and so did images of Santa Claus, hawking everything from potholders to perfume.

Shoppers pored over the shelves, looking for the perfect last-minute gift. Escalators with wooden treads *clack-clacked* loudly as they carried more people up to or down from the second floor. Voices and the tick of footsteps nearly drowned out Judy Garland singing "Have Yourself A Merry Little Christmas" playing over the store's speakers.

I wandered the aisles, drinking it all in, my eyes as

wide as the kids lined up to see Santa Claus. This store was long gone in my 2015 time, replaced by a bank and a dialysis center, but now I understood why my grandmother would get all giddy and nostalgic when talking about shopping at Pierce & Taylor.

I turned to my own shopping and picked up the first item I needed—a toothbrush—then made my way to the lingerie department for the second. I found a dozen shelves stocked with slips, bras, and every sort of contouring, shaping, and downright rib-crushing undergarment ever imagined. I chose a pair of cotton granny panties that would cover me from navel to mid-thigh. Not very sexy, but practical. And a bargain, at two pair for just under a dollar.

The last stop on my shopping spree, I doubled back to the toy department. Among the bins full of yo-yos, puzzles on sale, and a vintage version of Legos, I found the perfect Christmas present for Sully—a toy jeep. I pulled some coins from my coat pocket and asked the clerk to wrap it for me then tucked it into the bag with my other purchases. I grinned. Sully may not like it, but I sure did.

Finished, I headed down the aisle toward what I hoped was the exit. The store was massive, the aisles seemingly endless, and as Jake had reminded me, I had a terrible sense of direction, no matter what time period I was in.

I slowed my already slow pace, my attention caught by a scrawny man in a porkpie hat and frayed coat, picking over the baby dolls. Suddenly, the man snatched one up and squirreled it away inside his coat. A second later, he reached into the next bin and did the same thing with a small red firetruck.

I gasped, though, really, should I be surprised? Shoplifting wasn't a new thing. It'd been around since enterprising merchants first put their wares out for sale millennia ago.

The thief heard me and swung my way. He spat a curse and snatched up a metal ladder truck easily two feet long and hurled it at me. A flash of movement as a broad-shouldered man in a policeman's overcoat leapt in front me and raised his arm like a shield. The firetruck banged his arm then hit the floor with a heavy clank, its rubber wheels spinning madly.

The shoplifter fled. Instead of going after him, Sully turned to me. "Are you alright?"

My heart hammered. With his overcoat, his uniform, and his cap fit squarely on his head, he looked as if he'd just stepped out of a Norman Rockwell painting.

"I'm *not* alright. You could've been killed," I said and Sully laughed. "Well, you might've been seriously injured." I watched him pick the truck up off the floor and toss it into the air, catching it deftly. "Okay, maybe slightly bruised. But the thing is, the guy could've had a knife."

Sully stared after the shoplifter. The man raced through the crowd, his hat bobbing. "Nah, he's not armed."

"Shouldn't you go arrest him?"

"I should. But I won't. I bring him in, I'm in for an afternoon of paperwork." He shrugged. "Besides... There's a reason he's stealing toys at Christmas."

My belly executed a perfect pirouette. "Sully, you're a good man. A hero, even." Compassionate. Kind, too.

He scowled. "No, I'm not. Some folks just need a break." He looked down at me and his scowl dissolved into a smile that encouraged more butterflies in my belly. "You know, I came in to pick up a doll for Effie for Christmas. Though truth be told, I've already bought her three. Quite a coincidence, us running into each other."

"Is it?"

He lifted a hand. "Don't start with that fate and destiny booshwa again."

"Really, Sergeant Sullivan?" Why couldn't that man accept he might be in danger?

"Really, Beryl Blue." He offered one of his most charming scowls. "I bet even fate takes a lunch break once in a while. You should too. C'mon, there's a restaurant in the back of the store. Join me in a bite to eat. I'm starving after my recent brush with death."

"Wise ass," I said but didn't argue. It was pointless, anyway. He'd brush off each and every objection I could come up with as casually as dusting lint from his sleeve.

I took his arm when he offered it and let him escort me to the back of the store. I patted my coat pocket, feeling the stinger inside. Sully may consider the dire predictions about his future nothing but booshwa, but I felt better having a weapon within easy reach in case fate had anymore tricks up its sleeve today. Or Rasmussen showed up. I hadn't seen even a glimpse of Niels since I'd chased him out the door of Scotty's bar, but that didn't mean he wasn't lurking in the shoe department, waiting for a chance to pounce.

We reached the lunch counter, a long table of Formica and chrome. Two waitresses in pale green dresses and white aprons hustled up and down a narrow aisle between the counter and the kitchen beyond. I sank onto a swivel seat next to Sully, joining several other customers who hunkered over coffee and Cokes and an early lunch. All very retro and cool, though I couldn't help thinking of what the lunch counter would come to symbolize a decade from now, as the battle for civil rights took center stage.

I removed my hat and shrugged off my coat, letting it fall over the seatback. Sully unbuttoned his coat and swept off his cap, tossing it onto the counter.

"Merry Christmas, Linda," he said to the curvy blond waitress with crooked teeth who approached us. "We'll both have coffee."

She responded with a dreamy sigh and fanned herself with her order pad as she hustled away. Sully turned to me with another big smile.

"What's got you grinning like that?" I asked. His giddiness got me grinning too.

"Why shouldn't I smile? I just survived certain death from a toy firetruck, I'm having lunch with the prettiest girl in town, and it's almost Christmas. Tomorrow's Christmas Eve, you know."

"Tomorrow is also my birthday."

His left eyebrow shot skyward. "What? Why didn't you tell me?"

"I didn't realize it. It was April when I hopped into the oscillator yesterday, August where I landed for my mission, and now it's December here. It's hard to wrap my head around these calendar hops."

He laughed. "Wrap your head around? You future people sure talk strange."

"So says the guy who was singing Flat Foot Floogie with a floy floy or something like that this morning."

He clapped a hand to his chest. "Oof. You got me." He turned to the waitress, who'd returned with our coffees and set them down in front of us. "Thanks, Linda. I'll have the tomato soup and a hamburger, with extra pickles. What about you, sweetheart?"

He addressed that question to me. I goggled at the array of sandwiches and meals listed on the sign board hanging above the rectangular order window that looked into the kitchen. What *wouldn't* I have? It all looked delicious and so tempting. And at low, low prices. I mean, twenty cents for a hamburger? That price would make a fast-food restaurant of my era weep with competitive envy.

After a thorough look-see and Linda tapping her toe with impatience, I chose a roast beef sandwich and potato chips. The waitress whisked herself away and Sully swiveled his chair to face me, his eyes sparkling.

"Tomorrow's your birthday," he said.

"I believe we've already established that fact."

"How old are you gonna be?"

Who knew? Jumping around in time sure did a number on my internal birthday clock. Would I still be twenty-six or did I jump ahead six months straight to twenty-seven, do not pass *Go*?

I reached out and touched the dimple in his chin. "You know a lady never tells."

Sully snorted a laugh. "You're a real piece of work, Beryl Blue." He picked up the sugar dispenser and tipped it over his cup. "What d'ya say we do something special to celebrate your special day?"

"Like what? Go on a cruise?"

"Already been on one of those. It's called a troop ship." He splashed some cream into his coffee and stirred. "The cruise over there was no fun, but the trip home sure was." He lifted his cup and looked at me over the rim. "I'm thinking we should celebrate closer to home. There's a party tomorrow night. A Christmas party. One of those boozy shindigs the Chamber of Commerce puts on a couple times of year. They invite all of us at the station. I never go, but I'd like to go now. Will you be my date?"

He couldn't be serious. Or... could he? "You want me to go out with you in public?" Sitting here with him now was risky enough. "What will I wear? My minidress?"

"*I'd* like that, but all that leg might give the ladies of the gardening club the vapors." He sipped his coffee, his eyes crinkling in a smile. "We'll find you a dress to wear. Cecelia might have something in the back of her closet."

My belly fluttered again. I supposed he was happy to have me here with him, but did he have to be so sweet and smiley and so... adorable? He acted like I was the girl next door he'd been panting to date since the high school pep rally before the big game and not the woman who would lead to his doom.

Fortunately, Linda saved me from answering when she came by with our lunches, my roast beef on white bread and a mound of potato chips and Sully's tomato soup and hamburger, hot off the grill.

Sully applied himself to the soup. I picked up half of my sandwich and nibbled on it at first, then devoured it as if I hadn't eaten for a year. The bread was soft and fresh, the roast beef plentiful.

Sully finished his soup and pushed the bowl away, watching me eat with affectionate, slightly mystified amusement. "You like that sandwich, huh? Don't they have roast beef in your time?"

"Oh, no, we do. It's just, everything seems to taste better here. Breakfast. Dinner last night." I bumped his shoulder with my own. "Maybe it's such a pleasant dining companion."

Laughing, he started in on his burger and we chatted while we ate, unhurried, shifting topics. He asked what it was like to have a Christmas Eve birthday. Special and annoying, I replied, like showing up to your own surprise party and someone else getting all the presents. I asked about living with his brother. He said he enjoyed the company and liked sharing expenses, but he wanted his own place at some point. We both agreed Effie was the most adorable child ever born.

The easy conversation took a turn when the romance fan in me asked about Pat and Cecelia's wedding.

"They got hitched at the Baptist Church over on Elm Street." Sully nodded when the waitress came by with a coffeepot. She refilled both of our cups and moved along. "Cecelia looked beautiful, of course. She wore a nice dress. Pat called the color coral pink, like seashells he'd seen in the South Pacific. Her nurse friends came, and her family drove down from Vermont. Me and Pat's boss from the hardware store, Mr. Flynn, were the only ones on the groom's side of the aisle."

"Really? Just the two of you?"

He nodded. "Did it bug me none of Pat's buddies

showed for his wedding to a colored girl? Hell yeah, and I'll tell 'em so if I ever have the bad luck to run into them." He gulped his coffee, his scowl in angry mode. "I don't get people like that. One thing I learned while freezing my ass off in the war, everyone bleeds red. We're all the same. That's all I need to know. All I needed to know when Pat started keeping company with Cecelia."

I nibbled on a potato chip, weighing his words, his uncomplicated explanation of a complicated issue. "I wish everyone understood that."

"Me too." He finished his burger and wiped his hands with a paper napkin. "But something else the Army taught me. It's hard to change a man's mind once he's made it up. All you can do is fight. When Pat met Cecelia, I figured he was in for a long, tough road, but I told him I'd be right there with him, fists ready. I'll fight for him, for her, and especially for Effie."

Pride flushed through me. It wrapped around every nerve ending and lit me up. Such a Sully thing to say. Such a Sully thing to do. Defending his family, sticking up for what was right. Always.

He swiveled to face me again. "Now let's talk about you. What have you been up to today? Did you go to a movie?"

"Movie...?" I said, confused. Sully the soldier might be adept at pivoting from one intense topic to another, but it took me more than a second to shift gears. "Oh, the movie. No. I went to the newspaper office instead."

His eyebrow moved up a fraction. "For what?"

I pushed my empty plate away and told him about the want ad.

His eyebrow rose much, much higher. "That's awful complicated. Is it gonna work?"

"Not so far. Maybe not at all."

He reached over and ran his fingers lightly down the back of my hand and along my ring finger. "Would it be so bad if you had to stay here?"

He caught me in his gaze, his expression filled with something I'd never seen before. Fear, I thought. Fear of losing me. Fear of me leaving him. The doubt that had scratched at me all morning came back for an encore. I resolutely pushed it away. I *had* to leave. I had to leave him. I knew that. Sully knew that. If I could defeat fate and keep him alive, I'd stay. Forever.

But...

I pulled my hand away, out of his reach. "It's not that simple."

"I s'pose," he murmured, holding my gaze a beat longer before he sat back and put on his poker face. He looked toward a countertop display case near the coffee machine and the pies and cakes rotating on the shelves. "I'm thinking about a slice of fresh pumpkin pie for dessert. How about you?"

A WHILE LATER, both of us stuffed full of pumpkin pie, Sully helped me put on my coat then tucked his policeman's cap under his arm and led the way toward the exit. More people thronged the store, searching for the perfect gift. A boy wearing earmuffs wove in and out of the crowd as he held a toy airplane aloft, making propeller noises. The line to see Santa had grown and snaked through the aisles, children dancing from foot to foot in impatience.

"Cripes," Sully muttered, scowling at the traffic jam. "It's like a convoy without a commander, only slower."

He took my hand and with his expert navigation, we soon made it to the front of the store. The revolving door flung us out onto the sidewalk and into the cold. We stopped to say goodbye in front of one of the store's display windows, decorated with holly-jolly exuberance, including miniature reindeer and elf figurines, a smiling Santa, and a toy train toot-tooting along tracks laid out in a circle.

Sully drew me to him for a kiss, his lips lingering on mine. The perfect kiss at the end of the perfect lunch in this perfectly splendid if a little chilly moment in time. Except for that dark cloud hanging over our heads. I'd let my guard down during lunch and had slacked off on watching for Rasmussen or any other dangers.

I broke off the kiss, eager to send Sully on his way.

He drew back and gazed at me steadily, as if reading my thoughts. "Don't fret, sweetheart. I've been on alert the whole time. Even at lunch when you thought I was mesmerized by your charms, I kept watch. That's something else the war taught me. Never let your guard down. You gotta be aware of the simplest things, like a change in the wind, or a different smell in the air. See that fella over my right shoulder? The one with the face like a mouse? He's a pickpocket known as Lenny the Dip and he's waiting for me to move along before going to work. He's the only threat within five miles at the moment."

He cupped my face and gently stroked my cheeks with his thumbs. "And don't forget I've got a whole precinct full of cops just down the street to keep watch over me. Now, you go on and catch the bus and I'll go catch Lenny." He kissed me one more time. "See you when I get home."

I floated to the bus stop in a daze. Sully rivaled Winston Churchill in his ability to deliver a reassuring speech. But it was the last word that had fallen from his enticing lips that sent a shiver of both fear and excitement skipping down my back.

Home.

A welcoming word. A safe, comforting, and loving word. Something I'd never really had. At least, nothing permanent. I'd had a home for only a short time with my parents, and then equally as brief with my grandmother. Or rather, the woman who'd taken me in after they'd died, the woman I would come to know as my grandmother. I'd had a home with her, but then I'd lost it and wandered around untethered afterward. I had friends in Futureworld, dear friends, but even there I still felt adrift.

Without realizing it, this place and this time had begun to feel like home. A real home. A place where I wanted to stay and live for always and always. With Sully. He was where I wanted to be.

The bus pulled up and I climbed aboard. My spirits dropped along with the coins I dropped through the slot in the farebox. Home with Sully could never be more than an impossible dream, no matter how much we both wanted it to come true. Despite his fine speech and encouraging kisses, the threat to his life and our future was still there.

And until we could figure out a way to stop it, the threat would always be there, hanging over us both.

JOSEPHINE THRUST Effie into Cecelia's outstretched arms, then stuffed a paper bag filled with clothes into mine.

"It's not much," she said, waving off my thanks. "But it'll keep you from having to wear trousers all the time."

She left, and while Cecelia rained kisses over her delighted daughter's face and got reacquainted after their day apart, I opened the bag and inspected its contents.

Josephine's sister Althea possessed both a generous soul and good taste. She'd packed the bag with lots of fashionable goodies including a couple of cream-colored blouses with tailored collars, a pleated plaid skirt, and two dresses, one minty green with dark green flecks and the other, a violet blue with short sleeves and a pencil skirt.

"How lovely," Cecelia cooed, balancing Effie on her hip. "Tom's eyes will pop when he sees you in that blue number."

Yep, they would, and a dress like this would offer one less stumbling block to attending the Chamber of Commerce shindig he'd mentioned at lunch. I had something dressy to wear and I had Sully as my eager and willing date. All I needed was the courage to put away my fears and venture out into public with him.

If I was still here tomorrow. *If* Glo and Jake ever got my message. I knew exactly squat about sending messages across time. Maybe it was like sending messages to Mars and there was a considerable delay on both ends.

I hung up the rest of the clothes in Sully's bedroom closet and put on the green dress. It had three-quarter sleeves and was a little snug in the hips and bust, but it fit. *I* fit. Except for my 1960s flat heeled shoes, I looked and felt like I belonged here. The word *home* tried to push into my mind again. I pushed back, refusing to even think about it.

I stepped out of Sully's room to find Cecelia on the phone, and Effie in the parlor, wearing a cute red dress and confined to a wooden playpen more dangerous than the highchair of doom. She didn't seem to mind her imprisonment. She hung onto the playpen's top rail, bouncing on the balls of her feet and squeaking happily at her mother.

"That was Tom." Cecelia hung up the phone and stood from her seat at the telephone table. "He's picking up dinner from the chop suey place near the police station. He knows I hate to cook, and with Pat working tonight, it'd be peanut butter and jam sandwiches for all if he didn't bring something home." She flashed a fond smile. "Tom's so sweet."

"Sure," I agreed, though sweet was one of the lesser adjectives beginning with *S* I'd use to describe Big Red. Sarcastic and sexy duked it out in the battle for adjective supremacy.

She gave my dress an admiring once-over. "Don't you look lovely."

Sully thought so too. "You're as pretty as a picture," he said when I met him at the door. "I'm glad I hurried home."

"You like?" I asked, running my hands over my hips, smoothing the soft fabric. I would've blushed if I knew how.

"Hell yeah, I like." His gaze shifted to his bedroom door. "Let me show you how much I like."

Behind me, Cecelia cleared her throat. "Did you want to put those bags down first?"

"What? Oh." He glanced down in surprise at the two brown paper takeout bags he held, stuffed full and smelling of ginger and pork fried rice.

Minutes later, we dug into an array of delectable dishes spread out over the table, chop suey with shrimp and mushrooms, chicken chow mein, and something I'd never seen on the menu at my neighborhood Chinese takeout, fried oysters. Sully had liberated Effie from her highchair and plopped her on his lap. She tried to grab anything within reach, but her uncle multitasked with ease, keeping her from upending his beer can and shoving her hands into boxes while feeding her noodles and managing to get a few bites of food of his own.

"Did you catch Benny the Dip?" I asked Sully, giving one of the oysters a try and immediately putting it back on my plate. I liked most seafood, but fried oysters? *Not* a fan.

"It's Lenny the Dip, and no, I didn't get a chance." Sully moved a box of fried rice out of reach of Effie's grabby hands. "For some reason, seeing me patrolling outside the store encouraged Lenny to keep his hands to himself. He didn't pick a single pocket." Cecelia laughed that delightful musical giggle and he gave her a crooked grin. "How was your work today? Has old Mr. Crotchety made any improvement?"

"Tom!" She laughed again. "I'm forever going to regret telling you about my patient's complaining ways."

"What hospital do you work at?" I asked. Ballard

Springs had three or four hospitals back in the day, though in my millennial life, they'd all been merged into one conglomerate under a massive corporate umbrella.

"Oh, I don't work in a hospital. Most of them prefer to employ only single women, not us old married ladies. As for colored nurses..." She shrugged. "I'm a private duty nurse for an elderly gent who lives on the north side. There's not much wrong with the fella, just age. Aches and pains we'll all have the pleasure of experiencing, the good lord willing."

"Lord willing, we'll have the strength to bellyache about it the way he does, too," Sully said. "That's called an eggroll," he added when I reached for one.

He went on to describe the delicacy as if I'd never heard of eggrolls or ever eaten Chinese food before. I let him lecture. I was usually the one going all know-it-all on him, mostly because being from the future, I *did* know it all. Most of it, anyway.

After dinner, we gathered once again in the parlor and listened to the sitcom *Fibber McGee & Molly* on the radio. Cecelia knitted in her rocking chair. I sat on the couch. Sully sat on the floor at my feet with his back against the sofa, legs stretched out as he helped Effie stack wooden alphabet blocks on top of one another. Well, Sully stacked. Effie waited until he'd built a precarious pile then, gurgling with glee, she knocked them all down. Her patient uncle would give her an approving grin, then start construction over again.

I rested my hand on his shoulder, watching them play, all kinds of complicated feelings rolling through me and the word *home* bubbling inside me again. I wished Time Scope had invented a way to freeze time so I could stay in this moment forever, with a child's laughter filling the warm room, my leg pressed against Sully's side, occasionally feathering my fingers through his thick hair. I longed to stay in this cocoon, safe and loved, with the night stretching out before us and Sully's bedroom only steps away.

The radio show came to an end. Fibber and Molly and the entire town of Wistful Vista and the thirty-piece orchestra that had somehow crowded into the McGee's parlor sang "'Twas the Night Before Christmas," then the whole mob headed off for a long winter's nap.

Cecelia's knitting needles clicked as she tucked her knitting into a sewing box next to her chair. She stood and came over to the sofa. "Time for the little one to be in bed," she said and hoisted Effie up off the floor and into her arms. They both waved night-night to us as they toddled from the parlor, headed for their rooms in the back of the apartment.

Sully waited until they were out of sight before turning and looking up at me with an impish expression. He ran his hand slowly up my calf, stopping to tickle the delicate spot behind my knee, tempting me to swoon.

"Time for us to be in bed, too," he murmured.

I shivered, caught in his gaze. I couldn't freeze time. Our time together would end. It had to end. But until then, I could make every moment count.

I bent down and kissed him.

9

—————

"Happy birthday, sweetheart."

Sully woke me with a kiss. It was early, the room still shrouded in darkness. The radiator clanged with determination, though it did little to ease the winter chill hanging in the air. But here in the bed, under the covers with Sully, I was warm and comfortable and secure.

"*Mmmm*... I could stay here all day," I said. "In fact, maybe I will."

"Lazybones. I s'pose that means you won't meet me for lunch again today."

"No. I'm staying here, and you know why. It's the safe thing to do." Exactly the wrong thing to say. He adopted that mulish scowl I knew and loathed. "Please, Sully. I know you're on alert and watching out for danger twenty-four-seven, but why tempt fate?"

"Why not?" He shifted and drew me closer. "I'd rather get into the fight than cower in a foxhole and wait for it to come to me."

Oh, Sully. The word *wait* didn't exist in his vocabulary. *Don't wait* were his operative words. Don't wait, seize the day and rush right in, take the bull by the horns and all those other cliches. The man of action, needing to take action and confront the risk head on. One of the reasons I loved him, and the major reason I feared for his life.

"Tell you what," he said, a sly smile curving his lips. "You stay put here today, and we'll go to the party tonight."

Ah. He hadn't brought the subject up again, but I knew he hadn't forgotten. Now he had leverage. I might as well agree. After landing in a cell at his police station, and running into him at the store yesterday, I figured fate would find a way to whisk me to that party, anyway. Kidnapping, fairy godmother and a pumpkin carriage, time skip, even. I glanced toward the closet, where the blue dress that fate had so thoughtfully provided hung inside, waiting to make its debut. Somehow, someway, I'd end up Sully's date tonight.

If I couldn't find a way back to Futureworld first.

"Yes, I'll go with you, you stubborn, impossible man," I said finally. "On one condition—"

"I wear a flak jacket and a helmet and ride around in a Sherman tank. I know, I know." He reached over and brushed a tangled lock of hair from my eyes, his fingers warm against my skin. "I promise to be careful, as long as *you* promise to try to relax and have fun."

He kissed me, a slow kiss that quickly turned hot and heated and ended with us both relaxing and having fun and me getting the best birthday present I'd had in a long, long time.

AFTER SULLY LEFT FOR WORK—GRINNING but running very late—I put on the pleated skirt Josephine's sister had loaned me and paired it with one of the blouses, a tuck-in with puffy sleeves and sharp collar points. I stepped out into the kitchen in time to wave hello to Jo and bye-bye to Effie. Pat had already left for classes at Camp Davis, with Cecelia heading out the door next.

Within moments, the apartment fell silent. I helped myself to eggs and bacon again, ignoring the hit to my cholesterol for the second day in a row.

I reached for the newspaper, still on the kitchen table where Cecelia had left it. I flipped through the pages to the classified ads in the back, kind of hoping I wouldn't find mine. If it was somehow missing, that could explain the lack of response from the future.

I scanned the columns of ads, looking for the category where I'd placed my message. Not help wanted, not items for sale, or a dozen other categories that filled the newsprint. I found it way at the bottom—*Clairvoyants*. It was the smallest block of ads, but the most unusual, sure to catch some temporal researcher's eye. And the perfect fit for someone who truly knew the future and could kick all the other mystics' butts in the authenticity department.

In between Madame O'Toole the remarkable card reader and The Marvelous Mystique, offering palm readings daily, I found my cryptic and slightly desperate message: *Madame Beryl Blue knows the future. Find me in Ballard Springs, Franklin Street, 1947. Holiday special; come by Christmas.* Simple and terse, but I'd hoped Alice or one of her team could figure it out. Clearly, they hadn't. A day later, no one had burst out of the vortex to rescue me, and it looked like no one would.

I got up and went to the kitchen window. The frosty temperature left the panes coated with a thin sheen of ice. Now what? I was all out of options. Except one. A drastic one that would shatter my world but would protect Sully. *Leave.* If I couldn't time skip, I could just walk away. Leave Ballard Springs, leave Sully, and disappear into 1947 for good. Without me here, he would have no one to save from Niels, or whatever other terrible event I'd need saving from that would lead to Sully's death.

But how could I do that? How could I leave his kisses and his embrace and his tender touch? How could I ever leave *him*?

Questions I couldn't answer, nor did I want to.

I returned to my breakfast and pushed my worries away by cleaning up. I turned on the box radio that sat on top of the refrigerator, or the icebox as Sully called it, hoping to find some music to listen to as I cleaned. After a crackling moment of static, an announcer implored listeners to stay tuned for *The Guiding Light*, coming up next. A soap opera, I soon discovered. In fact, the same soap I semi-remembered from afterschool TV in my middle school days.

I did the dishes and swept the kitchen floor, then reached for the newspaper to put it away. As I folded it, I spotted an ad for Bell Telephone System on the back page. I perked up. The ad read, *Busiest Christmas for Long Distance.* A smiling Santa Claus warned readers that call volume would be heavy on the holiday, so dial up the relatives early to be sure your Christmas greeting would get through. I perked up some more, getting an idea.

ET had phoned home, why couldn't I?

I could literally call home, as in dialing up my grandpa Hank. If he was still alive in this time period. And still hiding out in Illinois. And had stayed put in Chicago for the last twenty-plus years.

A ton of *ifs*, but my only option available at the moment.

I darted to the telephone desk in the dining room and stared at the hulking phone on top, unsure what to do next. I searched my memory for the early days after my parents died, when Grandma Blue and I still lived in the three-decker. We had a clunky rotary dial like this one, but I was too young to ever have used it. I'd seen people operate these kinds of phones in old movies, though. How hard could it be?

I sat down at the desk and picked up a handset that weighed about a hundred pounds. I put it to my ear, hearing the deep, steady hum of the dial tone. The dial had ten finger holes. I found the one marked "O" for Operator, pulled the wheel all the way around until I hit a metal stop, then let go. The dial emitted a soft *z-z-z* sound as it spun back into place.

Simple. All I had to do now was wait as it rang.

"This is the operator. Number please," a nasal voice answered.

It took a few seconds for my twenty-first century mind to process an actual human voice on the other end of the line. "Uh... number? I don't know. I mean, I'm not sure. I'm looking for someone. In Illinois."

"Hold please while I connect you with long distance," she said, like *duh, you should've known that.*

Several clicks and a moment of dead air later, her nasal-voice twin answered and demanded my party's name and address. A hundred female voices chattered in the background, some of Ma Bell's army of operators named Ginger or Gertie, working hard to get the calls through.

I hesitated. Hank had used the name Henry Gill in 1925. Would he still use that alias so many years later? I took a stab and offered up his details.

I held my breath, waiting, picturing the operator of these pre-Google days running her finger down a long list of names in a telephone book a thousand pages thick. Finally, she came back on the line. Every nerve and muscle in my body tensed. If I could talk to Hank, problem solved.

"I'm sorry, there is no one of that name in that location."

I replaced the handset in the cradle, truly hanging up a phone for the first time in my life. I'd reached a dead end. Problem unsolved. Disappointment and elation went to war in my emotional suitcase. I was stuck. Here with Sully.

Maybe for good.

THE THUMPING SOUND of dirt and slush being stomped off shoes sounded in the back hall, followed by the creak of the rear door opening. Pat, home already. Well, it was Christmas Eve. His classes had probably gotten out early.

He pulled a string suspended from the light fixture and the narrow back hallway lit up. He unwound his scarf and hung up his coat then stepped into the kitchen. His face telegraphed his surprise at finding me in front of the stove, though believe me, no one could be more surprised at this domestic turn of events than Beryl Blue. I'd found an eggplant and parmesan cheese in the icebox and some breadcrumbs in the cupboard in the pantry and had set out on an ambitious venture to put them together for dinner.

Pat came closer and peered at the eggplant sizzling in the skillet, inhaling deeply. "Looks delicious."

"No, it doesn't. It looks like toxic sludge. But it'll fill you up even if it doesn't taste great. I'm no Julia Child."

"Julia who?"

"Right. Wrong decade." I put the lid on the skillet and lowered the flame. "Cecelia's not the only one who loathes KP. My kitchen skills begin and end at scrambling an egg. But I wanted to make supper for everyone tonight as a way of saying thank you for letting me stay."

And to soften the blow when they discovered I might be stuck here for the duration.

"You think I had a choice in you staying?" Pat said as he opened the fridge and pulled out a can of Narragansett. "When Tommy wants something done, it gets done."

"Truer words were never spoken." That gushed out with tons of affection. "Has he always been that way? Bossy, playing Mr. Fix-It? Taking care of everyone?"

"Yeah. Always. Even when he was a kid." Pat sank into a chair at the little table and opened the beer. He tossed the metal opener onto the tabletop, next to a pack of Chesterfield cigarettes. Unopened, I was pleased to see.

I sat down across from him. "Tell me about those days. What was Sully like? Did he ever have fun as a kid, or has that scowl lived on his face forever? You must have a story. I can hardly get two words out of him about growing up."

"Tommy doesn't like to talk about those days, or any days. He's not one for looking back. Never has been. He's the perfect infantry man. He's focused on what's ahead, moving forward, looking for the next opportunity. Or threat." A fond smile touched his lips. "I remember back in thirty-eight, we were lucky to get jobs bussing tables at the Parker House in Boston. A swanky place with chandeliers and rich folks rubbing noses with Mayor Curley. Trouble came one night in October, when Orson Welles put on a radio play about Martians invading. You ever hear of that? Scared everyone shitless. Pardon me. Cece nags me not to curse, not with a little one in the house, but I'm a Navy man and can't help slipping up."

I murmured, "No problem," and he nodded, reaching for his cigarettes. He sliced me a furtive glance, then sat back and crossed his arms. I felt a touch of satisfaction. Maybe he could quit smoking, with a little pressure.

"Anyway, people didn't know it was a radio play, even though it was Halloween. Fellas were shitting—s'cuse me again—messing their pants, thinking Martians were landing on Boston Common. Not Tommy. He was cool, said he'd get to the bottom of it. This one customer went berserk, shouting we had to build a barricade on Tremont Street. He attacked a waitress who told him to shut up. Tommy set him right." He chuckled. "Bet that fella's jaw still smarts. I couldn't have been more than sixteen. Tommy was nineteen going on forty. Always thinking, always ready to stick up for others. That girl, me, Ma, and the rest of the world."

He took a fast swig of beer and his expression darkened.

"Then there was Pop. Built like a brick shithouse and mean as a wild bronco. Tommy always challenged him. I think he enjoyed it in a way." He eyed me with a wince. "No disrespect. My brother doesn't pick fights. But he don't shy away when the fight comes to him. He goes all the way to the mat. Especially when he went against Pop."

"That's how he got the scar across his nose."

His gaze turned sharp. "Told you that story, did he?"

Not without me having to crowbar the details out of him. "He's told me a little."

He gave a cynical laugh. "He must really like you." He sat back and drummed his fingers on the table, his eyes on me. "It happened long before Orson Welles scared the pants off the world. Ma and Pop were fighting, like usual. They were two people who should never have been married. They hated each other, it seemed, or maybe the booze made them like that. And Pop never got over the war. The first world war, I mean. It was like he was stuck in no-man's-land between the trenches. Angry, scared. He took it out on her. She let him, so he wouldn't go after us."

My heart ached. Literally ached. Sully had shared precious few details of his past, and now I knew why he didn't look back.

"I don't even remember what they fought about that night," Pat said, his voice low and strained. "She usually just took it, but when Pop came at me, she snapped. Lunged for him with a knife, like a banshee out for blood. She woulda drawn blood and more if Tommy hadn't been there. He threw himself between the knife and my pop. He was thirteen, maybe fourteen. He got cut. Blood everywhere. Ma screamed when she saw it. She threw down the knife and ran away. Look what you done, Pop says to him, like Tommy was to blame for every miserable moment of our lives."

"Oh, Pat." And, oh, Sully. You poor kid.

"I thought he'd lost an eye. I thought—" His voice caught. "I thought he'd die. Maybe he woulda if someone hadn't called the cops. They took him to the hospital and hauled the old man off to the drunk tank. Ma never forgave herself."

He noisily cleared his throat and grabbed the cigarettes and lighter off the table. His chair scraped the floor as he shoved it back and stood. He started across the room toward the hallway.

"Hey, Pat?" He stopped, eyeing me with a stung expression. I swallowed guilt and sorrow. "I'm sorry. I didn't mean to dredge up old wounds."

"I know. But now you know why he doesn't look to the past, and why he runs toward the fight. The only time *I* ever ran was to get away. I ran from our folks to join the Navy while Tommy stayed home and took care of them. Even in the war, I hid below deck on my tin can, away from the action. He ran toward the danger. He always sticks his neck out." He shrugged. "I never had that kind of courage in me."

"That's not true. I think you're just as brave."

"You mean me and Cecelia? I don't see me marrying a

colored girl as brave. I see it as fate. I love her, with all my heart." He eyed the cigarette pack in his hand then crushed it in his fist and tossed it back onto the table. "*She's* the brave one for taking on an old seadog like me." His strained features relaxed and his voice shifted. Tender, loving, so like Sully's. "Now if you'll excuse me, I've got to go pick up my other sweetheart. She should be waking up from her afternoon nap about now."

"Pat," I called and he turned back again. "You're a good man."

He nodded. "You're not so bad yourself." He gazed at me with an open, almost affectionate look. "By the way, I hear there's snow in the forecast for tomorrow."

10

Sully burst into the apartment well after dark, bringing with him the smell of the cold outdoors. He flung off his coat, tossed it and his cap in the direction of the coatrack, and pulled me into his arms.

"I missed you." He kissed me with a smack that echoed throughout the house. He let me go and glanced in the direction of the kitchen. "That smells good. What is it?"

"It's eggplant parmesan," Pat called from the parlor, where he was playing horsey with Effie. Cecelia gave an assist by holding their daughter on his back while he crawled around the room whinnying like a drunken nag that had just won the Kentucky Derby.

Sully's eyebrow quirked. "Eggplant what?"

"You'll like it," I said. "I cooked it." Both eyebrows shot up now, whether impressed or alarmed, I couldn't tell. I moved on to the domestic portion of the conversation. "Did you have a good day at the office, dear?"

"I had a dull day. How about you?"

"I figured out how to use the telephone. Successfully."

"Congratulations." His jocularity faded. "Does this mean you reached your people?"

He always said *your people* like they were aliens, though I supposed to him they were. "No. All I reached was a dead end."

"You'll find them eventually." I could've been mistaken, but his voice said he hoped eventually meant never. "I'm sure the party tonight will cheer you up."

A nervous sizzle tweaked my belly. Nervousness Sully's superhuman ability to read me picked up on in a flash.

"Hey, sweetheart, don't fret. We'll have fun." He stepped closer, his gaze in pep talk mode. "You just said you can't get in touch with your people. You may be here for a while. Maybe forever. While I'm fine with that, I know there's a risk of you staying and it scares me."

"Oh really?" After what Pat had told me earlier, I doubted anything could scare Sully.

"No. I admit it. I'm scared. I don't want your life in danger, but we can't have this... prophecy hanging over our heads every minute. The risk is always going to be there. We need to go out. I *want* to go out. Tonight, with you. If something happens, I'll deal with it. If we bump into your time traveling friend, I'll punch his lights out and be done with him. If nothing happens, we'll have a grand time." He crooked a finger under my chin and tipped my head back, flashing that special smile. "Especially me. I'll have the *best* time, because I'll be with the smartest, most exciting, and most beautiful girl in town."

I sighed. "It's such a Sully tactic to offset your bullish need to plow into danger with bald-faced flattery."

"Is it working?"

In a way. Perhaps his insistence we attend this shindig despite my worries went beyond his need to face the threat head-on. Maybe he simply wanted to show me off. Gee Beryl, slow on the uptake. The man was *proud* of me.

And he was right. A dark cloud would hang over us both as long as we were together, whether Ras was the threat or something else. I couldn't cower and hide forever. And what's more, I didn't want to. This place and time may very well be my new home, and we had to go on with our lives and fight the fight if and when it came to us.

But I wouldn't go unarmed.

"Sergeant Thomas Sullivan," I said, three parts affection, one very large part exasperation. "I have never seen anyone more determined to get into a fight than you." And now I knew why. He flashed his signature *I won* grin, and I linked my arm in his. "Come on, let's hurry up and eat. We've got a Christmas party to get to."

No one keeled over from the eggplant, and Pat went as far as to ask for seconds. We polished it off, along with the leftover pork fried rice, and afterward, Cecelia shooed us away and she and Pat cleaned up so Sully and I could get ready.

He took his best suit out of the closet and went into the bathroom to shave while I put on the blue dress in his room. Made of a soft, light fabric more suitable for a spring evening out than a winter event, the dress had a chic bow at the waist, short sleeves, a knee-length skirt that hugged my hips and a snug bodice that highlighted my other assets. I accessorized with an elegant, scallop-shaped handbag Cecelia loaned me, with a strap worn around the wrist and just big enough to hold my stinger. As usual, I left my hair to do whatever it wanted.

Everyone turned as I joined them in the parlor. Sully's eyes didn't exactly pop when he saw me in the dress as Cecelia had predicted, but he did stare in a stunned kind of way that got me shivering in delight and sending Jo's sister a million mental thanks for her generosity.

"You look beautiful," he said, his voice husky and appreciative, his feelings for me shimmering in every word.

"You clean up pretty good yourself." I spoke with equal heat and meant it. He looked edible in his soft gray wool suit, his hair brushed and gleaming in the light.

"One thing's missing." He stepped in close. "Your birthday present." He pulled a jewelry box out of his pocket. "You didn't think I forgot, did you?" He opened the box to reveal a small, pale green tear-shaped stone on a silver chain.

"Sully, it's gorgeous."

"I stopped by Abodeely's Jewelers before I came home. Slipped in the door right before they closed up for the holiday, but the old fella in charge was happy to help me out. He showed me some shiny things, flashy things. Nothing caught my eye until I saw this stone. And when he told me what the stone is called, I had to buy it. It's called beryl." He grinned. "I never knew there was such a thing."

I laughed. "I didn't either."

"Guess we both learned something new." He took the necklace from the box. I scooped my hair off my neck as he stepped behind me and fastened it. "Mr. Abodeely said that in ancient times, beryl was known to bring happiness and protect travelers from danger." He leaned close to my ear and whispered, "The perfect gift for my guardian angel."

I spun around and kissed him, my heart squeezing. *How?* That question again. How could I ever leave this man? Even if my future people showed up this very second and offered to whisk me away. Even with fate's threat hanging over both of our heads and my so-called beryl powers of protection unable to stop it. How could I ever go?

"I love it," I said, swallowing tears. "And I love *you*."

More than I could ever imagine or hope for. I kissed him again and hugged him too, never wanting to let go.

SULLY'S CAR puttered toward downtown. We didn't encounter much traffic, no surprise for Christmas Eve. He slowed the car as we passed the Higgins Library. *My* library. An imposing, Victorian gothic building with a mansard roof and dormers on all four sides. The polished iron banisters on the front steps leading up to the entrance gleamed under the streetlights. A massive wreath adorned with red ribbons hung on the heavy mahogany front door, closed and locked up tight for the holiday.

A host of memories and emotions flared inside me. I'd gone there for the first time with my parents when I was about four, and I'd spent every moment I could steal in the place thereafter, when I was growing up and working there as an adult. And it was where Sully and I had fallen in love.

"We'll go and visit," he murmured, as the library receded from view. "We'll stop in after Christmas. When it's open again."

"A nostalgia tour?" That seemed so unlike him, the man who didn't look back.

He glanced my way, his eyes shining. "Making new memories."

"I like the sound of that."

I slid across the seat closer to him and he slipped his arm around me like people could in the olden days before bucket seats. His embrace warmed me, and I snuggled against him, determined to put all my worries away for the evening and enjoy myself. Make new memories and have a grand time, as Sully put it. It *was* my birthday, after all.

Minutes later, he parked near a four-story brick office building with pretty lights in the windows. I waited to get out until he opened the door and held out his hand to help me from the car, one of those old-fashioned gestures that made him feel good and me feel special and a little ridiculous. The smell of snow hung heavy in the air. He escorted me inside and out of the cold. He hung up our coats in a cloakroom off to the right and our shoes clicked softly as we climbed three flights of stairs to the fourth level and what Sully had quaintly called the all-purpose room.

Christmas music greeted us at the top of the stairs, accompanied by the noise of conversation, laughter, and the clink of glasses and cutlery. The din cranked up in volume as we entered the spacious hall, with wood-paneled walls and plentiful windows. Brass wall sconces fitted with electric candles ringed the room, providing a festive blaze of light. A string quartet of four slender white men dressed identically in plaid sportscoats and bowties plucked out a soft tempo version of "Jingle Bells" on a small stage at the far end.

"Let's get some eggnog." Sully settled my hand in the crook of his arm and we waded in.

A hundred or more revelers filled the room. Women in Christmas red and men in gray flannel suits mingled in groups, chatted while sitting in folding chairs, or sampled eggnog and munchies from the refreshment table. Others gathered around the bar, imbibing copiously.

A dizzying array of nodded greetings, smiles, and a few introductions were made as we crossed the room, including other cops, several politicians, and the owner of Sully's favorite deli and his wife. I smiled and exchanged pleasantries, immersing myself in the holiday cheer as if I belonged in 1947, and truly relaxing for the first time since I got here.

"Not *this* song again," Sully said with a groan as the band launched into a cello-heavy rendition of "White Christmas." "I hear it every day. Aren't there any new Christmas songs?"

I giggled at his Grinch-like scowl. "Better get used to it, Sergeant Scrooge. It'll be around for a long time."

His grinchy scowl got grinchier. "It doesn't even snow where Bing Crosby lives, why's he singing about it?"

A fifty-something woman in a navy-blue tailored suit with impressive shoulder pads and a poinsettia corsage cut us off before we reached the refreshment table. She aimed a cheerful, "Merry Christmas," and a gaze filled with mischief at Sully.

He looked around as if searching for a convenient window to leap out of, but good manners got the best of him. "Good evening, Miss Sanborn. Beryl, this is Harriet Sanborn, director and head librarian at Higgins Library," he said as if introducing his personal undertaker.

I might have guessed without Sully dropping that info. She wore her salt-and-pepper hair pulled back in a telltale bun.

"Pleasure to meet you," she said, her eyes twinkling as we shook hands. "Sergeant Sullivan is one of our favorite patrons, and the most frequent."

She winked at him. Actually winked. I enjoyed her twinkly teasing immensely, enjoyed Sully's flushed-face reaction even more.

"Merry Christmas," he mumbled then quickly steered me away as if he had a bunch of overdue books and she was after him to pay the fine.

"Hey. I wanted to stay and talk library gossip with Miss Sanborn. Why'd you drag me away? She seems to admire you a lot."

He grunted. "Admire me? She's *laughing* at me, not admiring me. All those library gals laugh at me. They've been laughing since I brought them that damned suitcase."

"You mean *my* damned suitcase?" And by that I meant the vintage piece of luggage discovered in 2132 that had triggered my journey to Point Bailey and my last adventure with Sully.

"Yeah, *your* damned suitcase." We'd made it to the punchbowl, filled with eggnog most likely spiked with rum. Sully picked up one of the tiny crystal cups and adopted a rueful expression. "I did as you wanted. Went straight to the head librarian and asked her to stow the suitcase in the library for safekeeping for an unknown amount of time. Miss Sanborn looked at me like I had two heads. Who could blame her after the pack of lies I told her? I said it was evidence to a crime we were investigating and too sensitive to keep at the stationhouse."

"Very resourceful, sergeant."

"Very booshwa, Miss Blue. Now Miss Sanborn and all the girls at the library giggle when they see me come in. It's gotten so a fella can't check out the newest Agatha Christie without causing a riot."

"Well, this is one girl who won't giggle at you." I offered a saucy smile. "At least not about that."

Sully replied with one of those unfortunate drunken wolf leers and applied himself to ladling eggnog into the little cup. He handed it to me, and I sipped the vile liquid, managing not to squinch my face in disgust. Barely. I did *not* like eggnog. If I wanted an egg, I'd poach one. If I wanted rum, I'd drink a daiquiri, preferably strawberry and absolutely frozen, not this thick and slimy concoction made even more vile by the sprinkle of nutmeg on top.

But drink I did, watching Sully as he pored over the midcentury party snacks laid out on large silver platters —stuffed olives, Ritz crackers topped with cream cheese and garnished with festive red pimentos, deviled ham finger sandwiches, and a cherry-red Jell-O mold filled with grated carrots. Sully placed some of each treat on a small plate, but steered clear of the Jell-O. And so had everyone else.

Happy and content, I nibbled on a Christmas tree-shaped cookie when a high-pitched shriek suddenly cut across the room. I snapped out of my mellow mood and into a ten-alarm time cop alert. I dropped the cookie and thrust my hand into my bag, scrabbling to get hold of my stinger.

The source of the squeal wended through the crowd and tapped up to us on red pencil heels a second later. Millie. Sully's ex-girlfriend.

"Heavenly days," she burbled, her gaze popping between us. "Of all the people I never expected to see tonight, it's you two."

I relaxed my grip on my stinger as she kissed Sully's cheek then turned her gaze on me. She looked me over critically. I returned the favor. Tall, with an athletic build and patrician features, and as gorgeous as when I'd first met her in Point Bailey in 1946, Millie wore a below-the-knee red skirt and a white silk blouse with a floppy bow at the neck. Very stylish. For a maternity top, anyway. Seems Millie had been busy since I'd seen her last.

Sully greeted her as warmly as one says hello to an ex then turned to me. "You remember Beryl, don't you, Mill?"

Her clipped nod and frozen smile told me she remembered both me and how much she despised Sully calling her *Mill*. "I see you've finally returned to Tom's side," she said, in a tone that defined the word *arch*. "Where have you been all this time?"

"Just kicking up my heels in the twenty-second century."

Sully's eyebrow shot up. Millie's went in the opposite direction. "Beryl, you're such a kidder," she said, more confused than amused.

I eyed the sparkling rock and the gold band on her

ring finger. "Looks like some things have changed for you since I saw you last." I shifted my gaze to her sizeable baby bump. "A *lot* has changed."

Giggling, she straightened the poinsettia clinging to her golden hair like a drowning man to a life raft. "Oh yes. Roy and I met last fall. It was love at first sight." She caressed her belly lovingly. "We two will be we three in the spring. Oh, you positively must meet my husband." Her head swiveled as she searched the room. "Now, where did he get himself off to? Ah, there he is. Roy?"

She waved to a multitude of men in gray flannel mingling near the bar. One of them detached himself from the group and dutifully trooped over to us.

Millie seized his arm. "Darling, you remember my friend, Police Sergeant Tom Sullivan? This is his..." She tipped her head, looking like a perplexed sparrow. "Well, I hardly know what to call you."

I didn't know either. I kicked that around a moment. While I liked the alliteration of Tom's time-traveling twinkie, Sully's lover of the star-crossed variety seemed more appropriate. Soul mate, even, except that seemed too pompous and florid.

Finally, Millie went with a plain and simple, "I suppose I'll call you Tom's special friend. Beryl, this is my husband, Roy. He's in insurance."

That checked out. No slam on those in the insurance business. They had to put up with more grief and stereotypes than librarians ever would, but the guy couldn't look more like an insurance man if he tried. Average height, average build, nondescript features, horn-rimmed glasses, and hair slicked back with about two quarts of some kind of greasy hair tonic that smelled like cherries.

He looked like the cover model for a 1950s version of *Life Insurance Today* magazine.

We murmured our hellos and exchanged generic commentary about the weather. Millie's gaze bounced from me to Sully. "I'm so happy to see you two together at last. I guess you fixed whatever it was that kept you apart. You're both positively glowing." She flashed me a knowing smile and touched her belly again. "Will you soon be putting on the pounds like I am?"

I choked in surprise. Sully both scowled and blushed, if that was even possible. Roy chortled.

"Whoa, there," he said. "Don't put the cart before the horse, hon. Let the folks breathe. You already have lots of company who'll be changing diapers soon, no need to drum up new recruits."

He swept out his arm, gesturing to the many other women mingling and laughing, smoking and drinking and having a grand old time. A good seventy percent of them sported Baby Boom baby bumps of their own.

Including the woman in a moss-green maternity dress who strolled over to say hello to Millie, escorted by a tall, slender man in a sober blue suit and a pair of equally sober rimless eyeglasses. An ordinary, unremarkable white couple, the epitome of postwar conformity. People you might meet on the street or at the supermarket or at a party like this one. People who would blend in and not stand out.

Just as they had intended when they'd fled the future.

My mouth went dry, and my knees weakened. I had only one photograph and my hazy memories to go by, but I recognized them. The man, with a long ski-jump kind of nose and a friendly grin. The woman had hazel eyes, plump lips, thick chestnut hair like mine, and a curvy figure. So lovely.

And so very pregnant.

With me.

They were my parents, and they were here, in Ballard Springs. In 1947.

11

——————

Stunned. I mean... *stunned.*

More than any of the revelations about my past I'd been hit with, this one left me speechless. Lightheaded, gasping in disbelief. With a squadron of B-52s buzzing in my ears and a hammer banging on my brain.

When I was a kid, long before I'd ever heard of Time Scope and the temporal skip and a murderous bastard named Rasmussen, I wished with all my might to go back in time, to meet my parents. To see their faces and get to know them clearly and not in some vague memory of snatches of conversation, fractions of events, random smells.

Now, I'd gotten my wish. My parents were mere feet away. Alive. Real. I gazed into my father's dark brown eyes, the same eyes I saw staring back at me when I looked into a mirror. I could smell the light, flowery scent of Mom's perfume. They were so close I could reach out and touch them. Hug them.

And the only thing I wanted to do was run away. Well, perhaps faint or throw up first, but running away was at the top of my to-do list of reactions.

"Jane," Millie cried, making me jump. "I'm surprised to see you here tonight. Shouldn't you be resting? You look about to burst!"

My mother waved that off. "I feel fine. Dr. McFarland assures me this rugrat isn't coming until the new year."

The buzzing in my ears intensified. Big oops, Dr. McFarland. That rugrat wouldn't wait for the new year, she'd be born... I looked at the massive grandfather clock standing between two windows. *Gah.* Could I exist in the same space as baby me when I made my debut a couple of hours from now? That was one rule of temporal engagement Time Scope had failed to address in the training manuals.

"You okay?" Sully asked, from far away. Or close to my ear. I couldn't tell.

I shook my head, then nodded and shook my head again. This couldn't be happening.

Unaware of my current nuclear meltdown, Millie beamed like a gameshow hostess and performed the introductions. "Roy, this is the gal I told you about. Jane and I met right after she and Joe moved to town. I visited her as part of the Chamber's Welcome Wagon. Jane, I don't think you've met my old... er, friend Tom Sullivan." She turned to me. "Jane and Joe Smith, this is Tom's friend Be—"

"Betty," I said quickly. "I'm Betty... uh, Jones."

Millie gurgled in surprise and Sully's scowl went from concerned to confused. But what else could I say? Pretty sure I wasn't supposed to blurt out, hey, I know your real names are Felix and Mabel Blue, because I'm your daughter from the future who thought she was born on Christmas Eve 1991 and grew up a millennial only to discover she's a baby boomer, and...

Shit.

A whole lot of things made sense now. I knew why some of my earliest memories included wearing dresses and white gloves and patent leather shoes to church and the library, and riding in cars the size of a yacht. I knew why it had always seemed odd the nurse who'd tended me after mom and dad's murder was dressed in an old-fashioned uniform and a winged hat like Cecelia's. Why Jake, who'd lived for two years near my parents as their bodyguard, always dropped fifties slang like an Elvis impersonator.

I knew why a feeling of déjà vu had pinged my brain since I'd arrived in this time period, and why I'd felt like I fit in. Why the word home settled over me so comfortably, so familiar. Because I *was* home. I may have grown up in the 1990s, but I didn't go there until I was six, after my parents' deaths. I was born *here*.

I lasered in on my mother's baby bump. Tonight. Real soon.

I laughed. Uncomfortably. Or was that hysterically? Of all the lies I'd been told each time I'd asked about my past, this was the biggest. The worst. And I didn't understand why. I had a lot of questions for Grandpa Hank if I ever saw him again. Even more questions for Jake and Glo when I got back to the future. If I ever got back.

While my brain hummed and my insides churned, Millie rambled on. "Joe's a professor. He teaches at the state college. Philosophy or some such."

"Physics," my dad, aka Joe, corrected.

"And you?" I asked Mom, struggling to keep my voice steady when all I wanted to do was scream. "Do you also teach?"

A hesitation and a flash of pain crossed Mom's face, then she laughed as if she found that the most ridiculous question she'd ever heard. "Me? Heavens no. I take care of the house, and soon..." She touched her belly. "Soon I'll be taking care of him."

Okay, first, don't be so sure you and dad will be passing out *it's a boy* cigars. Second, there she stood, inches away from me, my brilliant mother, who'd led the team in inventing time travel, now hiding her true self behind a façade of housework and pinning diapers on a line. My whole being sizzled with rage. I hated Rasmussen more than ever for what he'd done to her. What he'd done to all of them.

"What is it?" Sully murmured. His fingers brushed mine as he tried to take my hand. "You look like you saw Marley's ghost times two."

I pulled away and gave a curt head shake. He scowled as I plastered an attentive smile on my face and pretended great interest in Millie's announcement that the final houses on her suburban cul-de-sac were nearing completion.

"They're pretty little Cape houses like all the rest," she bubbled. "Joe, won't you come take a look? I know you'll love it, and living in a three-decker must be so cramped. You'll need more room when the baby comes. The price is a bit steep at four thousand, but you'll have a yard and even a garage."

"We like our place just fine." Dad exchanged a look

with Mom. A look that said they preferred paying rent over a mortgage and a paperwork trail that could lead Rasmussen right to them.

"We like the convenience of being close to downtown —*ooh!*" Mom's eyes widened then she hunched her shoulders as what had to be a contraction squeezed her belly.

Dad reached to steady her. So did I, an instinctive, automatic action. I took her hand and held on tight. A sudden flood of memories rushed through me. Memories of all the times I'd held her hand when I was a child, walking down the street, in the grocery store, the many times she'd taken me to the library and we climbed the front steps together.

"That was a doozy," she said, taking several deep breaths and standing straight again. "Like an aftershock from an earthquake." She gazed at me with a smile. "This little one's awful feisty."

Tears pushed at my eyes and I could barely breathe. This wasn't happening. Couldn't be happening. Feeling like I was going to both faint *and* hurl, I released her hand as if it had suddenly caught fire and backed away.

"Need to visit the powder room," I blurted and fled.

"Beryl, wait," Sully called, a verbal scowl I barely heard as I pushed through the partygoers and out into the hallway. I hurried toward the stairs. My destination wasn't the bathroom, it was the front door and escape from this *Twilight Zone* episode fever dream.

A tall figure in a plain brown suit stepped out of the shadows at the stairwell and I skidded to a stop, shock and fear freezing me in place.

Rasmussen.

"Happy birthday, Beryl," he said, as dutiful and insincere as a greeting from a coworker I didn't know very well. His gaze strayed over my shoulder, toward the sound of laughter and conversation and music coming from inside the all-purpose room. "Sounds like they threw you a party to celebrate."

My hands trembled violently, but I managed to open my handbag and whip out my stinger. I stepped to the center of the hallway, putting myself between Rasmussen and everyone I loved in the room beyond like a barrier. A terrified, shaky barrier, but a barrier, nonetheless.

"I won't let you hurt them," I said. My weapon whined as it powered up.

He chuckled. "Didn't Hank teach you anything about the nature of time? I can't kill them now, even if I wanted to. Their fate is in the future." He held up his hands, palms up, showing me he was unarmed. "I'm here to see you. To offer you one last chance."

The stinger's "go" light flashed. My finger twitched between the *stun* and *kill* buttons. "This again? Travel with you? To hurt Hank. You must really hate him."

"Is that what you think? I don't hate him. I simply want him to feel what it's like to lose something he loves. To lose everything, like he did to me."

Blunt, but the thought must've made some kind of sense in his warped mind. "That's quite a motive. What's in it for me?"

"Travel with me, and you'll get the one thing you've always wanted. Your family."

"My family?" My rational mind ordered me to shoot

him and get it over with. Instead, my grip on my stinger loosened. He'd hooked me. I wanted to hear more. And he knew it. A gleeful smile curved his thin lips.

"I was furious when you contaminated my vortex at Woodstock," he said. "You disrupted my escape, dislocated my calculations. Brought me to this year instead of... Well, where I intended to go. Then I realized this was the perfect place for *you* to be." He stepped closer. "I've given you the gift of time, Beryl. A chance to see the precious things you're going to lose if you don't join me."

I narrowed my eyes. "What're you talking about?"

"Your parents are supposed to die, in April, six years from now. Their fate is sealed, a fixed point in time. However, *I* have the power to change that. I'll return to the scene of the crime. I'll stop my younger self a moment before the deed is done." His eyes glimmered. "A minor adjustment, and I can conquer time."

I swallowed bile. He sure had a high opinion of himself. And seriously, a *minor* adjustment? The coldness in those words, like my parents' murder was a mere blip. Something that could be undone by unchecking a box in an online order.

"Spoiler alert, Niels, that's impossible."

"Is it?" His voice turned oily and smug. "Impossible perhaps for Hank. Not for me. Come with me. I'll show you what I can do." He touched his TDC. A pale-yellow light pulsed inside the device, giving his face a ghoulish glow. "All it will take is a simple command." He began to tap out a code. "A set of coordinates, and what's been done can be undone. I'll fix it. I'll fix everything."

He was playing me. Had to be. And yet... If anyone could figure out how to undo the past, it would be him.

The brilliant mind who'd unlocked the secrets of the temporal skip. If he could really stop his younger self from killing my parents, that would change everything. Change their life, my life, Sully's life.

Sully.

Hope fluttered in my breast like a hummingbird's wings. A selfish impulse took hold. If I went with Niels, Sully would be safe. My parents would live, and Sully would be safe. I'd have a home, a family. Fate would be defeated, and Sully wouldn't die. Traveling the centuries as Rasmussen's partner in time crimes seemed a small price to pay for those rewards. *If* he was telling the truth.

Did I want to take that risk?

The thunder of running footsteps and a roar of rage erupted behind me, startling me from my dithering. Sully sprinted down the hallway toward Niels like a lion going in for the kill.

Rasmussen swore, then banged on the controls of his TDC. A patch of blue shot out from the device. "You had your chance, Beryl," he spat, his eyes as hard and cold as frozen bullets. "Now, you die."

A fiery blur flew past me as Sully lunged for Niels, but too late. Rasmussen leapt over the railing and melted in a tornado of blue fire as he plummeted downward. Sully's hands grasped at thin air.

"Son of a bitch." Sully spun toward me. His face blazed red and his eyes sparkled with fury. And fear. "Why did you leave without me?" He didn't wait for an answer. He crushed me in his embrace. "Are you alright?"

"I'm fine," I said, my voice muffled against his chest. Fine, except for that dark and dire promise Niels left me with. *Now you die.* I shuddered and Sully held me tighter.

"Jesus, Beryl." He kissed the top of my head. "This is my fault. I should've listened to you. You were worried he'd be here..." He loosened his hold and rained relieved kisses all over my face, not one of which met my lips. "I knew something was wrong. You've used that powder room excuse before. I knew when you didn't come back, something was wrong."

The only thing wrong was he'd interrupted me before I could take Rasmussen down. Or run off with him into the unknown. What choice would I have made?

I stuffed my weapon back in my bag. "Thank you," I said and slid my arms around Sully's waist, hugging him tight. It didn't matter now. Rasmussen was gone. My chance to get him had vanished with him.

Sully scowled. "Thanks for what? Almost losing you? Letting that bastard get within five feet of you? For—"

The door from the party room burst open, cutting short his list of self-recriminations. Music and voices spilled into the hallway, and so did my parents, followed by Millie clucking like a mother hen, with Roy trailing behind.

"What's wrong?" Sully demanded. He released me and snapped into action.

I knew what was wrong, and I suspected he did too, but if he had any doubt, Millie clinched the deal with a loud and panicky, "It's her time. The baby's coming!"

"We don't know that," Mom said, panting, nearly breathless. "I'm not due for a month. Could just be more false labor—" She cut off with a soft cry and hunched into herself, seized in a fierce contraction.

"False labor my eye," Millie nearly shrieked. "That baby's coming."

The Rasmussen drama swept out of my mind on a rushing tide, replaced by a scorching sense of unreality. Like I'd fallen into a dream, a nightmare that held on tight and wouldn't let me wake up.

Sully straightened. "I'll call an ambulance." He flew to a nearby office and aimed a broad shoulder at the locked door to break it down and get to the phone inside.

"No. No ambulance," Dad bit off, throwing up his hand like a traffic cop. "I'll drive. We have a midwife. We'll be fine."

Sully nodded and backed off. Reluctantly. He joined Dad as he hustled Mom down the stairs, Dad on one side supporting her, Sully on the other.

"Wait," I cried. "Dad, listen to me. You're in danger. Rasmussen will find you. If you have a TDC, time skip now. If not, run, leave town. Escape *now*."

Well, I *tried* to say all that. Tried to shout a warning, loud and desperate. But the words caught in my throat like a logjam. Nothing came out but a choking gasp and a hiccup. I reached to grab Dad's shoulder, to shake him or stop him, or anything to get his attention, but my hand hit an invisible wall and bounced back. My ears buzzed like a horde of angry hornets had taken up residence in my head.

My insides twisted in frustration and I wanted to scream. I'd been able to talk to them and touch Mom's hand only moments ago, why couldn't I do that now? It was as if time or some other force had gotten in the way.

Still, I kept trying to sound the alarm. I dogged their steps downward, bleating incomprehensible sounds, growing more frantic by the moment. At one point, Dad glanced back, frowning. Though the scent of time travel had all but dissipated, I thought maybe he'd catch a whiff and put the pieces together. But his concern and questions were forgotten as Mom grabbed the railing and bent over nearly double. She breathed in and out from her mouth in measured breaths, appearing to relax into the contraction until it eased.

"Why is she breathing that way?" Millie asked, perplexed.

No one answered. With our anxiety off the charts, our little posse clattered down the rest of the stairs and out of the building into the frigid night.

Millie and her husband went back to the party as soon as my parents climbed into their car and sped away, but I stared after them as the taillights from their plain and unremarkable black Ford coupe grew smaller and smaller until they turned a corner and out of my life.

Sully took my hand. The night air smelled like snow and the temperature had dropped. His fingers were cold, but his grip was strong, anchoring. The only thing keeping me tethered to reality.

"Beryl," he said, his voice coaxing, concerned, his gaze probing. "What's wrong?"

I shook my head, utterly drained, both body and soul. Unable to answer. This was one thing he couldn't help with, one thing he couldn't hero his way into fixing.

I stared down the street. A few cars rolled through the intersection where my parents had turned, steam rose from the sidewalk grates and catch basins, and Christmas lights twinkled on downtown buildings. In just a few hours, at one minute before midnight, to be exact, I would be born. A quick labor, a fast delivery with no complications. We'd be a family for six and a half years. A happy family, despite the living in hiding thing.

Then Niels Rasmussen would find us.

And I'd given up my chance to stop him.

12

───────

Sully didn't press me for answers again. He didn't speak at all as we drove back to his place. He kept his gaze on the road, the dashboard light illuminating his concerned face.

I sat back against the car's seat with my eyes closed, grateful for his silence. I needed time to slow my racing heartbeat. To wrap my head around the strange and heartrending events of the last half hour, to process the whole time-tripping, temporal joke fate had played on me. To make any of it make sense enough to put into words.

The house was still when we got back, save for the ping of heat in the steam radiators. Pat and Cecelia had gone to bed, but they'd left the Christmas tree lit. Sully and I sat on the sofa drinking beer and looking at the lights. He'd turned on the radio and "Hark the Herald" drifted softly from the speaker as a live orchestra played Christmas music from the Commodore Hotel in New York City.

Finally, I found the words.

"Those people we met... Joe and Jane Smith. Those aren't their real names. Their real names are Felix and Mabel Blue. Well, I don't think their last name's really Blue. Or mine. That's probably an alias too. Nothing makes any sense anymore."

Sully took my hand, his touch gentle. "Sweetheart... focus."

I nodded and took a deep breath. "Those people. They're my parents."

Whatever he expected me to say, that wasn't it. "Son of a bitch."

"My thoughts exactly. There's more. You know how today is my birthday...?"

Sully's eyebrow shot up to his scalp and threatened to keep going.

"Yeah. Isn't that a joke? An unfunny, unhilarious, craptastic joke."

He slid his arm around my shoulder. "Go on."

I did. I told him everything. Well, not everything. I skipped the full resumé and got right to the important details. Most of it. I told him about growing up in the 1990s. About playing Oregon Trail on my Dell computer and getting mad when my pioneer avatar died of dysentery. I told him how I lived and breathed and squealed for 'N Sync. How I devoured the *Wheel of Time* book series and haunted the library for any and all new young adult titles. How I'd lost my grandmother to cancer and became an orphan almost nine years to the day after losing my parents in what I thought had been 1998.

And how I may have grown up a millennial, but I was born a baby boomer. Tonight, on Christmas Eve.

Sully probably understood only a quarter of what I babbled, but he listened patiently, a little stunned. But not surprised. He'd been through a lot in the war and as a cop too. He'd met me and my time-traveling cohorts. Pat Sullivan might be skeptical, but his brother believed. One hundred percent.

I concluded the Beryl bio with Rasmussen's part in the story. "He killed them, or will kill them, in a little over six years, at dusk on April twenty-fourth. Someone decided it was best to relocate me, I guess. Somehow my grandmother became my grandmother, but in the 1990s. Glo might be able to give me specifics. Jake too." And Hank. He knew more than anyone.

Sully grunted, looking as if he'd just been smacked in the face with a temporal shovel. Twice. "Did that rat bring you here to get a jump on himself? To kill your folks now?"

"No. I don't think he could, anyway. He said something like time won't let him. He just wanted to taunt me. Said he left me here to show me what I would lose if I didn't agree to his offer."

"Offer?"

"Ultimatum, really. He wants me to travel with him. He said he could undo the past if I became his partner in time crimes. If I do, he said he could save my parents. That he could go to the moment of the incident and stop his younger self from killing them."

Sully tugged his ear. "And you believe him? If he can change the past, why can't you do it? Or me. Or anyone. Why hasn't it been done? Why didn't someone go and cut off Hitler's nuts from the get-go?"

"Maybe somebody did, and it made the timeline worse."

"Worse? Couldn't get much worse than what happened. You said his offer came with an ultimatum."

I hesitated then blurted, "Go with him or he'd kill me."

Sully's knuckles cracked as he curled his fists into tight balls. "Over my dead body."

His protectiveness warmed me. And infuriated me. "Which could've happened tonight when you rushed him." He frowned. He did *not* like to be scolded. I knew how that felt, but, seriously, he could've forced fate's hand, racing to my rescue like that. I softened my tone. "I get it. You thought I was in trouble. But I had things under control. I had a weapon."

"Why didn't you use it?" He scowled, then he swore. "Because you were thinking it over. You were considering his offer. And I interrupted your negotiation."

"No, of course not."

His left eyebrow twitched in annoyance. "Beryl you're an amazing woman. Smart, resourceful, full of fun. But one thing you're not is a good liar. Or even a passable liar."

"Okay, I may have thought about it. For a second."

"That was one second too long."

"Wouldn't you, if it could save someone you loved?"

His expression turned fierce. "You know I would do anything to save you. Save Pat and Cecelia. Effie. *Anything*. But I would never make a deal with the devil, especially that smug bastard. He wants to use you, that's all. Like he did Dorella."

"Yeah, I get it." I rubbed my eyes with the heels of my hands, frustrated, exhausted. "He says we're a lot alike." Sully scoffed. "No, in some ways he's right. He lost everything he loved and worked for. The grief drove him mad, fueled his obsession with taking shiny objects as his own, no matter who he hurts. I could've ended up like that. I did, in a way, but instead of taking things, I ran. Ran from foster homes, from anyone offering love that could ease my grief. Anyone offering me a home. Niels is a temporal exile and so am I. I don't belong anywhere. I found a space at Time Scope, but even that feels like a temporary gig. So, I get what he's saying. We're both wanderers without a home."

"Hey." He took me by the shoulders and turned me to him, seizing my gaze with an intensity that got my belly flipping end over end. "You do have a home. Here, with me."

Now he'd done it. Activated the waterworks. The tears I'd been holding back by sheer will since coming face-to-face with my past rained down in a torrent, drenching my pretty dress and threatening to flood the parlor.

He reached out and brushed tears off my cheeks with his thumbs. "For a girl who says she never cries, you sure do it a lot."

"I can't help it." I sniffled. "Everything's such a mess, and here you are, my solid rock. You make everything so much better."

"Glad you think so highly of me. But I mean it. You have a place here, with me. Not because you're stuck and you can't find your people. I say to hell with them, anyway. They let you get lost and they're taking their damned sweet time finding you. *I* won't let that happen.

I'll keep you safe and protected. Stay with me. Be with me."

I blinked at him in surprise. "Sully, are you...? Is this a proposal?" My breath seemed to have left my body. "Are you asking me to marry you?"

He cleared his throat nervously. "Damn right. We'll make it official the Monday after Christmas. We'll go down to City Hall and get that piece of paper."

"Oh, ah..." Not exactly how I'd pictured getting the question popped. In fact, I'd never imagined getting close enough to anyone to consider marriage as the next step. The forever step. "Are you sure? I mean, wouldn't you want someone like Millie, someone of your own time? You know, that whole Greatest Generation, nifty '50s, *Happy Days* package. The wife and kids and the house with the picket fence in the suburbs?"

He snorted like an offended dragon. "What is that phrase you like to say? Do you even know me? I don't *want* Millie, or anyone like her. I don't know what a picket fence is, and if I had one, what would I do with it?" He cupped my face with his hands, his fingers caressing the tender skin behind my ear. "It's *you* I love, Beryl. You. Or haven't you noticed? I've fallen for the most impossible girl. A time traveler." He gazed deep into my eyes. "What do you say? Make a home with me. We'll make a great team."

A moment of panic squeezed my belly, followed by a wave of sensations. Joy, excitement, fear, but mostly love. How I loved this man. This honorable, courageous, and maddening man. I wanted desperately to stay with him. He'd asked me to marry him before, in 1943 when we'd first met, and my answer then had been a resounding no.

We were two people from different worlds, different eras, and our love could never be.

Now? I wasn't sure. Only one person from the future knew where to find me, and he wanted to kill me. There'd been no response to my advertisement. I couldn't figure out how to contact Grandpa Hank and I had no clue how to get in touch with Glo and Jake and Alice.

I gazed into Sully's eyes, so blue and earnest. So full of love. I smiled. Perhaps fate was trying to tell me something. Perhaps this was where I was supposed to be. With him. For always.

Sully broke into a grin and kissed me. Deeply, fully, and with great attention to detail.

He didn't seem to notice I hadn't given him an answer.

SULLY EASILY DRIFTED off to sleep after we made love, but I lay awake for a long time, watching the hands of the alarm clock on the bedside table move straight up, pointing to midnight. Christmas had arrived. So had the expected snowstorm. Outside, the wind picked up, whistling through the window cracks.

And across town, I'd just been born.

That sense of unreality gripped me again, as if I were living in a dream. Could I really do this? Could I live here without causing a major disruption in the timeline? Live in the same town as my parents without our paths crossing? What would happen if I encountered infant Beryl? I shuddered, remembering my inability to speak earlier, and that invisible force that had shoved me back when I'd reached for my dad.

I gazed at Sully. His chest rose and fell steadily as he slept, his expression relaxed, no scowl at all. He looked younger, far less careworn. Vulnerable, even. Temporal conundrums aside, could I live happily ever after with him, even with the sword of fate hanging over his head and Rasmussen waiting for all of us six years in the future?

I stiffened. Rasmussen. His threat from tonight echoed in my brain. *You had your chance. Now you die.* More words from long ago followed. *If I'd seen you in the car, you'd be dead too.*

The puzzle pieces slid together to form a neat but gruesome picture. Rasmussen's plan. A terrible, brutal plan that made some sort of sense in his disordered mind. He'd tried to kill me at Woodstock, but a chance encounter with a concertgoer had disrupted his aim. He'd tried to kill me, several times, in Point Bailey, but he'd been stopped then, too. He'd almost succeeded in taking me out in 1882, and maybe would have if I hadn't anticipated his attack.

Tonight, he didn't even try. He claimed to be unarmed but still could've come at me at any moment. Instead, he'd monologued about how we should travel together and fed me that bullshit story about changing my parents' fate. Why?

Because he'd already made up his mind.

I sat up. The blankets fell away. Cold air brushed my body, raising goosebumps. My blood thundered through my veins and pounded in my ears.

If I'd seen you in the car, you'd be dead too.

He'd said that in Point Bailey, when I'd discovered who he was and that he'd murdered my parents. Sharp, vengeful words that had cut me to the core then—and chilled me to the bone now.

Tonight, he'd tried to cut a deal with me because, as Sully said, adult me he could use, like wannabe Annie Oakley and the other women he'd traveled with until something or someone more valuable came along. An asset. A prize he could flaunt in Hank's face. And if he could corrupt me or bribe me or offer me the one thing I wanted more than anything else, he could use me to help him track down the other temporal ex-pats who'd fled into the past to escape his rage.

But young Beryl he had only one use for. To get his final, fatal revenge on Hank.

I pulled my legs up and hugged my knees, shivering in terror. My trembling woke Sully. He shot bolt upright, muscles tensed, his keen gaze searching the room. Looking for danger. Ready to fight.

"What is it?" he demanded.

I stroked his face, felt his warm, rugged skin and the bristles of his beard. "It's nothing. The storm's started and it's snowing. The wind woke me, that's all."

His eyebrow did a doubtful wiggle, but he didn't push for more. He pulled me into his arms and down against the pillows. "Whaddya know, we got a white Christmas." He pressed his lips to mine. "Guess that'll make Bing Crosby happy."

He yawned and within moments he fell back to sleep as quickly as he'd woken, his breaths coming in measured movements. I lay with my head on his chest, his arm around me. I buried my face in his neck, taking comfort in his warmth, the scent of his skin. My heart ached. I had to leave him, and soon. I couldn't tell him why. If I did, I knew he'd move heaven and earth and risk his own life to fix it. This was something he couldn't fix. I doubted I could fix it either.

But I had to try.

I shifted and stared up at a crack in the plaster that streaked across the ceiling like a lightning bolt. Or, like a blast from a zapper. I shuddered again. Rasmussen's sick, sick plan would take him more than six years into the future. To April twenty-fourth, the day his younger self murdered my parents. The day he'd missed me, a child huddled in the car's back seat and crying my head off.

He'd gone to finish the job. He'd gone to 1954 to kill me.

13

———

Christmas Day, 1947. The same yet different from any other year in the modern age. There were gifts galore, a child whose eyes sparkled in the lights, and plenty of food now that rationing was a thing of the past. But no TV, just radio and the "Carol of the Bells" and other Christmas favorites performed by a live orchestra.

After a quick breakfast of toast with apple jam, we'd brought our coffee to the parlor. Sully and I sat on the sofa, Cecelia took her usual seat in the rocking chair, and after he'd dressed the turkey and put it into the oven to cook, Pat sank onto the floor beside Effie. She looked adorable in a velvety green dress with a white collar and white belt dotted with bright red poinsettias, and she gurgled and goggled at the mountain of gifts Santa Claus had left under the tree.

I wore the blue dress again—it was too pretty not to— and let myself enjoy the day, and Sully's company. We stayed close, we touched, held hands, and kissed each other with a frequency that would've prompted Pat to holler "get a room!" if he wasn't so occupied with Cecilia and the baby. He occasionally tossed me stunned looks because, yeah, I'd called it—it snowed. A lot. Snow fell for hours, turning the world frosty white and proving to doubting Patrick I was what I claimed to be, a time traveler who knew the future.

Mostly. The future I so desperately wanted to know continued to be a nebulous, rippling uncertainty. What would happen if Rasmussen succeeded in killing little me? Would adult me wink into nothingness? Or would that create a paradox that would split off into another timeline where I'd still exist? And the primary problem troubling me, how could I stop him?

An answer to that last question had crawled into my mind and taken root. An idea. A daring, audacious idea with multiple parts and earth-shaking consequences. But an idea I couldn't shake. The answer had been there since that moment last year when I'd lifted a glass of synthahol and vowed to find a way to kick fate's ass and change Sully's destiny. It sat on the edge of my consciousness like a ripe plum ready to be picked, I just hadn't figured it out until now.

To save him, I had to save them. My parents.

And there was only one way to do that.

"Isn't it time we opened those presents?" Cecilia said, pulling me out of my temporal musings and setting off a gift wrap-tearing frenzy. Effie got into the spirit and gleefully ripped the paper off every package her parents placed in front of her. Cecilia oohed over her gift from Pat, an enamel brooch in the shape of a bouquet of blue flowers, forget-me-nots I thought. Pat gushed over a box with a sailing sloop on the cover and Old Spice aftershave and a shaving mug inside.

Sully's eyes gleamed as he handed over his gift to me.

"Oh," I breathed as I opened the small jewelry box to see a bracelet nestled inside, dotted with beryl green stones matching the necklace he'd given me last night. "It's gorgeous."

"Looks better on your wrist than that time machine. We'll get a ring for you next. Before we visit the city clerk."

My stomach did an uncomfortable backflip, but I nodded and smiled as if I thought that was a dandy plan. "Now it's my turn." I handed him the gift I'd picked up for him at Pierce & Taylor, a tiny package wrapped in plain brown paper. "It won't outdo your gift but remember, it's the thought that counts."

"You shouldn't have." He gave a dubious lift of his eyebrow as he peered at the diecast toy jeep he held gingerly between his thumb and forefinger. Made by a company named Tootsietoys, the jeep was about four inches long, painted Army green, and had what felt like real rubber tires.

"I know, it's ridiculous," I said. "But it reminds me of when we first met at that crappy little gas station, when you so sweetly offered to drive me into town in your jeep."

"Offered? You practically browbeat me into giving you a lift."

"True, but I had no choice. I needed to protect you, after all." Well, that was what Glo had told me. She'd dropped me on the side of the road outside Ballard Springs in 1943 and said I had to save Sully from an assassin or the future was toast. All part of the test and a gigantic lie, though I didn't know that at the time. I didn't know anything, except that the broad-shouldered redheaded soldier who'd insisted he could save himself without my help had taken my breath away.

And still did.

"I remember that jeep ride." Sully rolled the toy vehicle across the top of the table beside the sofa. "I remember you riding beside me, your hair flying, your nose in the air, telling me a load of booshwa about joining the WACs. I wanted to kiss you silly the minute I saw you. If it hadn't been for the other fellas in the back seat, I'd have pulled over and done it."

"Liar. You were obsessed about protecting my reputation. Your skill at avoiding being alone with me that weekend was impressive and legendary. No way would you have done anything like that. At least, not without my permission."

Like the first time we'd made love, when he'd practically jumped out the window to keep people from knowing he'd spent the night and thereby tarnish me as a fast woman in those prudish days. I supposed the world was still prudish, but Sully perhaps had changed.

He gave a *can't argue with that* shrug. "Well, I *did* want to kiss you." He glanced toward the others. Seeing they were occupied with opening a squeaky plastic duck toy for Effie, he leaned close and whispered, "Can I kiss you now?"

I said yes.

A while later, Pat called Sully's name, getting our attention.

"If you two can stop necking for a second, I've got a

surprise for everyone." His knees cracked as he stood up from the floor, leaving Effie near the tree, playing with her duck and her new Raggedy Ann doll. "It was too bulky to wrap, so I hid it under a blanket out in back. Tommy, give me a hand."

Cecelia and I exchanged mystified glances as the two men left the room. The door to the back hallway clicked open and shut, then they returned carrying a large, rectangular wooden box with a long cord and a plug dangling down. Sully pushed the radio aside with his elbow, clearing a space on the credenza, and he and Pat plunked the heavy thing on top.

"Is that a television?" Cecelia asked in surprise.

Certainly was, but an early form of one. About three feet wide and made of some kind of durable wood, it had a small glass screen flanked by inset speakers and a half dozen control dials lined up along the bottom in a row.

"Sure is." Pat picked up the cord and peered behind the credenza, reaching for the outlet to plug it in.

"Oh, Pat," Cecelia said. "It's lovely, but televisions are so expensive."

"Not this one. Mr. Flynn sold it to me on discount. Says next year's RCA Victor models are so much more advanced, this one'll be obsolete." Pat patted the top of the console. "But it'll do the job. It's got picture synchronization and an automatic station selector. Once we get an antenna, we'll be able to tune in television stations from all over the state." He hesitated. "When there are any."

Sully whistled, duly impressed. "Will we be able to watch the Red Sox games?"

"Yep. Goodbye radio. We'll be able to watch a lot of things."

Pat turned one of the knobs with a decisive click. Cecelia joined the guys gathered around the miracle box and the excited trio watched as a pinprick of light blossomed at the center of the thick glass screen and widened to show a picture of... snow. A fuzzy, crackling pattern of snow accompanied by a distant and echoing *s-s-s-s*, like a snake hissing a warning from inside a cave.

I watched them with fondness in my heart, a hollow sensation in my belly. If I was able to pull off my plan, everything would change. Sully would never know me. He'd never have any reason to sacrifice himself for me.

"Beryl?" Sully prompted.

"Hmm?" I'd been so busy feeling sorry for myself, I missed his question.

"I said, are these contraptions going to catch on?"

"Uh..." All three gazed at me expectantly. I supposed I wouldn't violate any temporal prime directive in answering the question. "Let's just say you might be the first family on the street to have a TV, but you won't be the last. If you're looking to invest, put your money in RCA. And IBM. Wait, that's more for computers—*no! Stop!*"

Okay, I may have overreacted, shrieking like that. And flying off the sofa like a missile being launched was definitely overkill. But when I saw Effie tug a handful of those icicle strips made of lead off the Christmas tree and steer the toxic treat toward her mouth, I didn't think. I just moved to stop her.

The three people gathered around the TV reacted too. Pat stiffened, Sully's gaze raced around the room, hunting for the threat, and Cecelia sprinted the distance between her and her daughter in a nanosecond. Propelled by a mother's super speed, she got to the girl long before I could.

"Evelyn Grace Sullivan," she cried and snatched the icicles out of Effie's hand. Startled, Effie let out a wail that shook the windows. Cecelia wrapped her in her arms, with both Pat and Sully closing in to comfort her.

As for me, I fell back onto the sofa. Cold prickles ran up my spine. Not from the baby's brush with poisonous Christmas decorations. That had shaken me up, but the name that Cecelia had used rattled me even more. *Evelyn*. Glo's middle name. A family name, she'd told me. Coincidence? Maybe. Except, as Glo herself liked to say, there were no coincidences in time travel.

A few minutes later, the drama had passed. Effie's tears had dried, and she drifted off to sleep in her playpen. Pat and Cecelia returned to their chairs and the gift-giving continued. Sully dug out a square box from behind the tree. Wrapped in white paper speckled with dozens of jolly Santa Clauses, he handed the package to Pat.

"For both of you," Sully said. "Not as fancy as a television but takes pictures that are more permanent."

Pat peeled off the wrapping paper to reveal a square yellow box with a Kodak logo splashed across the front. He threw off the top and gazed at the wonder within. "Tommy, you got us a camera."

The cold prickles returned to attack my spine again.

Pat found a roll of film in the box and loaded it into the camera, which he pushed into his brother's hands.

"Take our picture, will you?" He led Cecilia to the Christmas tree, where they posed, all smiles.

Understanding broke through. Everything came into focus and formed a picture of my friend and my boss, Glo, whose middle name was Evelyn. Glo, who chose Sully specifically for me. Glo, with a strong, determined jaw. Just like Sully's. I gaped at Pat, showing Sully how to operate the camera. Just like Pat's.

My knees went weak. Glo had a lot of pictures of her family hanging on the walls of her house and office. Some were current, but most were photos of her relatives from years and centuries ago. One photo flashed into my mind. Glo's several times great-grandparents, smiling as they posed in front of a Christmas tree dripping with icicles. An interracial couple from a time when marriages like that were rare.

I stared at sweet little Effie, snoozing in her playpen. I'd been barraged by a never-ending stream of shocking revelations and surprises these last days and weeks. But this one? The most stunning and unexpected. Pat and Cecilia were Glo's how-many-times great-grandparents.

And that meant Sully was her uncle.

I PHOTOBOMBED.

What else could I do? It would ruin Glo's wonderful picture forever, but it was the best and only way to tell her where I was. Though clouds of confusion had entered my brain, I acted swiftly and jumped into the frame as Sully pressed the shutter button.

My action resulted in an uncomfortable laugh from

Pat and Cecelia, and the most mystified eyebrow lift Sully had ever eyebrowed. It did *not* result in a flare of blue light announcing a time traveler's arrival. I frowned, disappointed. Like the ad in the newspaper, and my attempt to call Hank, my photobomb was a photodud.

As the delectable smell of the turkey roasting in the oven drifted to every corner of the apartment, we continued our snowed-in Christmas celebration. More pictures were taken, wrapping paper and ribbons were cleaned up, Effie's diaper was changed, and at one o'clock, we sat down to a magnificent dinner of turkey and homemade cranberry sauce. The TV had been turned off—there was nothing on, anyway—and on the radio, Gene Autry crooned his new hit song, "Rudolph the Red Nosed Reindeer."

After dinner, Cecelia dozed in her rocking chair, while Effie sat on Pat's lap as he and Sully played a vicious game of gin rummy at the dining table. No surprise to discover Pat was as competitive as his brother.

I watched them play. Or pretended to watch. Mostly, I anxiously chewed my bottom lip, still stunned at the revelation of Sully's connection to Glo and just about everything else that had happened since I'd dropped into 1947.

I fell so deep in my thoughts I almost missed the flash outside the front windows.

Cecelia's eyelids fluttered open. "Lightning?" she said, sleepily, looking around. "In the winter?"

Sully stiffened and his expression said it all. He knew what that light meant.

"Excuse me," I said, avoiding his gaze.

I grabbed my coat and hurried out onto the porch.

The temperature hovered around a frosty twenty-five degrees. More than a foot of snow had fallen and showed no signs of tapering off. All was silent and calm, but not bright. Though only midafternoon, the storm's clouds had darkened the day to dusk.

Tentative footsteps and a slight rustling broke the silence as Glo emerged from the shadows in the far corner of the porch. She looked like she'd just stepped out of the movie *Doctor Zhivago*, in a furry, pillbox hat and a heavy, midcalf length white coat with faux-fur trim that nearly swallowed up her petite frame. She held her personal commpad tucked under her arm.

"You ruined a perfectly nice family picture," she said, eyeing me with a fierce scowl. Sully's scowl. Why had I never noticed it before? The scowl, the determined jaw. The pieces of Sullivan that had come down the generations to be reborn in Glo.

"Sorry. It was the only way I could let you know where to find me. I tried calling Hank. Tried a newspaper ad. I was going to send a letter if I could figure out how."

"Sometimes it takes a minute for temporal messages to be received. And that letter thing never works." She craned her neck to peer into the house through the lacy white curtains covering the front window. Looking at her family. "This is... seeing them... It's... what would you call it? A real trip?"

Well, I'd only use that phrase if I was still at Woodstock, but I knew what she meant. "Trippier than my discovering you're related to everyone in that apartment? Including Sully. Did you know all along who he is and what's supposed to happen to him?"

She nodded stiffly. I did my best to swallow my anger

and the accusations that stormed inside me. I had painful questions that demanded answers and I didn't want to waste time on useless recriminations. She already seemed freaked out. It would do me no good to yell at her and upset her more.

"Tell me how it happened," I prodded. "How was Sully chosen? Your ancestor, your family. Why did you throw him into my path? Why is *he* the sacrificial lamb in this temporal Shakespeare drama?"

She looked away from the cozy scene inside the house and gazed out at the snow-covered street. "My great aunt Evelyn studied our family history as far back as the records allowed her to go. She discovered many interesting characters in our family tree. Some success stories, and one big mystery. An uncle from way back, a white man who was a cop. He died while on the job. My aunt searched and searched but could never find out what happened to him, or when it happened. Only that he died. That uncle was..." She drew a deep breath and faced me. "Or, that uncle *is* Tom Sullivan."

I shivered, frozen down to the bone, but not from cold "And you... what? Ensured his death by hooking him up with me?"

"Blame me if you must," she said, soft but firm. "But I've been working at Time Scope long enough to know, time is inevitable. As much as I hate it, this is what's supposed to happen. It already happened. It's going to happen, and always will happen. He dies, protecting you."

I ran a hand over my face. I hated these twisty temporal pretzel puzzles that had no beginning, no end, and a decidedly murky middle. I hated the finality of those two words even more. *He dies*. All the more reason to get out of here, now. But not to go home.

"Speaking of relatives... Imagine my surprise to meet my parents face-to-face. They didn't die in 1998, did they?"

"No." She shifted her gaze, looking everywhere but at me.

"Rasmussen murders them six years from now."

"Yes." Again, soft but firm.

"You knew that. All this time, you've known."

She finally looked me in the eye. "I did. Jake knew too, but don't blame him. Hank decided it was best not to tell you. He thought if you knew, you might try to save your parents. And that's—"

"Against the rules."

"Not just Time Scope's rules, Beryl. Against time itself."

That so-called fixed event. Something Rasmussen seemed pretty certain he could find a way around. "How did I end up living in the 1990s?"

"It's another long story."

"Which you're not going to tell."

Her lips pulled up in a grim smile. "Not at the moment. It's too cold. My face is going numb. Everything we did was to keep you safe. From him."

"I'm not safe anymore. Rasmussen is still on the loose, and he's going after me. Young me." Her eyes widened and I gave her a quick rundown on my encounter with Niels last night, highlighting the threat but leaving out his job offer—and his other offer, to change my parents' fate. "I know where's he's going, and I know what he's going to do. And I'm going to stop him."

"Out of the question. Too dangerous." She slid her commpad out from under her arm and started tapping on the screen. "I'll send Jake. Better yet, I'll send a team after him."

"No. No Jake, no team. Just Niels and me. *I* have to stop him. You guys are always talking about fate and destiny and how you can't mess around with it and all that crap. Well, this is *my* destiny. Not only that, it's *my* life. I don't need your blessing. All I need is a TDC and I'm on my way."

She studied me, her left eyebrow hiking upward Sully-style. "You've come a long way from the woman I picked up off the floor in your library and sent into the past. Kicking and complaining. Shaking in terror and almost puking at the idea of killing a man. You've grown up since you fell off that ladder. You've gained wisdom. I'm impressed."

Not sure I'd gained any more wisdom than I'd had yesterday, but I took the compliment with a nod. "Have I? Or have I just decided to meet destiny head-on? To stop letting Hank and Time Scope run my life. To take fate into my own hands."

My parents and Sully's fate too. I didn't want to be the woman Sully died trying to protect. I wanted to be the one to save him.

Glo heaved a sigh and reached into her coat pocket, producing a wristwatch TDC with a narrow leather band. She held it out but closed her fist around the device before I could take it from her.

"Beryl." She peered at me closely. "You're *only* going to stop Niels from hurting your younger self." Not a question. Or a statement. An order.

I looked through the windows into the parlor. The men had abandoned their card game. I heard the faint strains of "Auld Lang Syne" playing on the radio. Pat waltzed Cecelia around the room. They looked into one another's eyes with dreamy expressions. Sully sat on the sofa, with Baby Evelyn balanced on his knee. She bopped him on the nose with her Raggedy Ann doll. He took the battering with aplomb and an affectionate scowl.

A bittersweet sensation stung my chest. "No worries, Glo. I know the rules."

And I planned to break every one of them.

I took the device and it disappeared into my coat pocket in a flash. "I'll see you back in the future. Unless you want to come in?" I forced a lighthearted tone. "It's cold out here, and it's Christmas in there. Plus, there's real coffee. Why not join us?"

Longing tinged with sadness flickered across her face, a ton of emotion for her. "Maybe. After this is done. When Rasmussen is caught, extracted, and locked away. Then I'll think about it." She moved back into the shadows and tapped on her commpad. A sharp wind kicked up, and a pale blue light rose from the screen. "Godspeed, Beryl."

She punched a button and disappeared into a swirling tunnel of blue. The time tornado's churning wind swept across the porch and out toward the street where it joined with the storm's howling gusts.

It took a second to collect myself before I stepped inside. I shivered. From the cold, and from anticipation and dread of what would come next. Now that I had the means to time skip, I couldn't waffle anymore. I was going to do the exact thing Glo had warned against. I was going to catch up to Rasmussen—the younger version—and stop him before he could get to my parents.

If I succeeded, that would prevent the whole tragic chain of events from happening. It would reset time and change everything. My parents would live. So would Sully. Jake's guilt and self-recrimination would evaporate. Hank's grief would too. Even Glo's regret would be gone. She wouldn't have to choose to sacrifice a family member she'd never known.

As for me, I'd have a family. I'd be happy. Except for one thing. If this audacious and terrifying plan worked, if I succeeded in stopping Rasmussen and undoing time, I would never know Sully. We would never meet, never fall in love.

Never kiss.

But he would live. He'd have a normal life. A full life, with Millie or some other lucky woman and finally find out what a picket fence was. He'd have a family he cared for deeply, a family who loved him in return. He'd live in a world without me, a woman bouncing around in time with no home, nowhere to belong.

And that was all the reason in all of time to take this risk.

14

The telephone rang as I came into the apartment.

Now, I came from a world with a plethora of phones that beeped and pinged and vibrated to get your attention 24-7. But here, the shrill *b-r-r-ring-g-g* of the phone was rare. And the way the Sullivan family reacted, it could only mean bad news. Pat and Cecelia broke out of their clinch. Sully frowned. Even Effie turned to stare warily at the jangling beast.

On the third ring, Sully stood, handed the baby off to her mother, and snatched up the handset. He exchanged terse words with the person on the other end, then hung up and let out a relieved breath.

"Nothing to worry about. I've been called in. The power's out in half the city. They need some men to go door-to-door to check on the elderly and others who need help." His lips quirked. "I'm sure one of those doors will be the mayor's, and while we're there he'll ask us to shovel his driveway so he doesn't have to shell out four bits for the neighborhood boys to do it." His gaze touched on Pat, Cecelia, and then to me where I still stood in the entryway. "Sorry to cut Christmas short, but I got to go."

My spirits sank. I had to go too, but I'd thought we'd have a few more hours together before I left. I touched my coat pocket, feeling the slim contours of the TDC inside. Maybe this was the universe's way of telling me to make a clean break now.

Sully flashed me a scowl as he strode past to his bedroom to change. I hung up my coat and followed him, closing the door. I didn't speak. I watched him put on his uniform, missing him already.

"What happened? Was that your friend Glo?" he asked, buttoning his shirt, not meeting my eyes. "Are you going home?"

I hesitated only a moment. "Yes. I'm going home." In a sense. If my plan worked out, I'd have the home I was denied by fate. My chest felt hollow. But I wouldn't have him. "I have to deal with Rasmussen first."

That pissed him off. I could tell by the way he put on his tie and shoved the knot so tight against his throat it nearly strangled him. "*We* have to deal with him." He shrugged into his uniform jacket then put on his overcoat. "I've got to go in. Wait 'til I get back. We'll deal with him together."

Not a request. An order. Just like Glo. "Sully, I've got to do this myself."

"Why?" He strode up to me and seized my gaze, his expression stormy. "Is there yet another rule that says I can't help you?"

Bitterness fueled his voice, and why not? Our interactions over the years had been heavy on lies, liberally sprinkled with me quoting Time Scope rules and regulations. Putting him off, keeping him in the dark. "You... you wouldn't understand." I cringed to hear myself dropping that most evasive of phrases on him. And the most dismissive.

He growled like an aggravated bear. "I understand. Too well. We're too much alike, Miss Beryl Blue. When we met, you had this look about you. Haunted. Scared. Lonely. Like me. I'd spent my life running away from my past or the future or whatever the hell scared me most at the moment. When we were together, my fear went away. You put me on solid ground. You helped me. Isn't it time you let me help you?" He tucked a lock of my hair behind my ear. "I know you've got the ginger and the will to stop that creep, but you don't need to do it alone. You could use reinforcements. Help. *I'm* your help. You *do not* have to do it alone."

Another fine speech. A heartfelt speech that dug right down to my soul. *Alone* had been my mantra, my keyword and modus operandi my whole life. Beryl Blue, taking care of herself, by herself. Mostly by running away. Even running from Sully, though I had a good reason to run from him now.

He watched me closely, waiting for an answer. Only one response came to me. A lie. Next to running away, lying was what I did best. If there was a hall of fame for liars, I was the champion, MVP, number one, all rolled into one. I'd promised Sully I wouldn't lie to him anymore, but old habits die hard.

"Yes, yes, of course, you can help," I murmured. "I want you to help. I *need* you to help and I'll wait for you to get back."

His eyebrow of doom rose only a fraction, but it telegraphed volumes. Uncertainty, doubt, hurt, and something that cut me to the bone. Disappointment. "Could be hours before I'm back. The mayor's got a long driveway."

I couldn't bear it, couldn't look at him a second longer. I threw my arms around him and pressed against him, burying my face in the folds of his overcoat. "I'll be here. I promise."

His arms hung by his sides. After a moment, he embraced me. I smelled wool and Sully's familiar scent. Felt his heartbeat, and the strength and comfort of his arms holding me. If I could stop time, I would have frozen us together in this pose, in this spot. Forever. I took in all of him, deep, deep in my memory, to keep with me. Even if I flipped time and we would never meet, I knew my love for him would burn in my heart. For always.

Minutes went by before he loosened his hold. He slipped a thumb under my chin, tipping my head up to look at him. "Every time we say goodbye, I die a little," he said, his scowl turning affectionate. "I need a kiss to tide me over. To keep me warm 'til I get back."

I held back a sob. Oh, Sully, you perfect, perfect man. Romantic and tragic and so, so you. I kissed him. My lips joined his and we clung together for a long, long time. If I was successful, this was something I hoped I'd remember. His kiss, *this* kiss, our last kiss.

And how much I loved him.

I HEARD the muffled roar of Sully's car coming to life outside. I pressed my cheek to the bedroom window, looking sideways, straining to see down the narrow space between the apartment buildings to the street. Through the pelting snow, I caught come-and-go glimpses of him in the darkening day as he brushed off his car. A minute later, he climbed in and the headlights flashed on. The car slipped and slid as Sully pulled a U-turn, and the vehicle inched slowly down the icy hill.

I dried my tears and prepped to leave. It didn't take much time. I had nothing to pack, only memories. I'd worn the blue dress today and decided to wear it on my time trip. The style would fit better in 1954 than my sunshine yellow minidress. I folded that particular item and placed my equally anachronistic tights and suede handbag on top, tucking them all in the bottom drawer in Sully's bureau. They would probably disappear when I changed history, along with the pictures on the table beside Sully's bed, but I guess I thought I was leaving a little something of myself behind.

Lamenting my lack of pockets, I slid my stinger into the belted waistband of my dress, in the back, like tough guys did in the movies. Awkward, but the weapon stayed firmly in place as I walked to the parlor and encountered a touching scene. The Christmas tree lights blazed brightly. Cecelia had taken up her knitting again. Pat sat in his chair with his legs stretched out, holding Effie snuggled against his chest, her thumb in her mouth, while he read *Pippi Longstocking* to her.

Sadness, and an aching sort of loneliness gripped me. I'd come to care for all three of them in the short time I'd been a guest in their home, but if all went as planned, I would never remember them. I'd never know if Pat would succeed in quitting smoking, or if Cecelia would ever finish that mitten or scarf or whatever she'd been knit-one-pearl-two-ing since I got here. I hoped they would. I hoped Effie would grow up happy and healthy and with the strength to face all the bumps and bruises and challenges fate would throw in her way.

And I hoped that Sully would have a good life.

"I'm just gonna pop upstairs and wish Josephine and crew a Merry Christmas," I said, adopting a light tone. "I won't be long."

I backed out of the parlor, keeping the stinger out of sight. I slipped into the foyer and snatched the TDC out of the pocket of my borrowed coat then darted through the house to the back hall. I shut the door and pulled a string attached to a light bulb. A dim glow spread over a long, enclosed area, a dusty place, as frigid as the north pole, with a broad door to the outside and a window at one end and stairs leading upward at the other.

As good a place as any for a time skip. And protected from the storm.

I put all my worries and regrets behind me. Dry-eyed and full of resolve, I buckled on the TDC. The strap clung to my wrist, snug and familiar. And heavy, as the device powered up. The thrum of energy pushed down on my outstretched arm. Electricity pulsed over my skin and into my veins, prepping my atoms for the time skip. I activated the Interface voice controls and told Sarah to set the coordinates and begin the countdown.

A flare of cobalt blue shot out of the device, followed by a burst of wind that sent dirt and bits of paper skittering across the floorboards like terrified ants. The vortex came next, a tiny, swirling cone that blossomed from the TDC like a budding flower and grew into a raging tornado. April 1954, my parents, and Rasmussen waited for me inside the cyclone. I took one last look around, one last glimpse of Sully's world, then stepped into the vortex.

I hit *skip*—and slammed into a boulder. No, a boulder slammed into me.

Sully. My impulsive love, my determined hero. My complete and utter pigheaded fool had leapt into the stream. Snow dusted his overcoat and he breathed heavily, as if he'd just set an Olympic record to run here.

"Not without me," he said. He pulled me into his arms and squeezed me tight as the time tornado enveloped us both.

15

I imagined my face looked like Sully's did the first time I encountered the temporal cocoon. Somewhat surprised, somewhat scared, mostly *oh shit, what have I gotten myself into?*

We clung to each other as the vortex closed around us, followed by an ear-splitting *whirr*, like the hum of the world's loudest vacuum cleaner. Our bodies floated upward, our feet dangled inches above the floor. The whirlwind picked up to warp speed, a sensation both fiery hot and bitter cold. The de-atomizer kicked in next, or whatever the technical term was for the meat hook that stabbed through your back and speared your belly, giving a sharp tug and turning you inside out.

Then, *poof*. Sully's body melted, and so did mine, into a mass of pixels and atoms that soared through space and time, dissolving and reforming and agitating like clothes in a washing machine. Our beings joined, interlaced, then broke apart and came back together again in a surreal and supremely terrifying dance. I couldn't see or hear, but I could feel. I felt his fear, and also his love. Joining with me, supporting me, sheltering me. Protecting me.

A long time later, or in no time at all, the cyclone's clutching grip on us loosened. We separated as our bodies began to take shape. That's when things turned weird. A heaviness I'd never felt before elbowed into the stream. It yanked the vortex sideways then dragged us down. We plummeted at maximum velocity, until the stream ejected us from the temporal storm like a bouncer tossing rowdy drunks from a fancy nightclub. Abruptly, and with a shove that said *don't come back*.

I landed on my butt, coming down much harder than usual. Panting and in pain. My head clanged like a black-smith pounding out the anvil chorus. My passenger, on the other hand, hit the ground in a superhero pose—defensive crouch, his knee and one fist to the ground. Except for some heavy breathing and a stunned expression like an ox who'd taken a tranquilizer dart straight to the heart, he sprang up, alert and ready to plunge into action.

My hero.

My big, reckless, impulsive hero.

I scrambled to my feet and closed the small distance between us.

"Is this skip thing always like that?" he asked, gesturing to my wrist. The last anemic wisps of the time tornado hung over the TDC then sputtered out. "Like falling under the treads of a Sherman tank—*hey*."

I shoved him. Or tried to. He was as solid as an oak tree with its roots firmly planted in the soil. "Sully, why did you do that? Why'd you jump into the vortex?"

He scowled. "I figured you were lying when you said you'd wait until I got back. Not only because you're a bad liar, but because *I* would've lied, too. I told you, we're too much alike. I woulda lied like hell to keep you safe from danger. Woulda told you I'd wait but wouldn't. I got fifty yards down the hill before I realized that. I pumped the brakes, tried to turn around and slid into a snowbank, so I ran all the way back, scared you'd already left."

I stamped my foot. "You *know* I have to do this thing. You won't be safe. *I* won't be safe until Rasmussen is neutralized." I bent my arm and activated the TDC, frantically typing commands. "I'm taking you right back where we started."

He clapped his palm over the device and snorted. The snort of a man who'd never retreated in his life and wasn't about to start now. "Nothing doing. I'm gonna help you catch that son of a bitch whether you like it or not. He needs to be stopped."

"With *you* as the target that stops the bullet." I sighed, which became an aggravated hiccup-sob. "Why must you be so determined to get yourself killed?"

"It's my choice to make, Beryl." He thumped his chest. "*Mine*. I went to war. I had no choice. Uncle Sam drafted me, dropped me into a battle called the Bulge. Freezing my ass off. Watching guys die around me. My friends. Your uncle." His voice had gone bitter cold. "No one gave me a choice in any of that, but I gave it my all. With you, I'm choosing my path. Wherever it leads."

"Oh, Sully..." I breathed. His words set off a barrage of emotions in my chest, threatening to burst all over the place. He was all true-blue Captain America, the good infantry man, moving forward into the unknown. Willing to take the bullet if it would save someone else. Why did *I* have to be that someone else? "How could I *not* fall in love with you?"

"I don't know. It's my curse." He gave a crooked smile, knowing I'd given in and he'd won. Yet again. "Now, let's figure out what's next." He looked around. "Where are we?"

A quick scan told me we were not where I expected to be. I'd set the coordinates for the place where my parents' accident-not-an-accident had occurred—outside, near the entrance to Ballard Park, not indoors and certainly not here, in a large, hot room with a pitched roof and smelling of must, dust, and the distinct scent of books.

"We're in the Higgins Library. The attic, to be precise." Where the Beryl Blue, Time Cop story had begun. "Judging by the waning daylight, I'm guessing it's late afternoon. But when? What year?" I saw no computers or ancillary tech, like old keyboards or a broken mouse. Not even a videotape. No wooden bookshelves ranged across the center of the room, either. The shelves hadn't been installed until the 1960s. "Wait. Is that my suitcase?"

Sully followed my gaze toward the desk, and the Amelia Earhart brand suitcase tucked underneath, speckled with dust and cobwebs. "Yup. Right where I asked Miss Sanborn to put it. Is that a good sign?"

"I think so." Despite Sully's tailgating on the stream and that strange energy shoving us off course, we could've actually landed in 1954. But in the wrong place.

"One way to know for sure." He peeled off his overcoat and tossed it on the desk, then started for the door. "Let's go ask."

"Sully, wait. There's something you need to know before we go."

He froze, eyeing me warily. "Something bad I'm guessing. Bad enough you ran away instead of telling me."

True, but it stung to hear him say it. And to hear how much it hurt him. "I only just figured it out myself. And I'm sorry, but it's complicated. Remember how I told you I was in the back seat of the car when Rasmussen attacked my parents? And remember when we tangled with him last time, and he said if he'd seen me there, he would've killed me?"

He balled his fists. "How could I forget? That cold-blooded weasel bragged about killing a kid." His eyes widened as my meaning caught up to him. "He's going to finish what he started— *Jesus*." His complexion turned several shades of purple and he flew to the door.

I chased after him. "Slow down."

"The hell I will. A child's life is in danger." He snatched the door open. Or would have if it wasn't locked. He twisted and rattled the doorknob with such force it should've broken off, but it held firm. He frowned. "Something's kayoed the lock."

Something? Or someone? As in, Rasmussen. The gift that kept on giving. He knew I'd figure it out. He knew we were coming. That strange weight in the vortex dragging us down and driving us miles off target had to have been him.

"Sully, there's one more thing you need to know." I paused a moment then let the rest out in a rush. "I plan to kill Rasmussen, the original version. I'm going to kill him before he can get to my parents."

He frowned again. "No. No killing. No one needs to die, especially by your hand." He gave up on the knob and slammed his shoulder against the door instead. The wood shuddered from the onslaught, but barely gave an inch. "We'll catch that cretin and stop him before he can hurt you. Or young you, or... you know."

I conceded with a nod, though I wondered if fate, a demanding and ironic bitch, would make it that easy. "No matter *how* we stop him, we have to do it before he gets to my parents. That will save everybody. And it will reset the timeline. Sully... if we do this, if we succeed, it will turn back time."

There, I said it. Out loud. No going back now. After all the lectures from Jake and warnings from Glo and all the HR training sessions about screwing with the timeline being very, very bad, I was going to do it. I had Rasmussen to thank for that. He'd put the idea in my mind. My parents *could* be saved. The past *could* be changed.

"But here's the kicker." I swallowed heavily. "The wow finish to this whole temporal mess. If we succeed, if we upend time, everything will change. You and I... We'll never meet."

Sully stopped beating up on the door and swung toward me. "What? I don't get it."

Neither did I. I barely understood the concept of time travel. Start tossing paradoxes and causal loops on top of that, and I was lost. "If we stop Rasmussen, it will stop the chain of events before they happen. My parents won't die. We'll never meet." I brushed a tear from my eye. "Still want to help me fix that?"

He hesitated a moment before stepping closer and

taking me by the shoulders, his touch strong and comforting. "If it means you'll be safe, if it means you'll be happy, I'd go to the ends of the earth to make it come true." He released me and turned back to the door, doubling the force of his assault. "Now, let's go get that bastard."

THE WOOD around the lock splintered. It gave with a groan and the door flew open and bounced against the outside wall.

"There," Sully said with satisfaction then swept out his hand like a polite doorman. "After you, Miss Blue."

I touched his arm. "Let's get one thing straight, Sergeant Sullivan. We'll do this together. But you have to do what I tell you to. No theatrics, no heroic throwing yourself on the grenade. You got that? *I* call the shots."

He gave a sarcastic salute. "You are the bossiest woman I ever met."

A woman he would never meet if we got the job done right. "And you're the most stubborn. And pigheaded. Not to mention mulish and a million other adjectives I can't think of right now."

"That's why you love me."

He kissed me then took my hand, and together we raced from the attic to the mezzanine then down the stairs to the main floor. People swarmed the huge room, poring over books stuffed into the towering bookshelves, bent over newspapers in the periodicals area, and checking out their selected items at the front desk. Children darted back and forth or sat cross-legged on the floor reading books or magazines in their laps.

"Sergeant Sullivan?" A woman with a steel-gray hair bun stepped into the path between us and the front door. She wore a green skirt, a tan blouse, and an expression of utter shock. "Is that really you?"

"Miss Sanborn." Sully stopped so abruptly I almost crashed into him. "Tell me, what's the date?" he demanded with a minimum of politeness and a maximum of urgency.

Harriet's brow furrowed. "Date?"

"Today. What's the date today?"

"Umm... Why, it's April twenty-fourth."

My breath caught. The right date. And the right year, judging by the outfits the library patrons were wearing, like the cast of the fifties musical *Grease* about to take the stage. But I needed to be sure, so I chimed in, "And the year? Is it 1954?"

She narrowed her eyes. "Of course." Her gaze centered on Sully again and her suspicious expression turned fearful. "What game are you playing, sergeant? You disappear without a trace. You cause a mystery everyone in the city's been buzzing about for years, and you show up here asking the date."

"Sorry, no time. Thanks." Sully grabbed my hand again and we arced around her, sprinting across the room.

"Where have you been?" she called after us. "Everyone thinks you're dead!"

The library's heavy front door thudded shut behind us, cutting off that last word, but Sully heard it. He froze on the landing and gaped at his surroundings as if he'd just dropped onto another planet. Women in poufy skirts and men in skinny ties and rocket engineer style eyeglasses strolled past, brightly colored cars with tailfins cruised along the street, and across the way, a construction crew put the finishing touches on a modern new structure of glass that towered over the city's dusty older buildings.

Sully's head snapped toward me, and his scowl went nuclear. "Pat," he said, agonized. "Cecelia, and Effie. They think I'm dead."

I nodded but the grief in his eyes and voice robbed me of speech. This was one temporal consequence he hadn't thought of when he'd jumped into the vortex. To be honest, in the heat of everything that had happened in the last half hour, neither had I. A city cop had disappeared in a blizzard on Christmas Day. Never to be heard from again. Presumed dead. Even if Pat suspected me and my time travel shenanigans as the cause, he must be devastated at Sully's loss. And plenty pissed.

"I'll take you back." I activated the TDC. "I'll take you back home right now."

He chewed that over a nanosecond before he straightened and threw his shoulders back. "No. No going back. We'll finish this." His momentary panic and despair seeped away. His signature poker face clicked into place. "If what you say is true, Pat will never remember any of it." He jerked his chin in a westerly direction. "The park is three miles that way. Let's go."

16

Sully raised his hand to hail a cab. None stopped. He whistled. Still no luck. The passing taxis didn't even slow down. Even his police uniform didn't catch their attention. It was as if he was invisible. We had to go on foot.

We took off, running. He tempered his long stride so I could keep up with him as we raced down Main Street. I clutched my stinger to my side in an iron grip, ready for anything. Our feet pounded the pavement as we dodged window-shoppers and burst by pedestrians, headed for the scene of the crime soon to occur nearly three miles away. Not exactly an Olympic sprint, but we made good time.

At first.

The closer we got to Mill Street and our destination, the more things started to go wrong. I tripped over nothing and would've face-planted if Sully hadn't caught me. He stumbled. Several times. The man was as sure-footed as a mountain goat. He never fell or tripped over anything. When we turned right at an intersection and the crowd of pedestrians suddenly thickened into an impassable mob, I knew the truth.

Time was *not* on our side. The crowd, the taxis that wouldn't stop, our unusual clumsiness, the library's attic door that wouldn't open, and even the strange energy that had invaded the stream and shoved us off course. That hadn't been Rasmussen's doing as I'd thought. Somehow, time or fate or whatever force we were fighting had gotten wind of my plan to stop Niels and change the course of events. It was doing its damnedest to stop us.

I would do my damnedest not to let it.

We moved forward, not as fast as before. Sully played the cop card. "Clear the way," he boomed, putting his imposing size and uniform to work. "Make way, police business."

People jumped aside, but each time someone moved, another stepped into our path. With still two miles to go, time and fate doubled down. Some kind of force shoved against us. The same invisible wall that had closed in and kept me from reaching out to my father. Our movements slowed even further. The heaviness stole my breath. Each step forward felt like plowing through deep, wet snowdrifts.

I side-eyed Sully. "You feel it too, don't you? The push, the gravity slowing us down."

"Like an entire battalion pushing me back."

Thick, dark clouds rolled in, promising rain. I quaked inside. There wasn't much time. We had to hurry. But we couldn't.

We approached another intersection. A wall of pedestrians waiting for the light to change blocked us from moving forward. Sully craned his neck and scanned ahead for a way to break through. I took a moment to catch my breath, surveying our surroundings. Cars clogged the road. Stores and a tall brick apartment house lined the other side of the street. Next to us stood a sprawling, multi-story brick building with a sign over the front doors reading Ballard Springs Hospital.

A tall, slim, dark-haired young man near the entrance caught my eye. He walked toward the doors with a cocky sort of arrogance. He looked more like a young version of Paul Newman than Jake Gyllenhaal in his casual polo shirt, chino pants with a skinny belt, and his thick hair drenched in a greasy 1950s brand of hair tonic I just knew left an oil spill on his pillow every night.

Someone I hadn't expected to run into, but someone I was glad to see. A man who could help us.

Jake Tyson.

SULLY SPOTTED Jake a second after I did. "That devious snake," he cried and lunged for him.

I threw myself in front of Sully, seriously regretting telling him everything about Jake's lies, and how he'd used me—and Big Red—to test my fitness to take on the job of Time Cop. Sully had vowed to throttle Jake if he ever met him face-to-face and, well...

Here we were.

Main problem—this wasn't *that* Jake, the guy who'd conspired with Glo and Hank to send me back to 1943 and into Sully's arms. It took a second, but I figured it out. This was the man who'd been sent to the past to protect my parents. Younger, twenty-five-ish, fresh-faced, and full of confidence and dimples. The Jake from before. Before he'd failed to stop Rasmussen from killing them. Before he'd buried himself in guilt and self-blame and a strict adherence to the rules forever after.

"Sully, stop." I pressed both palms to his broad chest. "He doesn't know me. He doesn't know you. It's before we met."

Sully unwound, a little, but his furious scowl followed Jake as he reached the hospital's entrance, where he held one of the doors open for a lithe, pretty, golden-haired woman in a nurse's uniform and a cap like Cecelia's. The short straps of a boxy pink handbag rested in the crook of her bent arm, and she held a cigarette between her fingers with the casual poise of a long-time smoker.

Jake greeted her with a loving and shockingly flirty, "How was your day, babe?"

Her face lit up with a bright smile. "What on earth are you doing here?"

"Thought I'd surprise you with a ride home."

She took a deep drag on her cigarette and laughed, puffing out smoke. "You're the answer to a girl's prayers, Curly. My feet ache like the devil."

Curly. A bittersweet memory flashed. A way, way back memory, from when I was small. At a bowling alley with my parents, and a guy named Curly. He had a date, a sweet-faced blond who chain-smoked cigarette after cigarette.

The answers fell into place with a crash. Everything Jake had alluded to but refused to tell me when I'd asked, whether to spare me the pain, or to spare himself. Here was the woman he'd loved and lost. The woman he'd left behind when his mission ended, and he had to return to his life in Futureworld. The nurse who lived upstairs from my parents. The nurse who would take me in after they were murdered.

The nurse with a startling resemblance to my grandmother. Only, not her. At least, not yet. Here, now, she was Minerva Carter, twenty-two or twenty-three and absolutely gorgeous. She touched Jake's face and smiled into his eyes, clearly as smitten with Jake as he seemed to be with her.

My stomach flip-flopped. My knees got all wobbly. The rest of me wobbled too and I might have fallen into a heap at Sully's feet if he didn't reach out and steady me. Jake had been assigned to protect my parents and had lived in the past with them for two years. It shouldn't surprise me he and Minerva would be thrown together. And fall in love.

The light changed and the mob of pedestrians surged across the street. I stopped Sully when he tried to follow. I gestured at Jake, who took Minerva's hand and led her to a roomy-looking car the color of a robin's egg.

"Come on," I said. "Maybe he can help."

Time didn't like that and fought back. It took what seemed like hours to churn through the invisible fog cloaking us to get to Jake's car. He'd opened the passenger side door and helped Minerva inside like an official 1950s gentleman and not a cosplayer from almost two hundred years in the future.

He stiffened when he saw us, unable to hide his alarm. Whether from the sight of us moving toward him like jerky marionettes or Sully's uniform, I couldn't tell.

"What is it?" he demanded, serious, all business, no hint of dimples.

I got right to it. Or would have if I could speak. Like Christmas Eve when I'd tried to warn my parents, my mouth went dry and filled with cotton balls. Sully grabbed his throat as if a baseball had suddenly lodged in there.

Jake's gaze dipped to the stinger I held by my side. "Whoa." He threw his hands up like a shield. "Who are you?"

"B-B-B..." was all I could manage. Sully croaked like a demented bullfrog.

Astonishment lit Jake's face. "Temporal tongue tie. I've heard of it, but never seen it before. Something's wrong but you can't tell me. Temporal tongue tie will clog anything you try to say that could interfere with a fixed event."

He'd gotten all pedantic, but I could've hugged him for catching on so quick.

The passenger door was still open. Minerva poked her head out from the car. "Temporal what?" she asked, both curious and confused.

Jake brushed off her questions with a curt, "It's nothing, hon. We'll leave in a second." He closed the car door and pasted his gaze on me. "Did Hank send you? What's happening? Are the Smiths in danger?"

I nodded. Or tried to. Sully growled in frustration. We did our best to communicate with a frantic and herky-jerky game of charades. I mimed driving a car and shooting the weapon as best I could. Sully managed to lift his arm and point in the direction of the park, like a silent, traffic cop version of the Ghost of Christmas Future.

Jake's brow furrowed as he put the pantomime pieces together, then he said, "Get in the car."

I breathed a sigh of relief. In seconds, he loaded us into his vehicle and peeled out as we shot into traffic.

He gave Minerva a quick look. "Honey, there's something I gotta take care of. This could take a while. Maybe I should drop you off at home."

"Nonsense. If Jane and Joe are in trouble, I want to help. Why should you be the one to shoulder all the work?"

He flicked her a startled glance. "What?"

She trilled a laugh, sounding a lot like Grandma Blue, only much younger and several octaves higher. "Don't you think I know what you've been up to? You shadow the Smiths everywhere they go." She glanced back at Sully and me with an amused expression. "He told me he's a salesman for an international travel agency. Salesman, my aunt fanny. I may be a simple farmer's daughter, but even I know a salesman needs to meet clients. Or has a business dinner once in a while." She turned back to Jake. "You're a secret agent, aren't you? You're protecting Joe. He's not just a physics professor. He's working on nuclear secrets or some such, and you're keeping him safe from the communists. I've known that all along."

My lips twitched in a fond smile. I loved Grandma Blue with all my heart, but she'd always been kind of a know-it-all. Which she'd passed on to me. I supposed this was where it had started.

"Something exciting is happening." Minerva shifted and looked back at us again. "I wouldn't go home now for all the tea in China. Besides, you might need my help. If something goes wrong, you'll need a nurse on hand."

My amusement faded. If something went wrong, we'd need not just any nurse. We'd need her. *The* nurse. The nurse who'd been at the scene of what I'd thought all my life had been an accident. The woman who'd held me as my parents' car burned, and who I now knew would adopt me. The woman I called Grandma. But there were still some missing pieces to the puzzle connecting us together. Growing up, I'd known her as an older woman with a lined face and silvery hair. How did that come about?

"I'm Minerva, by the way." Her gaze hopped from me to Sully, waiting for a response.

"Don't bother." Jake met my gaze in the rearview mirror. "They can't tell you their names."

"Why not?"

"It's... it's complicated. Too complicated to get into now."

She accepted that with a knowing nod. "Ah, spy stuff," she murmured then turned her attention to the road ahead.

Jake sped up and seconds later, we buzzed up to an intersection. I slapped him on the shoulder and pointed for him to turn right. I hung onto the seat as he tore around the corner. The day darkened and twilight crept in. So did rain, drizzling from the sky in a fine mist. I clenched and unclenched my hands. I knew from the mission report Jake had filed that my parents were killed at dusk on a rainy evening. Would we make it in time?

Sully stared out the window with a grim look. I knew he thought about Pat and his family. Did they still live in that three-decker house? Did they have more children? Did they still search for Sully, hoping to find out what happened to him, desperate for answers?

I took his hand and squeezed it. "We'll fix this, Sully. I promise."

He turned from the window, looked down at my hand, then met my gaze. I caught a flash of doubt in his eyes before his expression smoothed into his usual impassive scowl.

About a half-mile down, I smacked Jake's shoulder again and indicated we turn left, onto Mill Street, a broad boulevard with two lanes on both sides that cut across the city and past Ballard Springs Park. He swung the car around the corner—and groaned. I sat up in alarm. Sully leaned forward and cursed.

A hundred cars seemed to come out of nowhere and clog the road.

Jake did his best. He wove in and out of traffic, squeezing by cars of all makes and models. "There's the park," he said, gesturing to a stretch of greenery ahead, past houses and corner stores and a barber shop that lined the street.

My heartbeat thrummed in anticipation and a bit of dread. The doubt I'd seen in Sully's eyes had taken root in me, growing stronger by the second. If we managed to catch up to my parents in time, would we succeed? What would happen then?

Sully craned his neck to peer past Minerva and out the windshield. "What kind of car are we on the lookout for?"

"An Oldsmobile 88 sedan, dark blue," Jake said.

"Curly, look." Minerva pointed, her voice rising in excitement. "I see them."

My own excitement accelerated. I sat up straight and spotted the car in a thicket of other vehicles, closing in on an intersection only a few blocks ahead.

"Hang on to something," Jake said and jerked the wheel to swing around a slow-moving Studebaker. He floored it. The car blasted forward and began to close the distance.

A grinding wail suddenly erupted from the engine, followed by a series of angry pings. The car bucked like a bronco auditioning for a Wild West rodeo show. Jake jammed the brakes, but too late. The vehicle bounced into the curb and stopped with a jolt. Minerva banged into the dashboard. Sully's arm shot out to protect me as we both sailed forward, but I still slammed the back of the front seat with a tooth-rattling smack. The car's engine let out a final, fatal wheeze and stalled dead.

"Son of a bitch," Sully spat. Minerva pressed her hand to her bruised forehead and echoed that sentiment. Jake pounded the steering wheel with both fists. Their frustration didn't compare to my own. Not even slightly. My parents were so close. I could see their car roll up to the red light only a few blocks away.

Sully eyed me. "Time to deploy the shoe leather."

We all hopped out of the car. Jake and Minerva pelted down the sidewalk like the devil nipped at their heels. Sully and I moved much slower. Drizzling rain splashed my face, the humid air pressed down, and so did time's cloaking device. My steps seemed to slog through thick mud. Sully wobbled like a drunken man unsure where to put his feet. A swirl of pedestrians thronged the sidewalk, hemming us in, impeding us further.

Ahead, the traffic light turned from red to green and vehicles accelerated. My parents' Oldsmobile moved slowly forward. The park's main entrance loomed in the distance, seeming hundreds of miles away.

"Hurry!" I urged Sully unnecessarily. "We have to get to them—"

A milk truck with Grove Dairy Home Delivery painted on its side blasted through the red light into the intersection. It missed my parents' car by inches but plowed into two others directly behind them with the brutal crunch of metal against metal. Tires squealed and horns blared as vehicles careened and skidded on the wet pavement in the chain reaction collision that followed.

To our left, a Buick with a deadly-looking torpedo hood ornament cut across both lanes—headed right for us. Pedestrians screamed and scattered. The driver, a squirrel-faced man in a fedora, wrestled with the steering wheel and gaped in terror as his car jumped the curb. Sully grabbed me by the waist and practically lifted me to throw me out of the car's path.

I stumbled but didn't fall, holding my gaze on him. He froze for a moment, and in that nanosecond of hesitation, my breath stopped. This was it. This was fate. At the last second, Sully hopped out of the way. The Buick slammed into a mailbox with a terrifying clang. The hood ornament speared the metal and the mailbox exploded into a thousand pieces. Letters flew everywhere.

"Are you okay?" Sully demanded, gasping for breath.

I threw my arms around his neck and hugged him tight, laughing like a wild—and very much relieved—

hyena. I was more than okay. He'd saved me and didn't die. *You could be in the path of a careening car*, Sully had said a while back, speculating on what fate had in store. He'd predicted it. He was right, and he'd saved me. And he didn't die.

Take that, fate.

I seized his hand and tugged. We could do it. We could still stop Rasmussen. Still save my parents.

"Help him," a woman behind us shouted. "Officer, don't go. He's injured!"

I turned to see a woman in a brown coat and a plastic rain bonnet covering her head. She gestured wildly to the Buick with the driver inside, slumped over the steering wheel. Blood poured from the man's head. More blood stained the spiderweb cracks in the windshield.

Sully's tormented gaze flicked from me to the injured man, and back to me. He wanted to help. He *needed* to help. But in the end, he hardened his features and chose not to.

He barked at the woman to call the police and report the accident, and we dashed away. We ran hand in hand, slipping on the carpet of now-wet mail strewn across the sidewalk.

We moved as fast as we could. Gravity's oppressive shroud pushed at us with ten times the force than before. I fought it every step of the way. Sully did too, breathing heavily, moving stiffly, like a wooden puppet whose strings were tangled. We inched forward.

The elusive Oldsmobile neared the destiny point. Jake and Minerva had almost caught up. I gasped to see a flash of blue light erupt near the park entrance, followed by a gust of wind. The younger version of Niels, Rasmussen

Prime, had arrived on schedule. I pumped my legs as fast as I could, fighting against the time web trying to hold me back.

I kept my gaze on my parents' car. We were so close. Only yards away. Hope and desperation surged through me. Sully had survived the car accident. Destiny *could* be defeated. Time *could* be rewritten.

A figure suddenly flew out of the bushes. Muscular arms clamped around me, pinning my own arms to my sides. Squeezing hard, cutting off my breath. Stopping me in my tracks.

Jake. Not the younger version who went by the name Curly here in 1954. My Jake. The one I knew in Future-world. That secret-keeping, follow-the-rules-at-all-costs son of a bitch bastard, Jake Tyson.

17

"You can't do this, Beryl," Jake said, his mouth against my ear, his voice urgent.

I squirmed and struggled to break free from his iron embrace. "No!" I cried, choking on frustrated sobs. "I can save them."

Sully rounded on Jake. "Let her go." His glower promised pain and hellfire if he didn't.

Jake's arms around me tightened and he dragged me back several steps. I let out a desperate wail.

"You coward." Sully's knuckles cracked as he balled his fists. "You're hurting her."

"I'm *protecting* her." Jake released me and turned me to face him, his fingers digging into my shoulders. "Don't you think I tried? I did what you're doing. Running, shouting, warning. Nothing worked. Only made it worse." His voice dropped into icy territory, as bitter cold as a January frost. "Look around. Look what happened."

He jerked his chin, gesturing to the vehicles littering the boulevard, smashed into one another, busted radiators hissing and sputtering steam, front ends buckled and cracked. People spilled from their cars, women bruised and hats askew, men bleeding, children crying.

"*I* did this. I tried to save your parents. Several times. I time skipped here, to this moment, and tried to undo the past. I tried to cheat fate. Fate fought back." His voice cracked with anguish. "I made it worse. So many people injured. Chaos. And your parents still—"

"You're lying," I shrieked, refusing to let him say that fatal word. Refusing to believe it. "You've lied to me from the beginning." I wrenched out of Jake's grip and swung to Sully. "You made it. You saved me from that car and didn't die. Time *can* be changed."

"We can try," Sully said after a moment's hesitation, vague, doubtful words from a man who was usually so certain.

"Beryl you can't change—"

I didn't hear the rest of Jake's warning. Rasmussen Prime darted out from the park as the Oldsmobile moved by the entrance. Several bursts of laser fire lit the twilight, followed by a blur of motion as Rasmussen fled the scene. My dad lost control of the car and it slammed head-on into a streetlight with a thundering *bang*.

I couldn't move, could barely breathe. Time had locked my feet in place, as if encased in invisible cement. I could only watch in horror as the rest of the terrible scene unfolded.

Oliver Bishop arrived and raced to help my parents. Too late. Smoke billowed from the car's interior. Minerva and the younger Jake had reached the Oldsmobile. Also too late. They exchanged frantic words. Jake was about to tear off after Bishop when Minerva pointed to the car.

Jake stiffened and dove toward the rear door. He yanked it open and pulled a screaming child with dark hair from the back seat. He handed little me off to Minerva, then took off after Bishop, who'd raced after Rasmussen Prime, beginning the chase across time that would end in tragedy.

For everyone.

Devastated, insensible with rage and grief, I ran to the smoldering car. Sully followed, with Jake calling for us to stop from behind. My feet moved normally again. The wall of gravity that had pushed us back had dissipated, and along with it, my last shred of hope.

At the car, Sully went to the driver's side to check on my father. The stuck door squawked as he tugged it open. Smoke billowed from the interior. Sully leaned in and pressed two fingers to my dad's neck. My stomach rolled and bile choked me as Sully looked over his shoulder at me and gave a mournful shake of his head.

I darted around to the other side to my mother. The door had popped open. I crouched and peered in at her. Dad was gone, but she hung on. Barely. Her eyes met mine. Tears and smoke clogged my throat, anguish pinched my chest. She tried to lift her hand to touch my face but didn't have the strength, so I helped her. Her palm against my cheek felt smooth and warm and I stored that touch in my memory bank to hold forever.

A sweet smile touched her lips. "Beryl. My girl."

My heart ripped from my chest as the smile faded and her hand went limp.

18

Gutted.

The only word for how I felt. Blinded by tears, consumed with grief. The world around me wavered and faded away. But I had no time to process that. To process anything.

Police sirens pealed from down the road, growing closer. A sizeable crowd had gathered to view the carnage.

"Won't someone help them?" a woman called, her voice strained and frantic. Several others echoed her cry, begging Sully to do something. He was still on the other side of the car. He met my gaze, his expression agonized. What could he do? They were gone. Fate had won. Destiny had been fulfilled. The tragic cycle had been set in motion and there was nothing anyone could do to stop it.

My gaze drifted to Minerva, standing out in the crowd in her white nurse's uniform, clutching little me tightly in her arms. Young Beryl wore a blue dress with white polka dots. I remembered that dress, and this moment. The girl had stopped crying, though her cheeks were still wet. She looked broken, confused, and filled with a deep, abiding sorrow. Sorrow flooded me too. Heartache and grief born this day that had burrowed down to the bottom of my soul and taken root, staying with me always.

Something flashed in the group of onlookers gathered behind Minerva. The glint of a knife blade in the streetlight beam. My stomach clenched. Rasmussen, the older version, the architect of all this pain, slithered through the crowd toward Minerva—and young me. He'd promised he'd do it, and here he was. He hadn't killed enough people to satisfy his destructive greed and need for revenge. He intended to take one more life.

Mine.

"Sully," I called, though he'd already seen the danger. His whole being coiled, the soldier he'd once been snapped into place, and he shot toward Niels. He slammed into Rasmussen full bore like a linebacker making a hard tackle. Niels yelped and Sully's grunt from the pain of impact could be heard for blocks.

The crowd shrieked. Young me wailed. Minerva hunched protectively and cocooned the girl in her arms. I flew up beside them and yanked them both out of harm's way. The air filled with the crack of Sully's fists smacking bone as the two men fought. Rasmussen's knife slashed wildly. It caught on Sully's sleeve, tearing a gaping hole in the fabric. More screams erupted from the onlookers. Little Beryl wailed again.

I armed my stinger and tried to aim at Niels. A futile effort, as both men were moving targets and I feared I'd hit Sully if I fired. Finally, Sully managed to grab

Rasmussen's wrist and snap his arm back. His grip loosened and the blade hit the pavement with a *ping*. Niels cursed and ran off, shoving through the panicked crowd and into the park.

Everything had happened in a matter of seconds. Too fast for me to comprehend. Except, Sully had defied fate. Twice. He'd saved me. Twice. He breathed heavily from the fight, rasping like a clogged radiator. His normally ruddy cheeks had paled to a pasty white, but he was alive. He hadn't needed my help to defeat fate at all. He'd saved me *and* little me.

I shifted toward my parents' car. But neither of us had been able to save *them*. That grief and sorrow that had taken root in young Beryl years ago flared inside me now. It stoked my anger and encouraged it to burn with a white-hot fury. I squeezed the hilt of my stinger and shifted my gaze to the park entrance, where Rasmussen had bolted.

I couldn't stop my parents from being killed, but I could put down their killer.

Sully reached for me, but I stepped back. Away from him and the comfort he offered. I didn't want to be comforted. Didn't want to feel at all. Didn't want to feel anything except rage. This dark and bitter fury, this consuming, primal lust for revenge I imagined shuddered through Rasmussen after he'd lost everything he'd ever cared about. The anger that had fueled his need for payback.

I wouldn't let Sully stop me. I wouldn't let fate stop me either. Or destiny or whatever other malevolent forces had been jerking me all across time. I wouldn't let any of that or anyone stop me. Not this time.

I clutched my weapon. I had no more doubts about whether I'd hit *stun* or *kill*. Hardening inside and out, I tore after Rasmussen, determined to stop him. Once and for all.

I DASHED along the pathway through the park. The rain had let up, but ominous clouds still hung overhead, reflecting my bitter mood. Sully raced after me, calling for me to stop. He usually outpaced me but fueled by fury and no longer stifled by time's shroud, I poured on the speed and easily left him behind.

I caught a flash of Niels ahead as he arced around a bend. He veered off the path. I splashed through a puddle and followed him into a clearing with a hill that sloped down to a large pond, the springs Ballard Springs was named for. A place I recognized, where Sully and I picnicked all those years ago when we'd met. Fate had a sick sense of humor, to bring us back to where we'd shared our first kiss.

To where I was going to kill Niels Rasmussen.

Niels aimed toward the pond. The normally clear spring water looked murky and gray under the stormy sky. I could see Rasmussen's fingers desperately working the time bauble on his wrist. He was going to skip and get away again. I didn't have a second to spare. The temporal wind had already whipped up and the time tornado began to form. He'd leap into the vortex before he ran out of dry land.

He was barely in range, but I slapped the *kill* function anyway. A blast of scorching juice surged out and seared into one of the rocks by the water's edge. It exploded like Vesuvius blowing its top. Shattered bits of stone rocketed in all directions. A jagged piece smacked the back of Rasmussen's head. Startled, he froze, disrupting his attempt to temporal skip. The vortex collapsed.

I closed the distance between us and stopped far enough away that he couldn't grab me.

"Don't you dare," I said as he reached for his TDC again. "Turn around, hands up."

He complied, slowly, and with a glare of pure fury. "Bitch," he spat.

Seriously? Of all the snarling, sneering, and sexist epithets he could have employed, he had to go with the trite-and-true first?

"That I am, Niels. Head bitch in charge, actually." I aimed straight for his heart. Or where his heart should've been. "And this head bitch says, this is the end."

"For me?" He looked pointedly over my shoulder. "Or for him?"

Sully had caught up and stood behind me, winded and drawing ragged breaths. I'd learned my lesson never to take my eyes off Niels for a second, but the hitch of satisfaction in his voice and the smug smile that touched his lips set off a clanging symphony of warning alarms in my brain.

Something was wrong. Terribly, terribly wrong.

I turned and got my first good look at Sully since he'd followed me into the park and raced after me. His eyes were glassy, his skin the color of ash. His breaths were labored. He trembled, unsteady. He'd unbuttoned his coat, revealing his uniform shirt underneath. Stained with blood. A *lot* of blood. It gushed from a gaping wound in his gut and spread across the shirt's once-white fabric in a raging river.

I froze in horror. Now I knew why I'd outpaced Sully and why he couldn't keep up with me. Now I knew why he'd cried out when he'd slammed into Rasmussen earlier. He hadn't howled with the pain of impact.

He'd been stabbed.

Niels had stabbed him. Stabbed him when... When Sully had saved me.

"Beryl... don't kill him—" His words cut off in a moan of agony. And then he crashed to the ground.

SEVERAL THINGS HAPPENED AT ONCE. A hard wind gusted across the water, followed by a blue tornado. Jake and Glo leapt out of the vortex and onto the scene. Rasmussen tried to flee but didn't get far. Jake caught him and took him down with a vicious volley of groin kicks and a bruising punch to the nose.

I barely heard the sounds of their fight. Barely noticed anything but Sully writhing on the ground.

Bleeding.

Dying.

I dropped to my knees beside him, numb with shock and disbelief. This couldn't be happening. None of it. All a dream, from the moment I tumbled off that ladder in the library's attic and fell into this warped time travel torture maze. I'd wake up in a minute and discover it had all been a nightmare of epic proportions.

Fate was a morbid bitch. A relentless bitch. Determined to get its way, no matter how long it took. And no matter who it took. Not even someone as heroic and good as Sully, a man who tried to do right, who only wanted to help people, especially me. My hero had run all this way, bleeding and in pain, to help me. To protect me. As he always did. And I'd been too consumed by rage and my need for revenge to notice.

I took Sully's hand in both of mine. It was sticky with his own blood. "Sully, stay with me." My voice trembled in a terrified, desperate moan.

His eyes wandered unfocused until he latched onto me. "There you are, Miss Blue."

Tears tried to fill my eyes, but I held them back. I wanted to see him clearly and tears would only get in the way. "I'm here, Sergeant Sexy."

His left eyebrow quirked up a fraction. "Tell Pat... tell him..." He couldn't rasp out another word.

I smoothed his hair back from his forehead. Sweat coated his clammy skin. "You tell him yourself. We're going to save you." Glo and Jake stood nearby, with Rasmussen now in handcuffs. I hit them with an icy glare. "We're going to save him."

Glo set her jaw, her expression filled with pain. Jake frowned and wouldn't meet my eyes.

"They can't do a thing," Rasmussen said with a rancid laugh. Jake held him firmly by the collar and blood streamed from his nose, but he seemed unfazed. "Don't you know? That's against the rules."

I told him exactly what he could do with the rules. Another person joined our group gathered around Sully. I looked up to see Hank.

"*You* can fix this." A panicked sob crawled up my throat. "I did what you wanted me to. What everyone wanted. I've upended my life and my century, and I run around time with no place to call home. I lost everyone. *Everyone*. But I am *not* going to lose *him*." My gaze bounced from Hank to Glo to Jake. People I'd come to rely on, and to trust. Fear and darkness pushed at the edge of my vision. "Do what you have to do. Break every rule in the book. Save him. Give me this *one* thing."

Jake scraped his hand through his hair. Hank and Glo exchanged unhappy looks. Rasmussen snickered again. I sagged. The time travel court had reached a verdict and adjourned for the day. I lost. Sully lost.

"Beryl," Sully said weakly, and the others faded from my view. I focused on him and only him now. "Kiss me." He tried to squeeze my hand and pull me down closer to him but he didn't have the strength.

I leaned in and pressed my lips to his. They were so cold. "I love you," I said when we parted.

"I know." He tried to smile, which turned into a scowl. That precious, precious scowl. "I guess I'll go now."

The tears came then. They spilled down my face in a steady stream. He couldn't go. I couldn't say goodbye. Couldn't bear to part from my gruff and grumpy Big Red, my hero of heroes who looked at me with such love. Couldn't part from his expressive scowls and judgmental eyebrow, those impossibly broad shoulders, and his stubbornness. The way he told me what I couldn't do and me doing it anyway. Or how he flexed his bicep to make his tattoo dance. His courage, his laughter, and that ridiculous wolfish grin he thought was sexy. How he protected me, even when I didn't need it.

And his kisses. His touch, his caresses, the way we made love. The only man who could convince Beryl Blue to stop running and find a home in his arms. Where I was safe and wanted and worthy.

He couldn't go. Because I couldn't live without him.

"Sully?" I whispered, then repeated, louder, more desperate as his scowl softened and his eyes closed.

Hank touched my shoulder, but I shook him off. Sully's breath stilled and the world crumbled. My heart shattered into a thousand bitter bits. Everything went black, and I didn't want to ever wake up.

19

"You're going on a trip with Uncle Curly and Miss Blue," Minerva said. "When you see me again, I'll look different, but I'll still be the same girl who loves you to pieces."

To underscore that sentiment, Minerva hugged little me and kissed her soundly on the cheek. Young Beryl looked unconvinced, but she didn't make a peep as Minerva handed her over to me. I took the girl's small hand and a strange sort of electricity shimmered from her fingers into mine, both unsettling and soothing and ultimately connecting us as one.

I led her from the parlor to the dining room while Minerva and Uncle Curly—aka Jake 1.0, the 1950s version with the dimples and greasy hair—said goodbye. Not a happy moment. One filled with the heartbreak of parting I knew only too well.

But it was part of the plan, a plan Hank had devised to keep little me safe. The two lovers would part. I would take young Beryl to her new home in 1998, out of

Rasmussen's reach. Jake-slash-Curly wouldn't join us. He'd return to his duties in Futureworld. In 2125, to be precise, several years before we would officially meet again, and my time travel journey would begin.

I didn't understand any of it, nor did I want to try. After everything that had happened, I just did as I was told.

"What do you like to watch on TV?" I asked little me, trying to make conversation while Jake and Minerva exchanged final kisses in the other room.

"Television's okay, but I like to read," she declared, her voice tiny but firm.

Oh, yeah, duh. I should've known that, or remembered that fact, actually. I'd been a reader since day one. Little me currently clutched a dog-eared copy of Julia Sauer's *Fog Magic*. More of a middle-grade reader's book, but with all the upheavals ahead in Beryl Blue's future, the moody story of a lonely girl's time travel adventure could be just the thing this six-year-old needed to read.

"Way to go, kid," I said. "I bet you'll even be a librarian when you grow up." She already looked the part, in her pleated skirt and bolero jacket and her hair pulled back in the messiest of buns. "Just stay away from ladders and time travelers," I added in a low voice.

But don't avoid gruff, broad-shouldered redheads. At least, not one specific redhead. When the time came, I wished for her to run straight into his arms.

She tipped her head and studied me with a solemn frown. A lump lodged in my throat. It had been six months for her since her parents had died. Long enough for the shock of loss to wear off somewhat, not long enough to be able to smile again. For me, it had only been two days since time had taken them from me and the grief stung me as sharp as a blade.

It'd also been two days since Sully had died.

Well, technically died. He'd bled out and flatlined and all the other things they get all dramatic about in medical TV shows. But my pleading and begging and threatening looks had spurred Grandpa Hank to action. As Sully had drawn his last breath, Hank said, "Screw it" and put in a call to Time Scope HQ's version of 9-1-1.

In a nanosecond, a temporal MASH unit materialized in the park. I'd watched through squinted eyes and clenched teeth as they descended on Sully with medical equipment an ER doctor from my former 2015 home could only dream of. I would never forget what they did to bring him back, and I hoped they'd never have to do it again.

Sully had hovered on the edge of death these last two days. The longest forty-eight hours in the history of time. He still wasn't out of the woods and could take a turn one way or the other at any moment, but Hank had finally told me there was nothing I could do for Sully but get in the way and he'd booted me out of the ICU. He'd given me this assignment to keep me occupied and now, here I was, escorting my younger self to her new home.

And if that wasn't the most meta, mind-bending, time travel headache-inducing form of temporal shenanigans to ever inflict on a person, I had no idea what was.

THE TIME SKIP to 1998 kept the shake-and-shiver to a minimum and except for a moment of wooziness, little me came through it like a champ. Better than not-so-little me. I'd never get used to time travel, or at least the landing portion of the skip. I dropped out of the vortex with my usual grace, as if I'd just been shot out of a cannon and landed on my butt.

"Uncle Curly!" young Beryl shouted when her eyes focused and she saw Jake. Not the fresh-faced kid of twenty-five she'd just said goodbye to in 1954, but an older, more mature, and much more cynical Jake who lived in the twenty-second century. The wounded and secretive man who'd tried to fix the past and had broken it instead.

Jake hugged the girl then introduced her to Grandma Blue. More than forty years had gone by for Minerva since she'd seen little me. She was sixty-seven now, slightly heavier, her golden hair streaked with white, but still bright-eyed and with the same warm and welcoming smile.

Young Beryl took the introduction well and within moments, the three of them crowded at the kitchen table with the mismatched chairs and cushions dotted with faded daisies. They nibbled on fresh-baked blueberry muffins and chatted like the old friends they were.

I watched, feeling wistful. I thought I'd prepared myself for the shock of landing in the kitchen of the bungalow where I'd grown up. And for seeing Grandma Blue herself. Not the young woman who'd tooled around Ballard Springs with Jake-slash-Curly and my parents years ago. I didn't know her at all. *This* was the woman I remembered. The woman who'd raised me. Who'd done her best for me. Who kept me safe from a monster. Jake gazed at her with love in his eyes. He'd kept me safe too, and so had Glo and Alice in their own ways.

But no one had protected me more than Sully.

I swung my gaze toward Hank, who leaned against the linoleum counter near the refrigerator with his arms folded across his chest. He looked way out of place in his 1920s bakery attire. The same clothes he'd worn when I met him back in 1925, minus the bib apron. Had he just come from meeting me or would he head there when our business here concluded? I put the questions out of my mind as quickly as they'd come. Dwelling on time travel brain teasers would get me nowhere except on the road to a splitting headache.

"Any word about Sully?"

Hank shook his head. "He's hanging on. That's all I know."

I wrung my hands together. That wasn't enough. I needed to know more. Any minute Sully could turn a corner, but which direction would he go?

At the table, snack time concluded. Jake took Grandma Blue's hand and helped her up from her chair. He led her and little me out of the kitchen and into the den, with its 1990s-style TV tuned to the afternoon soap *As the World Turns*, a footlocker filled with toys and books, and a cat named Dennis, whose crankiness made my Jenjen look like an amateur.

"She'll be alright," Hank said. "Moving her was the only thing we could do. She'll have a home here. As close to normal as we can manage."

Home. That word again. A word that should mean permanence but didn't. Not for me. I'd bounced around from decade to decade, era to era, across three centuries and still hadn't found a place where I belonged.

"Something's bothering me," I said. "Did I always bring the little tyke here? Or did you insist I do it just to get me out of the ICU?"

"No to the first part, yes to the second." He pushed off the counter and stepped to my side, gently touching my arm. "Don't fret, Beryl. If there's any change, if he takes a bad turn, I'll whisk you to him in a heartbeat."

I nodded. I knew that. It was the only reason I'd agreed to leave Sully's bedside. But I'd still fret, no matter how many times Hank, or anyone else, told me not to.

Jake came back into the kitchen and interrupted my worry-fest. He ran his hand through his hair, tangling it, looking emotionally wrung out.

Hank turned to him, a pained look creasing his face. "I have something to tell you. To tell both of you." He swallowed nervously. "*I* put the whole thing into motion. I warned Felix and Mabel about Niels. Oliver Bishop got a hit on his location, and I warned them. They were fleeing town because of *me*. If I hadn't raised the alarm, who knows. They may have stayed home and Niels never would've found them. Or maybe he would. I don't know. Time's funny that way. Maybe everything that happened was meant to be."

"Yeah, I get it," Jake snapped. "I still fucked up."

Hank rested his hand on Jake's shoulder. "No, you didn't. You call your attempt to save them breaking the rules, but really, you tried to fix a terrible wrong. You did what we all do. We fight destiny in any way we can. We plan, we think of every angle and possibility, try to prepare, and still, life happens. Accidents, bad choices, wrong turns. Cancer. Death. All of that. But life also gives us happiness, love, fulfillment."

Jake frowned, never, ever a good look for him. "Love?"

Hank sighed. "Yes, love. You love her, don't you?"

"Always." No hesitation, a firm, unshakeable declaration.

"Then go to her."

Jake's frown deepened to a contemptuous glower. "What're you talking about?"

"Go to her. You're punishing yourself for something that wasn't your fault. It's mine. I screwed up not telling you about Bishop and not warning you about Ras." His face tightened, the lines around his mouth deepening in pain. "I didn't tell you because I didn't want to add to your pain and guilt. I take responsibility for everything. It was *my* action that led to their deaths. *My* failure and short-sightedness that put Niels on his path of destruction. I thought I could keep them safe, keep them all safe. I was wrong. I screwed up." He sliced a glance at me. "I screwed up a lot of things. But I thought it was best to safeguard history." He sighed heavily. "I was wrong. I see now how wrong I was. And now I'm telling you to go."

"But the rules," Jake said.

"Oh, screw the rules. They can't be broken, but they can be bent." He flashed me one of his toothy grins. "We've been doing a lot of rule-bending lately. Take my advice, son. Go. You'll have to watch out you don't impact the timeline, of course. You can't talk about the future, and you can't buy half of Disney's stock, but you can be with her. You *can* be happy."

Jake's mouth opened and closed a dozen times. Choking chirps like a bird strangling on a piece of string came out but no words. Doubt, indecision, and hope lit his expression one after another like a busted traffic light. Then a dimplefest erupted on his face. The best look for him ever.

"Thank you." He bro-hugged Hank then kissed me loudly on the cheek. "Goodbye, Beryl."

He whipped out his commpad and shot to the door. Moments later, a blue light flashed outside, accompanied by a rush of wind.

Grandma Blue entered the kitchen as soon as he left. She came over to me and brushed a curl back from my face, gazing at me with a fond smile. "You grew up so pretty. And smart, too. Hank tells me you work for him."

I grunted, a pleased-but-not-going-to-admit-it response to compliments I'd learned from Sully. "I do my best. You taught me that." She'd taught me everything. Tears stung my eyes. Beryl Blue, the woman who never used to cry or allow herself to feel, now cried buckets and felt tons.

She nodded like she expected nothing less and turned to Hank. "Is Jake gone?"

"Yup. I doubt we'll ever see him again."

"I wouldn't be too sure," she said with a giddy grin.

What? *No.* But then again, yes... The memories clicked into place and so did the timeline. Grandma Blue's secretive weekends away. The tall, silver-haired gent with the dimples who occasionally took her out to dinner, dancing, and... bowling. That was Jake. He'd gone back in time to be with her, and they'd grown old together.

Stunned, and a little giddy myself, I pulled her into my arms and gave her a hug. Too tight, from the way she groaned, but it had been a long time since I'd seen her, and moody teenage me wouldn't hug her nearly enough, to my regret.

"Do me a favor," I said when I let her go. "Go easy on the kid about reading late into the night if she wants, so she won't have to pull that old flashlight under the bedcovers routine."

She raised an eyebrow that could rival Sully's in its skepticism. "I'll see what I can do. Will you stay for dinner? I'm making meatloaf."

Grandma Blue's special meatloaf, as dry as dust and always overcooked? I wouldn't miss it for the world. My stomach flipped, anticipating.

"We both will," Hank said.

She picked up her cigarettes and lighter from the table and returned to the den. I opened my mouth to order her to put the cigarettes down, but Hank touched my shoulder, stopping me.

"You can't change that," he said gently. "I would if I could, but there's only so many rules time will allow us to bend."

I scowled at him. I knew that. Damn him and damn fate. I'd have to live with her loss, live with *their* loss, and this empty spot forever. Jake had once said you never get over losing someone, you just get used to it. A hopeful, but ultimately empty platitude you found on a teabag. I doubted I'd ever get used to losing them. I knew I'd never get over it.

I sat down at the table and grabbed a muffin, picking at it sullenly. "There's another thing that's bothering me," I said, eyeing Hank. "Why Blue? You gotta admit, it's an odd last name. It's gotten me raised eyebrows and head scratches my whole life. Why did you choose it as my alias?"

"It is unusual. But I wasn't the one who chose it."

"Oh?" I stuffed a piece of muffin into my mouth. "Who did?"

He flashed one of his signature toothy grins. "What's your favorite color, Beryl?"

"Blue—" I barked a stunned laugh. "It's blue and always has been. Grandpa, you've got to be shitting me."

"Young lady, I never shit anyone."

A jaunty ragtime song filled the air. Hank held up a finger in a *wait a sec* gesture and slipped a commpad disguised as a 1920s vintage cigarette case out of his shirt's breast pocket. I shot out of the chair and to his side, watching anxiously as he skimmed a temporal text that splashed onto the screen.

"Is it Sully? What did they say?" I demanded.

He turned to me and waited several beats before speaking. Long enough for my heartbeat to rev into high gear and for me to consider grabbing him by the lapels and shaking the details out of him.

"He's going to be okay, Beryl." His voice wobbled with relief. "They've moved him from critical care. He's awake and he's asking for you."

THE TEMPORAL STREAM spit me out on the twenty-sixth floor of Time Scope's HQ and for the first time ever, I landed on my feet, with only minimum wobbling. I looked around. I was in the rehab and recovery clinic, a place for time tourists who shoot themselves in the foot while on safari or swoon at the feet of a historical figure they've run into on their trip.

And the place where I would find Sully.

I headed toward the clinic's main desk. This wasn't a hospital, but it sure smelled like one. It looked like one too, with medical supply carts clogging the hallways and bright lights overhead. Nurses and med techs zipped about and sailed in and out of rooms, taking care of their patients. They clustered at duty stations too, doing paperwork, chatting. Everything Cecelia did in 1947 and Minerva in the decades that followed, and even Florence Nightingale and her nursing sisters from way back when.

"John Doe?" I asked at the desk.

Hank's idea. I don't know why we had to be secretive about Sully's identity. Not like he was George Washington or MLK and everyone would know who he was, but I went along with the old buzzard's wishes anyway. Rasmussen, the only person who'd posed a threat to Big Red, had been neutralized and locked away in a secure cell where he couldn't hurt Sully or me or anyone ever again.

A pleasant young woman wearing one of Time Scope's signature jumpsuits adorned with a caduceus symbol directed me down the hallway to his room. Moments later, I stepped into a sterile scene exactly like the ICU unit where Sully had hovered near death for the last two days. White walls, white floor, and Sully wearing a white hospital Johnny and covered with a white sheet. The only difference—the thousand cords and wires he'd been hooked up to the last couple of days were gone.

He lay stretched out straight and very still. Ashen faced, worn out, exhausted. But alive.

His eyelids fluttered open, as if he sensed me there, and he looked at me with a slightly glassy-eyed gaze. "You took your sweet time getting here," he said.

I let out a laugh full of joy and tears. His voice was no more than a croak. The sweetest sound I'd ever heard.

"Traffic was a bitch," I said, earning a raised eyebrow. Just a fraction, but it made my heart leap. If he had the strength to eyebrow me, he was going to be alright. Truly alright.

He moved his hand, his motion labored, and patted the bed by his side. The med techs would probably warn me not to jostle the patient, but no way would I refuse the invitation. I sat. The mattress was pretty comfortable for a hospital bed. Wider and infinitely more comfortable than the bed in Ma's rooming house in Ballard Springs where we'd stayed in 1943 and first made love.

"What is this place?" He looked around then his eyes found mine again. "What happened?"

I knew I couldn't sugarcoat it. He wouldn't want me to. "You got stabbed. Saving me." I squeezed his hand. "Saving little me, actually. That's what that whole prophecy was about. You were supposed to die saving me, only not the adult version of me, the younger one."

He nodded, a feeble effort, though I doubted he understood what I was saying. Why should he? It was all an unending and unsolvable temporal riddle, like one of those choose your own adventure books I loved as a kid. A thrill ride of a read, but no matter how many different choices you make, how many times you tried to avoid the pitfalls of the plot, you ended up spinning round and round through the story to come right back to the beginning.

I leaned in and kissed his forehead. "Never mind. The most important thing you need to know is I browbeat Hank into saving you and bringing you here before you could die." Well, he *did* die, but I didn't go into that. "It was touch and go for a while. You drifted in and out of consciousness, on the edge of death for two days. But you being such an ornery and stubborn bull, you fought hard. And you won."

My voice caught on that last bit. So many times in those two days I'd thought he'd lose. That fate would win, despite Hank's intervention. Once he'd decided Big Red was worth saving, Mr. Time Scope had deployed a team of doctors and specialists to make it so. They'd helped Sully through the battle, but he was the one who had to win the war.

And he'd done it. Sully had not only cheated fate, he'd defeated it.

"I won 'cuz you wouldn't let me go," he rumbled, his voice stronger, clearer. "I dreamed I was in the forest near Bastogne. Cold as hell, fellas dead all around me. Blood on the snow. I wanted to lay down beside them." He paused, taking slow, measured breaths, gathering strength. "Then I heard you, calling me. Yelling at me. Something like, don't you fuckin' leave me." His lips twitched. "I thought, how can I leave a bossy girl like that? I followed your voice. You saved me."

Oh, man. Was I going to cry *again*? "Well, yeah, seems like we saved each other, sergeant."

He closed his eyes and fell silent. I thought he'd drifted back to sleep, then he murmured, "What's the catch?"

"What?"

He opened his eyes, his gaze sharp now. "The catch. There must be a price for saving me."

Yeah, the catch. There always was one with these future people. The deal we had to make with fate and time.

"Remember when Miss Sanborn said you were dead? You *are* dead, Sully. At least, back then you are." I shifted gears, a little less chipper, a little more serious. "As far as everyone knows, Sergeant Thomas Sullivan crashed his car into a snowbank on Christmas night. In a daze, he wandered off and disappeared. No one knows what happened. Maybe you took shelter in a cellar hole and froze to death, or fell into the frigid springs and drowned, your body never found." I did *not* mention the whispers about his running off with a pretty arsonist he'd sprung from jail. "Officially, you were declared dead, fallen in the line of duty."

Just as destiny and Alice's multitude of search engines had predicted.

He scowled, looking pained. "What about Pat? He think I'm dead too?"

"No," I said hastily. "Hank took care of that. Pat knows. Not everything, but he knows you're alive." I took a breath and dumped the rest out in a rush. "You can't go back. I think I can manage it so you can see Pat and Cecelia on occasion, well, maybe once, but you can't go back. You can't ever return to that life. You're a citizen of the twenty-second century now, courtesy of Time Scope, Incorporated."

I watched him closely, waiting for his reaction, some sign of regret or anger or heartbreak at hearing this news. When I'd been extracted from 2015, I felt as if a piano had slammed into my chest. But Sully? Nothing. Sergeant Poker Face as usual, giving no hint to how he felt.

I stroked his cheek and ran my finger along his bristled jaw. I noticed flecks of gray in his red whiskers. "Does it bother you that you can't ever go home?"

He gazed at me for several seconds then took my hand again. I offered no resistance as he tugged me down beside him. I gingerly rested my head on his shoulder, but he still sucked in a breath between his teeth.

"This is my home, Beryl," he said, gruff and with finality. "Here. Now. With you."

He managed to land a kiss on my eyelid before he dropped off to sleep again. I lay there, snuggled up against him, listening to his strong, steady breaths, watching his chest rise and fall, resting beside him through the night.

And where I planned to be forever.

EPILOGUE

I rinsed my breakfast bowl and placed it in the rack to dry. I looked up at Sully on the other side of the apartment, comfortable in one of the chairs. He was reading a book I'd picked up for him at my library, a World War II-set mystery he kept snickering at because of the historical inaccuracies. My cat—now *our* cat—Jenjen leapt up and perched on one of the chair's arms, eyeing Sully stoically. Sully ran his free hand down Jenjen's back and the evil thing purred his approval.

I strolled over. A short distance in this tiny studio, and even smaller with Big Red and his broad shoulders living here. We needed to find somewhere more spacious to live, but any move would have to wait until Sully had fully recovered.

"I'm impressed Jenjen's so friendly," I said. "He's usually ultra cautious with new people."

And by cautious I meant glacial. I'd had that cat for five years and never got a single purr out of him, not after feeding him or giving him treats. All Sully had to do was scowl at him and Jenjen had gone from suspicious death glare to devoted BFF in two seconds flat.

"I don't believe that." Sully scratched Jenjen behind the ears and the cat's expression turned rapturous. "Jenjen's my friend."

I watched their mutual admiration society meeting with a surge of affection for both cat and man, but mostly for the man. I thought about muscling his new friend out of the way and demanding Sully stroke me and make me purr, but I was already late for a very important date—my first shift at the library since I'd taken leave from both time copping and shelving books while Sully recovered in the clinic and the weeks of his recuperation here at home.

I bent and kissed the top of his head. "I've got to go."

He delayed my departure by dropping the book and hooking his arm around my waist, pulling me down onto his lap. Jenjen objected with an annoyed swish of his tail before jumping to the floor and stalking away.

"Poor kitty," I said. "I think he's jealous."

"Too bad. Let him get his own dame." Sully tightened his embrace.

I laughed. "Sully. Remember what the doctors said. You're still healing and need to take it easy."

He pouted. "I'm fine. I feel fine."

He looked fine, too. Hale and hearty enough to carry a ship's anchor up the side of a mountain and probably would do so if the opportunity arose. "I know. But the sooner they declare you all better, the sooner you can join the team and time cop to your heart's content."

He grunted his opinion of that then kissed me, his

lips lingering and igniting a firestorm inside me. I snuggled in and rested my head on his shoulder.

"Thought you were headed out," he said, his eyebrow popping up in amusement.

"In a minute. Something's been bugging me."

"Yeah?" He kissed me again. "What can I do to fix it?"

"It's not *that* kind of problem. It's a timey-wimey question. Would Jake even have gone to the rescue if we hadn't run into him? I mean Curly Jake. How else would he have known my parents were in trouble if we didn't warn him? Did we create a paradox?"

"Does it matter? It's done. It happened. We dealt with it." He pushed aside my shirt's collar and his lips brushed my neck. One of the million and one things I loved about him. He always had the answer. Though frankly, as his lips traveled downward, I'd forgotten the question.

I sighed. "Ah, you really are feeling better."

"Better than better." He loosened his hold and that wolfish leer I'd once loathed but now kind of adored lit his face. "I'll show you when you get back from work. Don't be long."

"You seem to be done in, Beryl Blue," Dewey-006.3 said, in a voice like Cary Grant's. Not that the west side library's resident book-shelving bot resembled Cary Grant in any way, shape, or form. Squat and square and with a tendency to wheeze as it tooled around the library, Dewey-006.3 had eyes similar to the rest of the bots I encountered here in Futureworld. Large, perpetually surprised, slightly menacing. I suspected the chief bot designer had a fondness for 1950s horror movies starring robots gone wild.

Creepiness aside, I enjoyed having Dewey as a work pal, mainly because its specially crafted hands attached to spindly metal arms could extend all the way up to the top of the tallest bookshelf. Keeping me and my fear of heights firmly on the ground and with no reason to ever climb a ladder at work again. Good from a safety perspective, but kind of bittersweet. The day I tumbled from that ladder in 2015 was the day my excellent time travel adventure had begun—and my life was never the same.

My TDC pinged as I put on my spring jacket, about to leave for the day. A message from Glo, asking me to pop by and see her when I came to HQ to pick up Sully, now fully recovered and undergoing a grueling course of time cop training. I hopped on a slide and opted to stand in one of the travel bays, rather than sit. Too keyed up. I always got that way when I knew I'd soon see Big Red. With the added bonus excitement of whatever Glo had up her sleeve.

I found her in her office, dictating a report to the Interface and not looking very happy about it.

"Look at it this way," I said. "As long as there's time travelers trying to mess with history, you'll have a job. *We'll* have jobs." I perched on the corner of her desk. "How was your visit with the fam?"

I didn't mean her mom and sisters. She'd recently time skipped to see Cecelia, Pat, and baby Effie in January of 1948. She'd gone to retrieve the items I'd left behind at their house and clean up any other anomalies, but she'd also gotten a chance to get to know her several-times-great grandmother.

"It was fine," she said, which was Glo speak for *I had an amazing time*. She really was the queen of understatement. She swung her chair to the right and gestured at the family photographs on the wall. "See anything new?"

I scanned the digipix and framed photos I'd seen dozens of times before, including the 1947 snapshot of Pat and Cecelia and a Christmas tree, now with the awkward addition of Beryl Blue's head photobombing in the left corner.

Just below that one, I spotted a color print of a woman in her early twenties, with her reddish-brown hair styled in an afro and flashing a peace sign at the camera. She wore a yellow minidress with white cuffs and collar.

"That looks like the dress I wore to Woodstock and left at Pat and Cecelia's. Wait." I gaped at Glo in surprise. "That *is* the dress. I thought you went to pick it up. And that's... Effie? She was at Woodstock?"

"I made sure she went to Woodstock."

"What? *Oh*." Effie was the woman in the yellow dress who'd bumped into Rasmussen, forcing his shot to go wild—and miss me. "Gloriana Evelyn Reid, you clever thing."

"*Somebody's* got to keep an eye on you. You get into so much trouble."

"That's what Jake used to say." I watched her straighten a pile of already neat and tidy folders on her desk. "You miss him, don't you?"

She fussed with her folders some more. "Damn right. I've lost one of the best security men I ever had."

"Not to mention losing a friend."

She scowled, looking so much like Sully I grinned.

"Yes, I lost a friend," she said, sighing. "On to business. I have an assignment for you if you're ready to get back to work. A time thief going after a rare manuscript in the twentieth century. Do you want the job?"

"Now you're just messing with me. I'm a librarian. I absolutely want the job. Where and when?"

"Boston, mid-1930s. You can wear a cute hat." She let that marinate a moment before adding, "You can also take Sullivan with you."

I beamed a smile that could blind the sun. "Does this mean Sully's been cleared for his first mission? He'll be happy to hear it." Understatement. He'd been agitating to get out into the field since the moment he'd woken up to find himself in the twenty-second century.

"I'm happy he's happy." She tapped her commpad and my wristwatch vibrated as the details uploaded into the TDC. "Now, get out of my office and back in the field where you belong. You've been on vacation long enough. Oh, and Beryl...?"

I stopped halfway to the door and turned back.

"How's he doing?" she asked.

"Good. He's adjusting. He misses his family." A lot. But Sully being Sully, he didn't dwell on it, preferring to move forward.

She nodded. "Tell him he's got family here. He knows where to find me."

I wasn't so sure about that. Sully was still finding his way around Time Scope's unending maze of offices and meeting rooms and cubbyholes. But her words touched me, and I knew he would feel the same way.

After we arranged our next bowling date with Alice, I left and headed for the training floor to find Sully.

Honestly, he could train the whole mess of them. But basic training was one of Time Scope's rules for new recruits, so the former soldier who'd fought his way across Europe nearly two hundred years ago had to endure pushups and PT all over again.

He'd had a little trouble learning to use futuristic weapons but he'd taken to fight training like the proverbial duck to water. My pulse raced as I watched him through a large window. His movements were lithe and swift, and deadly. Sweat matted his copper hair, slicked his forehead, and formed a dark V down the front of his formfitting tee shirt. His biceps flexed and I could just see his tattoo peeking out from under his sleeve.

A tall woman of about forty led the training. Jake's replacement. I remembered my days in that big room, nowhere near as skilled or coordinated as Sully, or anyone else on the team. But Jake had been patient. A prickle stung my heart. I guess I missed him too.

The trainer blew a whistle, ending the workout. The trainees gave each other *good job* slaps on the back, exchanged a few words, then filed out of the gym toward the showers. As if he sensed me watching through the window, Sully stopped and looked back. He grinned and blew me a kiss as he followed the others from the room.

I studied the mission specs Glo had sent while I waited for him to shower and change, which he did quickly, as eager to be with me as I him. He stepped out of the locker room, looking timelessly fashionable and unbearably hot in jeans and a black tee shirt that hugged his pecs and broad shoulders. His hair was all 1940s, though, still damp and combed neatly, with lines like a furrowed field.

"Hey," he said. He smelled of soap and Sully. My heart slammed into my ribs and my pulse rate kicked up to a surely fatal speed. Heat flared from head to toe. I would never need a radiator or have to pay a heating bill ever again as long as he was around.

Would it always be so? I had no doubt. "Hey yourself, Sergeant Sullivan."

He gave me a quick kiss and steered me toward the elevator. "What have you been up to?" he asked as he punched the button for the ground floor and the doors slid shut.

"We have an assignment."

His left eyebrow shot upward. "We?"

"We. Us. We're partners."

We reached the ground floor, and, as we strolled across the lobby to the exit, I gave him a summary of the mission.

"Apparently the Boston Public Library has a ton of books that belonged to John Adams. And our second president liked to add his John Hancock in the margins of those books in the form of annotated notes. That makes them valuable. Our temporal book thief thinks so too and wants one or more for her very own. We've got to stop her."

"Boston, 1933?" he said. "I was about fourteen then. Spent some time at the library. Any chance we'll run into me?"

"I hope not. I don't think I could handle two of you."

He scowled, filled with affection. "Have I mentioned you're a real piece of work, Beryl Blue?"

"You have. But tell me again."

"When do we leave?"

"As soon as you want to go."

"Now?" His eyes glimmered in anticipation, the man of action, anxious to get to work.

"Sure. After we grab a bite and feed Jenjen."

We reached the door. He vaulted forward to open it for me. I grinned, dizzy with happiness. A shocking state of affairs for Beryl Blue. The woman who ran away, who belonged nowhere, who had no home or family. Now I overflowed with both in a dozen time periods. Glo and Alice, my bowling buddies and the gal pals I never had in my old life. Hank, my new-found grandpa. Even my parents and Grandma Blue, the treasured loved ones I'd lost but could visit in my memories always.

And Sully. My family, my love, my one and only. My home.

We walked outside hand in hand. Together. Headed for the past and into our future.

Thank you for reading *Every Time We Say Goodbye*!

Thank you for reading *Every Time We Say Goodbye*! I hope you enjoyed Beryl and Sully's time travel adventure. If you did, please help others find this story by leaving a review.

Don't forget to sign up for my newsletter for the latest news on what's happening in the Beryl Blue, Time Cop world, what's next for me, plus exclusive content, free books, and all kinds of other goodies. Just stop by my website to join the fun!

www.janetrayestevens.com

ACKNOWLEDGMENTS

Beryl Blue's journey from shelving books in 2015 to skipping about in time with the impossibly broad-shouldered Sully would never have been possible without the help and support of so many others—writers, friends, and especially my family.

A huge thank you for your time and talents to Suzanne Tierney, Jeanne Oates Estridge, Lea Kirk, and Lauren Sheridan. Thanks also to Sharon Healy-Yang, Jean M. Grant, Tracy Brody, Christine Gunderson and the rest of the Sunday Accountability Group, Reina Williams at Rickrack Books, most excellent cover designer Elizabeth Turner Stokes, Melissa–The Literary Assistant, and an extra shout out to the extraordinary Kari Lemor.

ABOUT THE AUTHOR

Meet author Janet Raye Stevens – mom, reader, tea-drinker (okay, tea guzzler), and author of smart, stealthily romantic adventures. Derringer and Silver Falchion Award finalist and winner of RWA's Golden Heart® and Daphne du Maurier awards, Janet writes mystery, time travel, paranormal, and the occasional Christmas romance, all with humor, heart, and a dash of suspense. She lives in New England with her family.

www.janetrayestevens.com

Made in the USA
Middletown, DE
14 October 2023